COPS

G.A.HAUSER

COPS

Cover design by Syd Gill

Cover models; Benjamin Godfre and Rogan Richards

Edited by Natalie Cushman

ISBN Trade paperback: 978-1482-7368-2-3

WARNING

This book contains material that maybe offensive to some: graphic language, homosexual relations, adult situations. Please store your books carefully where they cannot be accessed by underage readers.

© First The G.A. Hauser Collection LLC publication: July 2013

ABOUT THE PHOTOGRAPHER

MICHAEL STOKES

Originally from Berkeley, California, I moved to Los Angeles in 1983 where I studied at Santa Monica College and swam on their swim team. In 1984 I became a flight attendant for Western Airlines, which was later taken over by Delta. In 1993 I graduated Cal State Long Beach, first in my class and Phi Beta Kappa with a BA in Fine Art, emphasis in filmmaking and photography. My short films were showcased in film festivals around the world, but I put my creative desires to the side to sell real estate. By the late 90's I was one of Long Beach's top-producing real estate agents. Feeling unfulfilled, I retired from real estate in 2005, subsequently renewing my interest in photography.

Now living in Los Angeles, I have been published in multiple anthologies, fine art photography books, magazines, book covers, magazine editorials and underwear campaigns.

I shoot portraits, catalogue, fashion and fine art, and my work has been featured in countless blogs. I still swim on a swim team, and I compete as a United States Masters swimmer. Feel free to add me on Facebook for updates and previews of my latest work and projects.
My first coffee table book is out as of November, 2012 and is now available on Amazon.

http://michaelstokesphoto.com

DEPARTMENT OF JUSTICE
FBI ANTI-PIRACY
WARNING
FIDELITY
BRAVERY
INTEGRITY
FEDERAL BUREAU OF INVESTIGATION

Chapter One

Officer Mickey Stanton held a gun in his hand.

He was drenched in perspiration and the drops kept stinging his eyes. Wearing his dark LAPD uniform, Kevlar vest, and a gun belt that could weigh down a body tossed into the Hudson River by the mob, he was boiling hot.

The room was so dark he had his flashlight held under his gun but didn't keep the light on. Keeping a light on made you a target. He glanced back. His partner, Jeff Chandler was leaning on a wall right near him, also running with sweat. Jeff had a gun in his hand, his flashlight held tightly under it, pointed towards the floor. They nodded at each other to continue searching the pitch-black premise.

Mickey raised his gun and flashlight and spun around a corner, lighting the graffiti covered room. The minute he spotlighted the area, two dark forms emerged, weapons drawn and opened fire.

Taking cover, Mickey crouched low, "Get down!" he yelled at Jeff, then returned fire knowing at this close range, he hit the two men square in the chest.

He felt Jeff beside him, and he too was unloading his clip into the two dark figures.

When Mickey's finger pulled on the trigger and nothing happened, he knew he was out of ammo. Mickey waited, his breathing like the huff of a bellows from his nerves.

"All right! End scenario!" was yelled out behind them.

Taking off the eye protection, Mickey used the wall to help him stand, sliding up the dirty plasterboard with his shoulder. A light was turned on and Jeff was beside him, wiping the sweat running down his face with his forearm.

A supervisor stood near and pointed to a few pink colored paint spatters on one of the dark-suited men who wore face shields and helmets. "Hit. Hit. Hit."

Mickey puffed up in pride.

The supervisor counted up the blue paint spatters next. "Nicely done, Chandler! Two shots to the chest, one to the head."

Jeff elbowed Mickey to tease him, as if he was a better sharp shooter than his partner.

The two darkly clothed men were part of the SWAT team, helping with tactical training. They wore pure black with face guards, and were shooting paint pellets back. And if you got hit? It stung and left a lovely dark bruise. Not to mention, you failed the course.

Both of the 'decoys' were spattered in pink and blue dots from Mickey and Jeff's paintball guns.

"Get over here." The supervisor called Jeff and Mickey into the lit front room, inspecting them for any paint hits.

"Good job." He didn't find any.

Holding the paintball gun at his side, and sliding the flashlight into a loop on his belt, Mickey held up a hand for a high-five from his partner.

Jeff slapped his hand. The two of them were filthy from the training, but were getting through the tough tactical drills.

"Out." The supervisor pointed. "Don't tell the next two officers a fucking thing. Got it?"

"Yes, sir!" Jeff saluted and laughed as he and Mickey left the structure, which was nothing more than plasterboard and plywood, but pitch dark for the nighttime training.

They walked passed the other officers awaiting their turn to get ambushed. SWAT loved to fuck with patrol, so they made the training as stressful as possible. And it was.

Before Mickey and Jeff could even take a pit stop, they were directed to lay the paintball guns down, and go collect their duty firearms, their Glocks.

"Fuck, I'm beat." Jeff kept wiping his face with his arm, but he was so dirty all he was doing was smearing his skin with the chalky brown dust.

"Last exercise. Then we go home." Mickey unlocked a small locker and removed both his and Jeff's pistols from it. They were unloaded, the slide locked back. Jeff stood and swayed from exhaustion as he replaced the empty bullet magazines into their holders on his gun belt. Mickey noticed him struggle from fatigue, so he secured the snaps for Jeff and then put his own magazines into his holder on his duty belt as well. They carried the opened guns with a box of ammunition to another area at the training ground.

As they approached Mickey could hear round after round going off, as the officers who went before them fired their guns.

Looking up at the sky, seeing it was dark and very few stars were showing through the ambient light, Mickey estimated the time to be near midnight. Late. He and his partner Jeff worked the day shift, so this was killing them.

They stood back as the range masters had another pair of cops already working their training routine.

Mickey gestured to a gun cleaning area and the two of them used it to lean against and rest. He noticed Jeff check his knuckles. Mickey lit his flashlight on them and spotted blood. "How'd you do that?"

"Fuck if I know. Probably got nailed by a rogue paintball." Jeff went to suck the torn skin.

Mickey glanced around and put Jeff's hand to his mouth, doing it for him. "Mm." Mickey released it quickly.

"My cum, my sweat, and now my blood?" Jeff shook his head.

"I love everything that seeps out of you, ya bastard."

The team at the range had finished their practice. Jeff and Mickey were being signaled over.

They were instructed, “Face down range. Load up.”

Taking out one empty magazine, they filled it, pushing the bullets into the spring loaded shaft.

Mickey kept an eye on Jeff. The training was brutal. It was supposed to be.

Jeff managed to get his magazine filled and stood by.

The ranger master said, “Guns loaded and ready to fire.”

Both men made sure they were physically standing with the pistols pointing downrange and loaded a clip into the gun, racking the slide, chambering a live round.

A full magazine, a bullet loaded, they were ready to roll.

“Holster.” They were handed ear and eye protection.

They jammed their guns into their holsters, snapping them in. First they put the ear protection on, then took the goggles.

“This is a failure drill.” The range master pointed to an old beat up patrol car, probably out of service for years. “Get inside, I don’t give a fuck who pretends to drive or who’s the passenger.” He then pointed down range. “You have five seconds to shoot. Door shut and secure, get out, use the door as cover and fire.”

Mickey nodded. So did Jeff.

As they walked to the car, Mickey asked, “Which side?”

“Don’t fucking care. I’ll be lucky if I hit the target.”

Mickey nudged him to the passenger’s side. Once they were both in the car, the doors were checked by another range master.

“Ready!” the second range master yelled to the first.

With the headset blocking out most of the noise, Mickey could hear his own huffing breaths like a loud bellows. They stared down range at the targets which were on a mechanism and dimly lit. As soon as the targets began to face them? They had to get the hell out of the car, use the door for cover, and shoot two rounds to the body, one to the head.

Jeff reacted first, but Mickey spotted the targets turning at the same time. He threw open the door, got to one knee and blasted three rounds while using the patrol car door to stabilize his arms. The targets turned sideways. No way to see what they had done in the darkness. They holstered their guns.

"Back in the car!"

"Fuck. I know I didn't get the head shot." Jeff sat down, closing the door.

"Shut up." Mickey kept his vision on the targets. They began to spin. He and Jeff hopped out and repeated the drill.

The blasting was loud, even through the ear protection. Two to the body, one to the head. The targets turned.

They holstered their weapons.

The range master lit up the lights to the range and made sure both men had their guns secured in their holsters before he walked down range.

Mickey took off both the eye and ear protection, so hot and sweaty he was about to keel over.

If they did not make the shots, they had to redo the training.

Jeff leaned on the top of the car with his elbow and Jeff heard him saying, "Please, God…please."

The range master stood by the targets marked them with chalk then gave the other range master a thumbs up.

"You're done. Clean your weapon and go home."

Jeff blew out a loud breath and he and Mickey headed to the cleaning station.

Two other men walked passed them, spattered with paint from the last scenario.

Mickey cracked up with laughter when he noticed it and they snarled, "Shut up, Stanton."

Shaking his head, chuckling, Mickey stood at the cleaning station and removed the gun from the holster. Facing a barrel full of sand, he released the magazine, then opened the slide, ejecting the bullet from the chamber, then he inspected it, making sure the gun was empty. Keeping the slide locked back he waited for Jeff to do the same. Once Jeff did, perfectly, they took the guns apart and cleaned them, standing side by side, under florescent light.

"Done with the torture for a few months," Jeff said as he used a brush to clean the barrel.

"Yup. Fucking hate this training."

"Gotta do it. Keep us sharp."

"I know." Mickey made sure the Glock was cleaned properly, using a little oil on the right spots for the slide. "Wanna fuck you."

Jeff chuckled.

Mickey assembled the gun, stuffed a magazine inside it, drew back the slide and released it, chambering a round, putting the gun into his holster. He had made sure his magazines were full of the proper copper-headed rounds, before he placed them into the holders on his duty belt. When he was done he tidied up the area, tossing out the tiny cleaning rags.

Then, in the bright light, he looked at his hands. "Damn. I've been wiping my fucking face with these things?" He walked over a dispenser of disinfectant cleaner on the wall and used some to rub into his fingers.

"You sucked my dirty knuckle, ya pervert." Jeff pointed his gun towards the barrel, loaded a bullet into the chamber, and holstered his weapon. He took a look at Mickey and laughed. Mickey assumed he was chuckling at how filthy his skin was considering what Jeff looked like at the moment.

"Where you goin'?" Mickey grabbed after him as Jeff turned to walk away.

"To our patrol car. Let's go."

Mickey walked beside him, not able to see anyone's faces in the darkness as uniformed men and women came and went from different training scenarios. They climbed into their patrol car and Mickey started it, turning on the air conditioning full blast, tugging at his Kevlar vest, and leaning towards the dashboard to get cool air to shoot under it.

After illuminating the dome light, Jeff lowered the visor and inspected his face in the mirror, wiping at the dirt, then looked at his knuckles. Mickey shut off the light and reached between Jeff's thighs.

"You want to suck my sweaty dick?" Jeff laughed at him. "You dirty, dirty, cop."

"Grrr." Mickey gave Jeff's crotch a squeeze.

"Not here, Mick. Head out."

Mickey put the car into reverse lowering the volume on the police radio. They were not officially 'on duty', and were logged onto a training detail. But, if another cop needed help? They would go, no matter when or where the help was needed, so, they listened to the nighttime transmission from dispatcher to on-duty cop.

Jeff straddled and it caught Mickey's eye.

He and this stunning ex-Seattle cop had been having sex since they were assigned to the same car. Eight-Adam-One, the West Bureau. Did anyone know they were lovers? If they did, they hadn't pulled them apart yet.

They tried to be discreet. Being a homosexual in the police was not quite accepted by all. And some of these Neanderthals didn't even want to work with women or minorities. But gay cops? No way. If they knew, you'd never get backup.

So, for the time being, he and Jeff kept up the straight act. Besides, they didn't want to be split up. And of course, if word got out they were lovers, they would be.

Mickey pulled the patrol car into a dark church parking lot, deserted on a Monday night. He backed up to the corner fence, shut off his headlights and looked at his man.

Jeff gave him a wicked smirk. "Do you know how badly I need a shower?"

"Uh huh." Mickey, the bigger of the two of them at six foot and nearly two hundred pounds, turned in the driver's seat, facing his prey.

Seeing Jeff's dimples as he laughed, Mickey cupped Jeff's jaw and urged it towards him. He could smell the gun cleaning fluid on his fingers, mixed with the disinfectant he had used.

Jeff didn't hesitate to return the kiss. As their lips connected, Mickey whimpered and went for Jeff's leather belt, the one holding his pants up, not his utility belt. Jeff reached into his open zipper and exposed his cock.

Mickey had a good look at it and then thrust his tongue into Jeff's mouth once more before diving onto his lap.

~

On duty, in uniform, in the patrol car. How often had they done crazy things like this? Jeff had lost count. But part of the excitement for them was the danger, the adrenalin rush. They got off on it, and each other.

The dirtier the better.

He grabbed a Mickey's blond hair in his fist and pulled and pushed Mickey's head, orally fucking him. "That's it, you fucking pig. Suck me."

Mickey snarled with his mouth full and drew deep, right to Jeff's pubic hair.

"Oh, Christ," Jeff said, shivering and feeling the suction from Mickey grow stronger. He thrust harder into Mickey's mouth, the awkwardness of his gun belt, his vest, the patrol car's mobile computer, the noise of the police dispatcher, all making this contact sublime.

He came, throwing his head back and grunting as Mickey breathed loudly through his nostrils as he sucked everything out of Jeff.

Mickey sat up abruptly and went for Jeff's mouth. The violence was what got them off. Two alpha dogs vying for supremacy. Mickey had Jeff pinned to the seat by one hand and was thrusting his tongue into Jeff's mouth.

Jeff could taste his own cum and smell the scent of his sweat on Mickey's skin. They were so excited they could barely get enough air into their lungs.

Mickey sat back and flipped his erect cock out of his uniform pants, looking around the deserted area. Jeff tucked himself back in and before he had even zipped his pants, Mickey had him by the back of the neck and forced him down to his lap.

Jeff opened his lips and closed his eyes, drawing all of Mickey's cock into his mouth, tasting the saltiness of his perspiration, and loving every minute of it.

Mickey held onto Jeff tightly and jammed his length into his mouth. Jeff moaned and even though his hands were filthy, he held the base of Mickey's cock, jacking it into his mouth.

"Fuck! Fuck!" Mickey came and when he did he whacked his hand against the driver's side window glass with a bang. Jeff squeezed him a few last times to milk him, and then sat up, staring at Mickey's cut cock and the way it poked out of his uniform pants.

Mickey slouched low as he recuperated, his cock growing soft quickly.

Jeff sat correctly in the passenger's seat, fastening his pants and making sure the butt of his gun didn't poke him in the gap between his vest and utility belt.

They took a moment to rest. It had been a hell of a long day. Half a day of answering calls for service, and a full night of training.

And while they stared into space like burned out zombies, the dispatcher kept sending LAPD cops all over the city to fight battles that simply had nothing to do with them, yet it was up to that thin blue line to keep the peace.

~

Mickey parked the patrol car in the lot at the station. Jeff was so tired his head kept nodding as he fought sleep. Mickey shut off the car and gave Jeff a punch on the shoulder to rouse him. Jeff sat up and blinked a few times to shake himself out of the deep haze, then opened the car door and walked to the trunk. Mickey popped it open for him from inside the car and got out, shutting the door and adjusting the heavy belt on his hips. Jeff took his kit out of the trunk and they walked to the entrance of the police station where the late shift teams came and went around them.

Using a security code, they entered the domain of the boys in blue, and went straight to the locker room to change.

"How was training?" one of the officers passing them in the hall, asked.

"Brutal." Jeff shook his head.

"Fuck," the cop said tiredly as he continued heading to the streets.

Jeff stood in front of his locker, trying to function, to kick his brain into action and remember his combination. He opened it and began shedding the heavy equipment, putting his duty gun into a waist pack and stripping off the filthy LAPD uniform to get it cleaned. His T-shirt which he wore under the vest was sticking to him he was so drenched. He pulled it over his head and tucked it into a bag to take home to wash. Now wearing a pair of cotton shorts and flip-flops, and a dark blue tank top, Jeff clipped the waist pack on his hips and removed his badge from the uniform shirt to attach to his wallet. Once he was done, he looked up and could see his partner appeared just as fatigued as he was. Mickey was wearing a white tank top and camouflage shorts, his black waist pack hung heavily against his right hip, sagging low from the weight of the gun inside it. He too had his uniform in a ball, ready to dry clean and a bag with his T-shirt in it.

Jeff shut the locker door and they stopped to relieve themselves and then stood at the sink to wash their hands and face.

Seeing how gritty he was, Jeff shook his head and couldn't wait for a shower. They left the uniforms in an area for pickup for dry cleaning inside the station and headed out.

Without the heavy uniform and vest, Jeff felt comfortable in the cool night air. Mickey was silent beside him while Jeff held the keys to his car as they left the area of patrol cars to head to where they had parked their civilian vehicle.

Jeff sat in the driver's side, tossing the sack with the T-shirt on the floor by his Mickey's feet as Mickey did the same. Jeff put on his seatbelt while Mickey combined their shirts into one bag, then slouched low.

Mickey asked him, "You okay to get us home?"

"Yeah." Jeff put his hand on Mickey's thigh as he drove them to the townhouse they shared in Anaheim.

He could see it was Mickey's turn to struggle to stay awake as he sank in the bucket seat beside him. Jeff had no idea how he managed to get them home safely, but he did.

Parked in his assigned spot at the complex, Jeff shut off the car and climbed out while Mickey picked up the bag at his feet and struggled to get upright and out of the low slung car. Jeff followed Mickey to the front door and leaned on Mickey's back as he opened the lock and entered their townhouse.

Jeff made a direct line to the second floor to the bathroom in their bedroom. He unhooked his gun-pack, laid it on the dresser then stripped, his clothing falling at his feet. Standing outside the shower, he held his hand under the spray as the water heated up.

Mickey entered, naked, and began brushing his teeth at the sink while Jeff watched him. Mickey caught his gaze and the shock of those sky blue eyes sent chills down Jeff's spine. He lowered his head and entered the shower, forcing himself to function when he was truly dead on his feet.

The shower door opened and Mickey, standing behind Jeff, tenderly washed Jeff's hair for him. Moaning in pleasure, Jeff propped himself up on the tiled wall. It was something they did. Though at times they battled like wildcats, made love like wolves in heat, this tenderness had become part of their routine.

Mickey nudged Jeff to rinse, and once he did, he returned the favor, shampooing Mickey's conservatively cut blond hair. Mickey also used the wall to prop himself up as Jeff massaged his scalp lovingly, then scrubbed his back and even his pits, using his fingertips to soap up the tufts of hair.

He heard a low growl from Mickey. Sexual.

Jeff ran his hands along Mickey's sides to his hips, staring at his perfect ass. Since they played in the sun on their days off, Mickey had tan lines. A pure white butt and brown back, legs and arms. Jeff, tired as he was, ran his soapy hand up Mickey's ass crack. Nothing turned him on like his cop partner. Nothing.

Mickey was fearless, a warrior on duty, and a pussycat when it came to their shared showers.

A low rumble of longing came from Mickey and Jeff spotted him clench his fists. Jeff rested on Mickey's back. "If you can get it up again, I will be in awe."

Mickey spun around, stiff with an erection and showed his teeth in a sensual snarl. "Be in awe, Chandler."

"You are un-fucking-real, Mick." Jeff swapped places with Mickey in the tub, allowing Mickey to rinse the soap and shampoo. As Mickey did, Jeff slid opened the shower door and grabbed a towel.

The water was shut off and Jeff looked up from rubbing the towel over his hair. Mickey's eyes had that gleam in them…again.

"Are you shitting me?" Jeff laughed, knowing that leer a mile away.

Mickey took a step closer, puffing up his broad hairless chest.

Jeff laughed and stepped out of the tub. "Jerk off. I'm wiped." Jeff tossed the towel over the rack and leaned on the sink to brush his teeth.

Dripping wet, Mickey stepped out of the shower and stared at Jeff while he pulled on his own length. Jeff peeked at him as he spat into the sink and rinsed his mouth. "No fucking way."

Mickey never took no for an answer.

Jeff gave him a wicked smirk and left the bathroom. He counted to three in his head and by the time he hit number two, Mickey had tackled and pinned Jeff to their bed. Mickey was on Jeff's back, using his knees to spread Jeff's legs.

The man outweighed him by almost thirty pounds of pure muscle and was a couple inches taller, but still, if Jeff really wanted to battle Mickey, he would. He *had* battled him many times before. This was all just part of the game.

"Get off me, you asshole!" Jeff tried to move out from under Mickey's weight.

Mickey growled near his ear and used a police hold, taking Jeff's arm behind his back to subdue him. Jeff knew the tactic, how could he not? Pain compliance. "Fuck you! Fuck you, Stanton!"

Mickey replied, mocking him, "No, fuck you, Chandler."

Jeff felt Mickey poking his finger into his ass.

Each time Jeff made a move, Mickey inflicted pain on his wrist to keep him still. Jeff watched Mickey reach for the lube. Jeff panted and felt his own cock throbbing. Yeah, it was hot. Even though he was spent, his dick was always interested.

The bottle tip was stuck up Jeff's ass. Jeff blinked and tried to jerk away as Mickey squeezed it, forcing lubrication inside Jeff.

"You fucking prick! Fucking asshole prick!" Jeff tried to prop himself up and get out of the hold, but the pain increased and he had to lay still. Mickey tossed the bottle to the floor and Jeff felt Mickey's fingers push inside him.

Jeff closed his eyes and chewed on the pillow, knowing he would not get sleep until his lover was fully satisfied, and there was nothing like a day playing tough cop to make Mickey want sex, again and again.

"Spread 'em." Mickey applied more pain pressure.

Jeff opened his legs and his own length throbbed under him.

Mickey aimed his cock and thrust in. Jeff gasped and gnawed on the pillow case like a dog with a chew toy.

"Ya like it, Chandler?" Mickey thrust his hips.

"Fuck you! Fuck you!" Jeff knew how to get his lover off quickly. "You dirty fucking pig. Get the hell off me!"

Mickey groaned and nibbled on Jeff's neck and shoulder, fucking him fast and hard.

"Dirty cock-sucking cop! Fuck you!" Jeff roared and felt his body light on fire from the internal friction. Mickey's cock went stiff inside Jeff and Jeff knew he was close. "Grab my dick, you motherfucking asshole!" Jeff clenched his jaw and tried to get out of the hold Mickey had on him.

But the minute Mickey heard what Jeff said, he released him and hoisted Jeff's hips up, grabbing his cock.

"Oh, God!" Jeff shouted and held onto the bedding in clenched fists.

"Come you, cocksucker!" Mickey jerked Jeff's cock as quickly as he fucked him.

Jeff felt the climax about to hit, strong and hard. He cupped the head of his dick and came, choking on the intensity while Mickey howled like a crazed werewolf and came inside him.

Jeff collapsed onto the bed, trapping his and Mickey's hands as Mickey panted and caught his breath, pinning Jeff to the bed.

"Christ, you fucking animal," Jeff said, moaning, "Let me sleep."

Mickey slowly backed off the bed, swaying and holding his cock as he stumbled to the bathroom.

"You suck!" Jeff yelled and grumbled as he had to get up to wash again. He met Mickey in the bathroom, cleaning up at the sink. "Douchebag."

"Fuck you." Mickey dried his hands with a towel and returned to the bed.

Jeff managed to scrub up once more, set the alarm, and dropped down under the sheet with his lover. Mickey hugged him tight and they both fell into a deep sleep instantly.

Chapter Two

The alarm went off and Mickey moaned in agony and slapped the clock to shut it up.

"God…no…" Jeff moaned beside him. "*…nooooo…*"

"Fuck." Mickey couldn't move and certainly was not looking forward to twelve hours on duty after the late training exercise.

What felt like seconds later, not ten minutes, the alarm clock again buzzed. Mickey nearly damaged it he whacked it so hard, but began to come around from a deep slumber.

"I can't. Don't make me." Jeff rolled over, hiding in the pillows.

Mickey sat up and rubbed his face and scruffy jaw. He shut off the alarm so it didn't buzz again and managed to stumble his way to the bathroom. He turned on a light and looked into the mirror. His hair was spiked and pointed at odd angles from going to bed with it wet, and his eyes were red from very little sleep.

Jeff brushed against him lightly as he passed behind him and stood at the toilet, holding his stiff cock, swaying as he tried to keep upright.

"We need time off." Mickey washed his face and cleaned his teeth before taking out his shaving kit.

"Fuck. I'm so burned out." After he relieved himself, Jeff turned on the shower and stepped in.

"At least the training is done." Mickey ran a razor over his jaw. "And we have three days off after today."

"Twelve hours. Motherfucker. The days are so long."

Mickey finished shaving and as he stepped into the shower, Jeff stepped out, drying off and taking his turn to shave.

Mickey rinsed quickly and shut off the water, standing for a second to drip and trying not to feel exhausted. “Coffee…”

“We should stop at Starbucks on the way to work.”

Mickey stepped onto the bathmat and dried his hair and back with a towel, watching Jeff running a razor through the foam on his jaw. They were both clean shaven with relatively conservative haircuts, although Jeff, the crazy ex Seattle cop, had his slightly longer than regulation. But neither of them liked the buzzed look of a jarhead.

Jeff splashed his face, patted it dry with a towel, and then left the bathroom.

Mickey ran a brush through his hair and got dressed in shorts and a T-shirt as Jeff did the same. As was their usual routine, they turned on their phones to check messages, since neither kept them on during their precious hours of sleep.

Reading text messages first, Jeff then headed to the kitchen and set up the coffee machine.

Mickey took a box of cereal out of a cupboard and then two bowls and the milk.

Jeff turned on a radio for the traffic and weather report and set two mugs on the table. He plopped down on a chair and filled his bowl with cereal. “Seriously, Mick, it better be a slow day.”

“It never is.” Mickey poured milk on his cornflakes and then stood up. While the coffee still dripped, he poured two full mugs and then replaced the carafe. He sat down and the two of them ate their cereal while listening to the traffic report.

“Already a crash on 10.” Jeff shook more cereal into his bowl.

“State’s problem, not ours.” Mickey read the cereal box.

“No. I mean the traffic getting in.”

“Shut up.”

“No. You shut up.”

Mickey gave Jeff a gentle, slow-motion ‘punch’ to his jaw and winked.

~

After stopping at a drive-through Starbucks, they each had double espressos sitting in the cup holder of Mickey's new white pickup truck. Mickey reached to crank up the CD blasting Led Zeppelin music as if he had even been born when the band was topping the charts. But, their tastes tended toward heavy metal, so Zeppelin it was.

Looking for a shady spot, Mickey parked in the civilian parking lot by the precinct and picked up his coffee.

Jeff did the same, hoping it had cooled enough to actually drink. He waited until Mickey was out of the car, then Mickey armed the truck with his key fob, sticking the key into his pocket.

Jeff shifted his heavy gun-pack to the front, so it hung over his pelvis more comfortably.

Sipping the coffee as they went, Jeff adjusted his sunglasses as Mickey did the same, since it was another scorching hot summer day in LA. And that meant trouble.

Heat made people short-tempered and hang out late in the evenings outdoors. Arguments broke out, booze was consumed, and in no time, shots were fired. On July fourth it was twelve hours of pure adrenalin and running call to call to call…at least they had that horrible night behind them.

Mickey opened the door for Jeff, waiting for him to enter first. It was pleasantly cool inside the station. On their way to the locker room, Jeff spied a bulletin board with the announcement for the upcoming sergeant's exam pinned on it. He hadn't mentioned his desire to test for it to Mickey, simply because if he was promoted, they would be separated, and not only from the patrol car as partners, possibly from the division completely. Jeff would go where he was needed, and that meant any district, and any shift.

But Jeff had been on patrol for so long, he was tired of it. Why hadn't he discussed it with Mickey? Because Mickey would be furious.

He hung back and Mickey noticed, stopping with him.

"Be right there." Jeff waved to him and Mickey kept walking.

Sliding his sunglasses to the top of his head, Jeff read the deadline and the requirements. He felt a pat on the back and looked over his shoulder. His sergeant, Sgt. Adkins, said, "You should test, Chandler."

"I want to, sir."

"There's a list of study guides. Just go to the secretary and she'll let you know what you need to work on."

"I assume its code, procedure…"

"Yeah. It's a ton of memorization. But you're not too stupid, even though you're ex–SPD." He laughed and smiled sweetly, then kept heading to his desk.

Jeff knew coming from the Great Northwest as a lateral transfer he took a lot of teasing from the natives from the City of Angels. And he finally had a tan. His pale white skin was pale no longer.

Sipping his coffee, he headed to the locker room and changed into a clean uniform, transferring his gun from the waist pack to his holster and knowing by the end of shift he was going to be a stinking, sweaty mess having to wear all the gear and long pants. Luckily the turnaround time for dry cleaning for their uniforms was quick, since during the summer, they sweat like pigs.

His ass received a discreet caress. He smiled at Mickey, who was dressed in his uniform and leaning beside him as Jeff finished getting ready. "Already wanna fuck you."

Jeff laughed and looked around the area. There were men getting changed around them, laughing and chatting together. Mickey and Jeff were partners for so long, no one would think it was strange for them to be best friends. Did anyone know they lived together? He had no idea. But neither he nor Mickey socialized with other cops on their division.

Mickey pulled something out of his pocket to show Jeff secretly. Jeff peeked. Mickey had tiny packets of lubrication.

"Oh, Christ, Stanton." Jeff cracked up. "Bad enough we suck each other." After he had pinned his badge to his shirt, he picked the cardboard cup off the top of the locker and finished the coffee, tossing it into the trash.

"Sex on duty. The final frontier."

Jeff couldn't stop laughing, tucking in his shirt, making sure his gun belt was snapped on with the leather keepers. He gave the handgrip of the Glock a tug, ensuring it was secured in the holster, and shut the locker door. "You're a madman." Jeff hung his sunglasses from his breast pocket.

"You fell for one. Don't blame me."

Jeff started heading out of the locker room, passing sinks with a mirrored wall behind it, and stalls and urinals opposite. He glanced into the mirror, first catching his own green eyes, then spotted Mickey's wicked smirk.

They entered the roll call room and took the same seats they had done since he and Mickey became a permanent two-man car. Everyone sat in the same place. Why? Jeff had no idea. He remembered when he was the newbie, he actually stood on the side of the room, not wanting a confrontation about sitting in someone's chair, yes, it was that territorial.

The room filled up with cops, gossiping, drinking coffee, and getting to their seats as roll call was about to begin. Mickey and Jeff sat side by side, as usual, at a table facing the front of the room. Flo and Chris sat in the row ahead of them, and immediately Flo spun around to ask, "How did your training go?"

Jeff showed his skinned knuckles. "Only this to complain about."

Flo raised up the material of her short-sleeved uniform shirt exposing a large black and blue bruise. "My medal of honor."

Mickey winced. "Fucking paintballs hurt."

She shrugged and tugged the sleeve down. "Wasn't considered life threatening so I passed." Flo pushed Chris teasingly. "He has to do it tonight."

"Shut up." Chris didn't turn around, sitting facing the front, his elbows on the table.

Mickey teased Chris, "SWAT's gonna kill ya on that tactical night search."

Jeff nudged Mickey to stop, but Jeff knew Chris was aware they were just joking with him.

"Shut up, Stanton." Chris still did not look back at them.

Ages ago, Chris had nearly caught Jeff giving Mickey a blowjob in the patrol car, but they had successfully convinced Chris he did not see what he thought he saw. That Jeff was merely picking up a pen he dropped when he raised his head from what appeared to be Mickey's lap.

Jeff didn't know if they were fooling anyone, but he also didn't think his personal life was anyone's business.

Two sergeants entered, holding clipboards and sat at the table at the head of the room.

Jeff yawned and knew no matter how much caffeine he ingested it would do nothing but make him have to pee.

~

It was Jeff's turn to drive, and Mickey's turn to write.

Once they were updated on anything new that the shift coming on duty had to know, they were let loose onto the streets to battle the chaos.

They walked through the parking lot which was filled with black and white patrol cars and located theirs by its ID number. Jeff sat behind the wheel, getting the engine running with the A/C as Mickey checked the contents of the trunk and placed his bag with his own items inside it. While Mickey made sure they had flares, first aid supplies, cones and a fingerprint kit, Jeff did a check on the shotgun. Each patrol car contained one, locked inside a holder behind their seat. It was fully loaded and ready to go if needed. Once they gave the car a onceover for damage, so they didn't get blamed if something happened on a previous shift, they dropped heavily in the seats. Mickey used the car's mobile computer to log them on, getting them ready for service.

Jeff lowered the vehicle's dispatch radio while he shut his personal radio off completely. He watched the changing of the guard as the weary LAPD cops left for the day and others set out to begin their long shift. He often wondered why civilians were so quick to judge the men and women in uniform, but in reality, there were a few bad cops that made it crappy for them all. And even worse, bad decisions made by the brass. But no matter what happened politically, the boys on the front lines bore the brunt of the verbal and political abuse.

"Eight-Adam-One."

Jeff blinked at dispatch calling them the second they logged on. "Jesus, that was quick."

Mickey picked up the mike, responding, "Eight-Adam-One."

"Eleven-twenty-five, location on your screen."

"Ten-four." Mickey leaned over to see the details of the call on the computer that was attached to the dashboard.

Jeff knew an eleven-twenty-five was some kind of traffic hazard, but that could be anything from garbage in the street to a disabled car.

Mickey said, "It's been holding for an hour. Probably nothing there."

Jeff read the address and noticed the complainant was just an anonymous cell phone caller. He nodded and drove out of the precinct lot, wondering what the day held for them. Patrol was like that proverbial box of *Forrest Gump* chocolates. But unfortunately, most of the bites were nasty and needed to be spat out.

~

Mickey scanned the traffic up ahead to see if it appeared as if anything was creating unusual movements in the flow. He picked up the mike and told dispatch, "Eight-Adam-One, ten-ninety-seven," letting her know they had arrived.

"Ten-four, Eight-Adam-One."

Jeff slowed the car down to a crawl and the two of them inched along the heavy congestion of vehicles to try and figure out if whatever was there earlier, had gone. Jeff said, pointing, "You think that was it?"

Mickey leaned closer to him to see out of Jeff's side of the car. A dead Irish Setter dog was in the road. "Oh fuck. Poor thing."

Jeff kept driving, then made a U-turn and blocked the spot where the dog was lying. They got out of the patrol car and took a look. It was freshly killed but in the heat, the flies were already circling.

Mickey felt sick for the owner, since the dog did have a collar on.

Jeff knelt down to inspect the tag.

Mickey keyed his mike, "Eight-Adam-One."

"Eight-Adam-One."

"Ten-ninety-one –David. Request animal control."

"Eight-Adam-One, roger."

Jeff stood up and shook his head. "Ginger was her name."

"We should get her out of the street." Mickey removed a pair of latex gloves from his pocket and put them on as Jeff did the same. "Some kid is going to be devastated." He stood near the front of the dog as Jeff moved to the hind quarters. Each held the animal's legs and carried it to the sidewalk.

Pedestrians passed and made sounds of upset, but kept moving.

They set the dog down gently and Mickey took off his gloves. "No need to wait. Animal control will find her."

Jeff snapped his gloves off and headed back to the car. They both sat down in their seats and tossed the gloves on the floor of the patrol car to throw out later.

"Fucked up way to start the day." Jeff waited for a gap in traffic to drive off.

"Breaks my heart, Jeff." Mickey stared at the still corpse.

"Clear the call. Let's go." Jeff merged into traffic.

"Eight-Adam-one," Mickey said into the car microphone, "Ten-twenty-six."

"Roger, Eight-Adam-One, is ten-twenty-six."

"Why do I have a feeling that is going to be an omen for a very fucked up day?" Mickey said.

"Shut up, Stanton."

"No. You shut up." Mickey whacked him on the vest.

~

Jeff kept scanning the area for traffic violations or suspicious people as he drove the now familiar territory of their district. When he first hit LA he was lost and had to rely on Mickey to direct him, especially when the call was urgent and he was under pressure. But three years later, he knew every alley, every hotspot for drugs, prostitution, crack houses…he knew it all.

And since, in Jeff's opinion, the court system was broken, he and Mickey arrested the same people week after week, in a revolving door of in-and-out-of-jail games.

Warrants were issued. Duh! Did the judge really think someone who lived in a crack house would show up for a hearing?

If Jeff thought about that aspect of the job, he'd lose it. So, he didn't. He thought about being a hero…or at least trying to keep people safe. He cruised the areas of town with the highest incidents of burglary or car theft. Between calls for service, he did what he could to act as a deterrent, but the staffing was low, and there never seemed to be a hiring boom for cops…anywhere.

The dispatcher called them after a lull which lasted a whole half hour.

Mickey answered and they stared at the computer as it beeped and a call for service with the address and details popped up.

"Eight-Adam-One, assist fire. Details on your screen."

Jeff tried to read it and drive at the same time. "Wow, she didn't broadcast much. What's going on, Mick?"

"Eight-Adam-One, roger." Mickey clipped the microphone back on the metal holder and read aloud the information as Jeff started heading to the address. "Says, it was originally a medical call but on arrival, fire backed out and is calling for police assistance."

"That's it?"

"That's it. It's at that cheap motel we get a lot of weird calls from."

"I saw the location. What the fuck?" The most dangerous incidents were usually the ones they knew nothing about.

Jeff pulled into the motel lot and there was one large fire rig already there, along with a medic unit. To their delight, they recognized two of the firefighters.

Jeff and Mickey hopped out of the car and approached Blake Hughes and Hunter Rasmussen, two LAFD men who they had a close personal relationship with. Hunter and Blake were gay and partners, and they socialized with them quite often.

Although when they met off duty, Jeff kissed each man hello, he could see many spectators and fire officials lingering so he resisted the urge. "Hey, what do you have in there?"

Mickey kept his eye on the unit door, which appeared slightly ajar.

Hunter said, "We got the call as a medical emergency, but when we knocked we heard something weird inside. We busted the door to get in, but the lieutenant had us back out and wait for you to clear it."

Jeff met Blake's serious gaze and nodded. "Okay. Back the fuck up. Get behind your truck." Jeff drew his weapon and he and Mickey cautiously approached the door, guns pointed downward.

Mickey keyed the microphone of his lapel radio telling dispatch, "Eight-Adam-One, ten-sixty-six, attempting contact."

Jeff, his finger indexed, off the trigger, started to drip from sweat from the heat and his nerves as he and Mickey had no idea what was behind the door.

"Roger, Eight-Adam-One, requesting back-up?"

"Negative." Mickey placed both hands on his weapon and nodded for Jeff to knock.

Standing on either side of the door, in case bullets began firing through it, Jeff hit it hard and yelled, "Los Angeles Police! Come to the door!"

A very strange sounding voice said, "Help me! Please!"

Mickey and Jeff exchanged skeptical glances. Jeff touched the doorknob. The lock had obviously been broken open by the firemen.

They exchanged another glance at each other and both got ready with their weapons. Jeff kicked back the door but neither of them entered. "Where are you!" Jeff shouted, "Come out now!"

"I can't! Help me!"

"Fuck." Mickey stepped in, searching the bedroom area of the small motel room, gun pointed at eye level.

"In here!" the voice yelled.

Both Jeff and Mickey pointed their weapons to a hall where a light was on inside a room to the left.

"Show me your hands!" Jeff ordered, loud and deep.

"Now!" Mickey aimed at the doorway.

Two bloody hands poked out through the open door.

Jeff felt sick. "Get out here! Now! Keep your hands were we can see them!"

"I can't! Please! Help me!"

Mickey kept his gun aimed and ordered, "Do not move your hands!"

A whimpering cry came from the inside of the room.

Jeff and Mickey walked closer, seeing those two hands, dripping with red. Mickey turned the corner first, gun pointing inside it. Then he lowered it and said, "Oh fuck."

Jeff immediately looked in. A man, naked, was seated on the toilet, a power saw was on the floor, bloody, and red spatter was everywhere.

"Help me!" The man was weeping and could not move.

Jeff holstered his weapon and ran outside, "Guys!" He waved to the fire crew.

Blake and Hunter raced in.

"He's cut himself." Jeff felt like throwing up.

"Suicide?" Blake rushed in.

Both Hunter and Blake halted when they saw what Jeff and Mickey had seen. Mickey holstered his gun and backed up, appearing pale.

Two other medics rushed in with a gurney and Jeff and Mickey searched the bedroom, seeing nothing amiss, but finding an envelope on the bed. Cries were heard from the man inside the bathroom, and soon he was on the gurney, getting wheeled out.

Blake said, "Just hold this towel on yourself!" to the man on the gurney.

Mickey covered his mouth in disgust and Hunter shot Jeff a glance of disbelief. The man was holding the towel over his own crotch as they rushed him out of the motel to the hospital.

Jeff took the paperwork out of the envelope. It was a letter to a psychiatrist. When he read it, he felt as if he was going to faint.

Mickey didn't look too good either. "We gotta bag that shit for the twenty-four hour hold." He left the motel room.

Hearing sirens blasting as the medic unit drove off, Jeff read how this man didn't want to have a penis anymore and was upset no one would help him. Jeff couldn't get through all of the wordy rambling of what appeared to be from a very sick man, and slid the letter back into the envelope to submit as evidence. Mickey returned, holding a camera and a few bags for the evidence collection.

Once photos were taken, including a toilet full of red water and a pair of scissors on the floor near the saw, Jeff gloved up and began collecting everything to place into evidence. Neither he nor Mickey said a word, each sick to their stomachs.

They dumped the items into the trunk of their patrol car and told dispatch, “Eight-Adam-One, ten-nineteen, with evidence.”

“Roger, Eight-Adam-One.”

Jeff tossed the gloves into a trash can by the motel and sat down, blowing the cool air at his face. “Not a suicide.”

“Nope.” Mickey kept his mouth covered as if he may be sick.

“What would cause a man to do that to himself?” Jeff shivered visibly and kept one hand over his groin as he drove.

“Fuck. I don’t want to think about it.”

They parked at the station and gloved up once more, just to carry the items to place into evidence, with the paperwork Jeff had found. Mickey headed to the write-up area to get the report done for a mental evaluation, and while he did, Jeff stopped at the men’s locker to wash his hands and face. He wouldn’t get that image out of his head for the rest of his life.

After he cleaned up, he relieved himself, holding his cock, staring at it, and shivering with disgust at the idea of trying to cut it off. He bit his lip in horror, and finished quickly, needing to get those thoughts removed from his brain.

Seeing Mickey still typing at a computer, Jeff headed to the secretary’s office and knocked on her open door frame.

“Hi, Jeff.”

“Hi, Missy. Sgt Adkins said you had all the paperwork for what I needed to study for the sergeant’s exam.”

“I do.” She opened a file and handed Jeff a packet, thick with information.”

“Crap. And this is only the instructions?” he tried to laugh as he replied but he was horrified at the amount of work.

“Yes. Sorry. You need to memorize all the LA city codes, the state and county codes…you know. Proper procedure, the works. It’s not an easy exam.”

“Ya think?” Jeff fanned through the pamphlet to see all the information he had to accumulate to get this studying done.

“At least now it’s on computer. I used to have to hand out the big book of study guides before. Weighed a ton.”

“Thanks.”

"Is Mickey testing?"

"Oh. Uh. I don't think so. And, don't tell him I am, okay? I probably won't make the list anyway."

The older woman made a gesture of locking her lips with a key and Jeff smiled as he left. He quickly brought the folder to his locker and hid it into a sack he used for his dirty clothing, then went to find Mickey.

Mickey was staring at the screen, but not typing.

Jeff pulled over a chair and read what he wrote. "What else can ya say?" Jeff shrugged. "Just leave it at that."

Mickey nodded and hit the print button. "And I was thinking of stopping at the fire station for lunch."

"Good idea. I just hope they aren't making sausages."

Mickey gave Jeff a look of disbelief then actually smiled. "What a job, huh, Jeff? What a crazy ass job."

"Well, we can at least tease Blake and Hunt about not having the balls to go in without their big brawny cop heroes first."

"Do you fucking blame them? When I saw those two bloody fucking hands?" Mickey winced.

"Stop. I can't deal with it. Seriously. If I don't make a joke out of this, I'll need a rubber room."

Mickey logged off of the computer and headed to the printer. He distributed the hard copies to the few who needed them, and the rest was sent electronically.

"Let me take a piss and wash my hands." Mickey held his hands up as he they were repugnant.

"Go. I'll wait here." Jeff watched him walk down the florescent lit corridor, knowing half of him didn't want to take this exam but the other half, wanted to get the hell off the front lines.

Chapter Three

Mickey heard his stomach grumble as they drove out of the precinct parking lot. "Head to the fire station."

"Yeah?" Jeff said, "I was thinking of hitting our favorite Mexican restaurant."

"Nah. We'll do that tomorrow. I need to see the boys." Mickey leaned his arm on the passenger's door-rest and pointed a vent at his face, hot from the heavy gear.

"Okay." Jeff drove to the firehouse while they remained on the last call, waiting to get to their destination before asking for a meal break. The last thing you wanted to do was spend your precious break time driving to get where you needed to be, giving you less time to actually eat.

He parked the patrol car on the side of the building, seeing the bay doors open and all the big red fire trucks inside.

Mickey picked up the mike and cleared their last call and asked, "Request code seven?"

"Eight-Adam-One, code seven."

Mickey hung up the microphone, turned his personal radio on, and checked his watch. He climbed out of the car and both he and Jeff headed through the open bay to the interior of the station house. The minute they walked in, Jeff sniffed the air and moaned, "Mm. Perfect timing."

Mickey checked his watch. "Well, it is six."

He heard laughter and loud chatter as he approached, and there was Blake wearing an apron over his uniform, at the stove, while Hunter, Hailey Barnet and Kim Lu helped set the table and cut up salad.

"Uh oh." Hunter spotted them approaching, "The cops are here. Hide the dope."

"Jeff! Mick!" Blake smiled happily, stirring a pot of tomato sauce.

Hailey laughed. "Do you guys have food detectors as well as radar detectors?"

"I can smell Blake's cooking from the West Bureau's parking lot," Jeff teased.

"Sit down. What can I get you to drink?" Kim asked, gesturing to the table.

"Water, thanks," Jeff replied. "Man, did you guys get over that last call already?" Jeff sat down. "You seem so normal."

Mickey nodded his head in thanks as Kim gave him a bottle of water as well, and then Mickey sat beside Jeff. He watched Blake strain the pasta in a colander in the sink.

Hailey laughed at Jeff's comment. "These three guys have been cringing and holding their groins since they came back."

"God!" Blake said, "Can we not discuss it while we eat?"

Jeff asked Kim quietly, "What did the ER docs say?"

"They can sew it back on. He hadn't taken it all the way off." Kim glanced at Blake.

"Gross!" Hunter shivered comically and put a basket of bread on the table. "Why? Oh, Christ why, would someone do that to themselves?"

Mickey looked at Jeff, shaking his head not to tell them, since they had read the letter left by the victim. "Don't."

Jeff picked up a roll and split it, buttering it.

Blake brought a huge bowl of spaghetti and meatballs to the table and said, "Dig in." He joined them at the table and they all ate with hearty appetites, despite the last call.

"Where's the lieutenant?" Hunter asked with his mouth full.

"Shit." Hailey hopped up. "I'll get him." She trotted off.

"Keep your L-T happy, boys," Jeff said, smiling.

A minute later Hailey returned and said, “He’ll be out in a minute, he’s on the phone.”

Blake wiped his mouth on a napkin and asked, “You guys see any of our friends recently?”

Jeff shook his head. “No. Between our shitty shift and getting mostly weekdays off lately, we haven’t. You?”

Hunter said, “We had Josh and Tanner over for a barbeque.”

“And you didn’t call us?” Jeff asked, his mouth full of pasta.

Mickey replied, “They did. We were working.”

“Dang.” Jeff guzzled the water and checked his watch.

They ate quietly for a few minutes, the two police radios and the fire dispatch muttering calls in the background. When you were a first responder, you learned to listen as you did everything else, so you knew when you had to drop and run.

“Been a fucked up day already,” Jeff said, “We started the shift with a dead dog screwing up traffic.”

“That is so sad.” Hailey pouted.

“Poor thing.” Hunter shook his head.

“Then we get this fucking guy—” Jeff began.

Mickey elbowed him. “Not while I’m eating, Chandler!”

“What? Mick, come on, we’ve gone on gross calls before.”

Hunter took more pasta from the bowl. “Not like that. No way. That’s a first for me and Blake.”

Kim shuddered and frowned. “It was sick. I never want to even think of that shit again.”

Mickey gave Jeff a look of admonishment. “Happy now? Now all we can think about is that scene.”

Hailey said, “And the red spaghetti sauce.”

“Shut up,” Blake said, laughing.

“Glad I’m not a guy.” Hailey smiled.

The rest of them kept quiet and Mickey wished he could forget the incident completely.

~

Hours after their lunch break with Blake and Hunter, Jeff stared into space as Mickey typed a report for an auto theft on their mobile computer. He was parked in the church lot they occupied when they wanted peace and quiet and…after dark, as a place to play.

The lot was expansive and surrounded by shrubs and trees, making it a good place to be left alone. By backing into the corner, you had a grand view of anyone or anything that drove into the area before they could come up close and disrupt them.

The sun was beginning to angle down but since it was July, it was still light at nine o'clock. Jeff was beginning to wear out from the long shift hours and rubbed his face, yawning. He placed his sunglasses on the dashboard. As Mickey typed beside him, Jeff closed his eyes and could easily nap. In the background the dispatcher was sending cops to domestic violence calls, traffic accidents, suspicious activity…everywhere and to everything.

Jeff didn't realize he'd dozed until he woke when he felt a touch to his thigh. Mickey had obviously finished the report and scooted closer. "Tired, baby?"

"I am. I'm exhausted."

Mickey reached for Jeff's jaw and turned it to face him. The kiss was tender and loving, a side of Mickey Jeff knew and enjoyed, but they tended to act quite the opposite most times.

After the kiss Mickey looked around the abandoned parking lot, rubbing his hand over Jeff's crotch. Jeff knew what his lover wanted. "I'm so tired I don't know if I can get it up."

Mickey dug deeper under Jeff's balls and scooted even closer so he could kiss his neck. "Bullshit."

Jeff chuckled as chills of pleasure began to build, and he did indeed feel his cock begin to swell.

"Wanna suck you, bitch." Mickey chewed on Jeff's jaw and earlobe sending chills over Jeff's skin.

"Dirty, dirty pig." Jeff smiled, still relaxed in the driver's seat, but now with his legs straddled as he enjoyed the crotch rub.

Mickey went for Jeff's zipper flap, pushing back the material.

"Some days I hate this uniform." Jeff looked down at the heavy vest, the weighty gun belt, long dark pants…

Mickey ignored him, working on getting the zipper down.

Jeff caressed Mickey's blond hair, seeing his determination to get at his cock. Something caught his attention. He tapped Mickey. "Mick, sit up."

Mickey instantly moved upright in the seat.

A car pulled into the lot, seemed to spot them, and made a circle to get out quickly.

"Go!" Mickey pointed, buckling his seatbelt.

Jeff hit the gas and grabbed his sunglasses as they skidded across the dashboard. He put them on his face and nailed the pedal to the floor, hearing the heavy engine of the powerfully built patrol car whine as it went from zero to sixty in mere seconds.

"Right turn!" Mickey pointed as he spotted the car. It was a dark sedan and they couldn't get close enough yet to get the license plate. Zigzagging around the traffic, which was always heavy in LA, Mickey leaned closer to the windshield as if trying to see the plate number. Then he began typing on the computer.

Jeff couldn't read it yet, and was focused on getting on top of the car without turning on his lights and sirens. The occupants hadn't done anything illegal at the moment.

"Stolen hit." Mickey grabbed the microphone. "Eight-Adam-One."

"Eight-Adam-One."

"Possible code thirty-seven, license plate number…"

Jeff could tell the occupant of the stolen car knew they were onto him as his driving became more erratic. Jeff turned on the overhead lights and sirens while Mickey got verification it was indeed a stolen car, and he broadcast the location they were chasing it.

"Eight-Adam-One is in pursuit, code-three."

The air became jammed with other officers offering to back them up, and Jeff kept pace with the stolen car enough to not lose it, but it was beginning to blow through red traffic lights and stop signs without hesitation. No way was Jeff going to allow them to get broadsided over a stolen car.

As the rest of the LA vehicle traffic either stopped short or tried to get the heck out of their way, Jeff slowed at the intersections because people simply did not pay attention. Mickey kept broadcasting their location over the air, describing the direction of the suspect vehicle.

Jeff changed the sound of his siren from wail to yelp to wail, to keep the rest of the civilian traffic alert. The stolen car rode over a curb, hit a parked car and kept going.

“Motherfucker!” Mickey said, “What the hell do we have here?” He advised the dispatcher the stolen car had just hit a parked vehicle and the location of the accident.

“How many in the car, Mick? I only see one. The driver.”

“That’s all I see.” Mickey held onto the dashboard with his right hand and used the radio with his left to keep dispatch in constant communication.

Behind him, Jeff could see three other marked units flying after him, all spinning lights and blaring sirens.

The LA traffic had come to a complete stop as this caravan of emergency vehicles flew like a crazy train down a broken track.

Jeff looked up ahead and noticed a State Patrol motorcycle cop spot the incident and he too flew after the stolen car behind their caravan of black and white.

“This asshole’s going to crash again and kill someone,” Jeff said, “Mick, he’s losing control completely.”

It was then Jeff heard their sergeant on the radio asking for their vehicle speeds. That was an indication he was worried too, even though he was not on the pursuit, or at least they didn’t hear him say he was with them if he had.

Then up ahead, Jeff spotted a billow of smoke and debris flying. “Fuck!”

Mickey told radio, “Suspect has crashed.”

Jeff and Mickey were the first to arrive, and the one man from inside the car emerged from the smoldering wreck and took off. Jeff threw the patrol car into park and ran after him, seeing a black semi-automatic pistol on the sidewalk as if the suspect had dropped it. Mickey picked it up as he ran, tucking it into the back of his belt and they began a foot pursuit.

The dispatcher called to them, "Eight-Adam-One, your ten-twenty?"

Jeff had no idea where they were. He was just trying to keep the man in sight.

Mickey got on radio, to reply as he ran, "Need containment! Westbound from scene of the accident! White male, twenties, approximately five-ten, slender, wearing a black baseball cap, green shirt and blue jeans…"

"Eight-Adam-One." Jeff keyed his mike as he ran, "Request K-9. Any K-9 officers available?"

"Eight-Adam-One, requesting K-9." The dispatcher then repeated the description of the suspect Mickey had supplied as well as their location.

Noise of a helicopter began to intrude on everything else, and Jeff had lost sight of the suspect.

Another unit asked, "Last ten-twenty for suspect?"

Mickey and Jeff stopped short and spun around, looking for a sign of the guy.

"Where'd the fucker go?" Jeff caught his breath, sweat pouring down his face.

Mickey looked up at a helicopter circling. He keyed his mike, "Eight-Adam-One. Any luck on K-9?"

"Eight-Adam-One. Affirmative. ETA twenty."

Another officer ran up towards them, catching his breath. "You want me to hold the spot for the track?"

"Yeah. We need to head back to the stolen car." Jeff wiped at the drops on his face.

"And this." Mickey put on rubber gloves and removed a gun from behind his back. "He dropped it at the scene."

Jeff shook his head in dismay and they started their walk back to the abandoned stolen car as units flooded the area for containment.

The sedan had crashed into a cement column of an apartment building's underground carport. Mickey stood behind their patrol car at the open trunk, and removed the clip and the single chambered round from the suspect's gun, placing it all into an evidence envelope. Jeff looked into the car which was still running, smoking and hissing. He shut off the ignition with a screwdriver that was poking out of it. While other units continued the hunt and they waited for a K-9 unit, Jeff and Mickey searched the car. Jeff popped the trunk and blinked in shock. "Mick."

Mickey walked to stand beside him. "Oh, no fucking way."

Inside the trunk was an automatic AK assault rifle with a huge extended clip, a ski mask, a sack loaded with bank bundles of cash, boxes of ammunition, metal containers and spare clothing.

Jeff shook his head and called for a supervisor to respond to the scene.

He heard Sgt Adkins reply, "Eight-Lincoln-Twenty, ten-four."

The CHP officer rolled his motorcycle closer to talk to them. "Lose him, boys?"

"Yeah. No clue if we got him contained." Jeff pointed to the trunk. "Looks like he robbed a bank."

The motorcycle officer leaned over to peek into the trunk. "Good catch. You'll find him. Good luck." He waved and drove off.

The sergeant pulled up nearby and exited his patrol car. He took one look into the trunk and said, "You boys found a live one, didn't you? Let me see if the FBI task force wants to have a look." He took his mobile phone out of his pocket and stepped aside.

Mickey and Jeff finished a search of inside the car, but there was nothing in the passenger's compartment but trash and cigarette butts.

As if they had been in the area, an unmarked unit rolled up and two plainclothes detectives stepped out. Nodding, as the sergeant filled them in, they walked towards the trunk and looked in. "Get this car towed to the evidence lot. We'll process it there."

Mickey acknowledged him and switched tactical frequencies to call for a tow truck.

Jeff kept his ear to his radio when suddenly the dispatcher said, "All units -code thirty-three- resident just came home to find intruder inside his apartment."

Jeff looked up at the windows of the apartments they were standing right in front of.

Hearing the address, Jeff said, "The fucker doubled back to get to his car!"

They scrambled to take cover and Mickey and Jeff crouched behind their patrol car, looking up at the apartment building right where the stolen car had crashed.

Sgt Adkins told dispatch, "Eight-Lincoln-Twenty requesting SWAT. All units maintain containment."

"Roger, Eight-Lincoln-Twenty. Is there a SWAT commander monitoring radio?" dispatch asked.

"Roger, code three."

Mickey took out his weapon and held it at his side, staring up at the apartment building as he did. "We were standing there? Like sitting ducks?"

"He dropped his gun." Jeff had both his hands on the grip of his pistol, crouched low, pointing it down.

"He dropped one gun. How the hell do you know he's not carrying an arsenal?"

The helicopter was annoying and loud as it circled. A noise of a truck engine came up behind them. The tow truck parked and the driver got out.

Mickey ran towards him and Jeff saw him waving at him to stay back. Jeff dabbed at his sweat and watched the tow truck driver go pale and park around the corner to wait.

A K-9 officer arrived and Jeff could hear his dog going ballistic in the back seat. He too parked and they all sat tight for SWAT's arrival.

Since this was a high priority incident, the radio air traffic went dead except for anything involving what they were doing right here, with this crazy man and the stolen car.

Mickey returned to crouch beside Jeff and Jeff could see the sweat rolling down his temples as they cooked behind their own patrol car, which was running, overhead lights still rotating.

After what felt like forever to Jeff, SWAT pulled behind them in their personnel carrier and waited to be briefed by the sergeant and the FBI task force. Jeff and Mickey stayed put. They had no idea which unit in the apartment building had been broken into.

"Bet the fucker is watching everything on the news." Mickey wiped at is face quickly, his hand still on his gun.

"Yup. Or out a window."

The sound of the SWAT team's heavy boots were heard running beside them. The dog was with its handler, jogging along with them, going crazy, ready to chew someone up.

They all stayed in place as SWAT made entry into the building the car had hit. In the dead silence Jeff could hear the roars of orders from SWAT, and the smashing of doors. Jeff closed his eyes to pray the fucker did not have another weapon.

In mere minutes, SWAT escorted a man outside in handcuffs, placing him into the FBI task force's sedan's back seat. Jeff and Mickey stood, holstering their weapons. The sergeant waved them over after discussing the arrest with a SWAT commander.

"Can you ID the guy?"

"Yup." Mickey and Jeff both nodded. They walked over to the sedan and looked into the back seat.

"Affirmative, sir." Mickey nodded.

"Ditto. That's him."

The sergeant handed them a piece of paper from his pad. "Here's his name and DOB for your report. Just write up the stolen recovery. The task force will handle the property in the trunk and we'll get a traffic unit to take the hit and run accident he also is responsible for."

"Let me give them the gun he dropped." Mickey headed to the trunk of their patrol car.

"Gun he dropped?" Sgt Adkins did not look pleased.

Jeff said, "After he hit the pole and fled, he dropped the gun on the sidewalk. Must have fallen out of his pants."

Mickey brought the weapon over and handed it to the sergeant.

"Good work, guys."

"Thanks." Jeff pointed down the street. "Let me get the tow truck driver over here to hook it."

"Okay."

Jeff walked down the block to where the man was parked and waiting, wondering what would have happened if…if the suspect had not dropped the gun. Since they had no idea he had doubled back and was right on top of them when they were searching the car, they simply would never have seen it coming.

"Go hook the car. Bring it directly to the evidence garage for processing."

"You got it."

By the time Jeff walked back to their patrol car, Mickey was sitting in it, running the suspect's name on the computer. Jeff moved their patrol car to get it out of the way for the tow truck driver and headed back to the station so they could write up the report.

Mickey read the notices off the computer, "Felony warrant; assault with a deadly weapon. Felony warrant; felon in possession, felony warrant, grand theft… total of warrants? Fifty thousand bucks."

"And yet he is out on the street." Jeff had no idea why the system was so screwed up. "Glad he dropped his gun, babe."

Mickey held Jeff's thigh and squeezed it.

Jeff cupped his hand over Mickey's and wondered how long their 'police angel' would keep watch over them. They had a lot of close calls.

Chapter Four

While Mickey worked at a precinct computer, typing up the report, Jeff sat opposite him, behind a divider, looking up the information for what he had to do to test for sergeant in the upcoming exam. He read the dry information; city codes, department rules and regulations…state penal code…

Jeff rubbed his face and if he and Mickey didn't live together, Jeff could actually begin studying over their days off to kick-start this grueling exam.

He had to tell Mickey.

He shut down the computer and was very glad they could hold this call until the end of shift, because Jeff simply could not motivate himself to get up off the chair, let alone go out and answer more 911 calls.

He heard Mickey talking and gathered up the energy to stand up, walking around a small divider to see several men in plain clothing patting Mickey on the back.

One spotted Jeff and smiled. "Officer Chandler."

"Yes?" Jeff crossed his arms and leaned on the desk where Mickey was working.

"The money in the back of the suspect's car matched the serial numbers of a bank robbery committed in East LA early this morning. Well done." He reached out his hand. "We got a full confession. Fucker doubled back to the car to get his AK, when he spotted you two returning. That's when he kicked in a side door at the apartment house, gained entry and also broke through a private door to a unit. When SWAT nailed him he was using the apartment owner's phone to call his girlfriend, crying he was going to be locked up for years." The officer made a face at how pathetic it was. "They're only going to charge him with trespass for that break-in, since he had no intent to take anything."

"Typical." Mickey kept typing.

"I need statements from you both, how you located the car, right up until we showed up."

Mickey and Jeff exchanged glances, knowing they spotted the car when it pulled into the church lot. Where they were hiding. About to have oral sex.

Mickey said, looking at Jeff, "We located him while we were cruising down Wilshire."

"Just looked hinky, so we ran the plate." Jeff got the silent message from Mickey so he played along.

"Love it. Write it up." The man patted both Mickey and Jeff in gratitude and Jeff sat at the available computer beside Mickey and booted it up.

Mickey said quietly as he typed, "I was sitting beside my gorgeous partner, and about to suck his big delicious dick when…"

Jeff laughed and shook his head. "Okay, so driving down Wilshire."

"Well, that is where we were."

"Got it." Jeff tapped keys, typing the statement. "It'll never go to court. He'll plead."

Mickey laughed sarcastically. "He's probably already out on bail. We're the morons who are still working and risked our lives."

Jeff thought about it. "No. With that many outstanding warrants? He's a flight risk."

"You have much to learn, Chandler." Mickey finished typing his statement and said, "Ya wanna read it? Make sure we jive?"

Jeff scooted over and Mickey took a quick sniff of his hair then backed up, crossing his arms.

Jeff read the statement and nodded. “It’s what happened.” He rolled the chair back to his computer and finished it up, hitting print and send.

“I’m done. I don’t want to do another thing tonight.” Mickey yawned and looked at his watch.

“We can milk this for a bit.”

“I know what I wanna milk.” Mickey grinned wickedly.

Jeff swatted his shoulder and walked to the printer, getting the paperwork for their sergeant and lieutenant. He placed all the associated information into an envelope and put one on each of their desks. When he returned to the computer, Mickey tilted his head to Jeff and they left the station, walking back to the patrol car.

“Let’s park somewhere for the rest of shift, and we’re done.” Mickey sat in the passenger’s side.

“You got it. But not the church lot.” Jeff started the car and shut off his personal radio as the one in the car came on.

“That’s our spot.”

“Maybe we need a new one.”

“If you cruise around too much, we’ll get flagged down for some petty bullshit. I can’t write up one more report, Jeff. I’m fried.”

Jeff tried to think as he drove. “Fuck it. We’ll go back to the church. What are the odds another stolen car will pull in there?”

“After the shit calls we’ve had today?” Mickey moaned.

“We’re done. No more.” Jeff pulled into the lot and as he usually did, backed all the way into the corner and tossed his sunglasses on the dash. “Déjà vu?”

“Too tired to kiss me?”

“Never.” Jeff scooted closer, putting his arm around Mickey’s shoulders and they pressed their lips together.

Mickey caressed Jeff’s hair opening his mouth for a deeper kiss. What began as tender and sweet love, soon morphed into hot passion. Jeff felt Mickey’s hand between his legs and straddled wide for him. Yeah, they could fuck, would fuck, when they got home, but playing on duty was simply too hot to resist.

Jeff peeked at the parking lot and entrance occasionally as they kissed. Mickey was facing him, so it was up to Jeff to keep an eye on the surroundings.

Mickey took Jeff's hand and brought it to the spot over his uniform pants where he had grown erect. Jeff traced the length of Mickey's cock with his fingertips, then rubbed his palm over it.

It throbbed as he squeezed it, and Jeff moaned against Mickey's mouth.

He couldn't test for sergeant. Where would he be without his Mickey to play with?

Mickey shifted heavily in the seat beside him. It was so tight between their size and the equipment in the car, it was like trying to make out in a matchbox.

Mickey tugged on Jeff's bottom lip playfully between his teeth and went for Jeff's groin with his hand.

Jeff spread his legs wider, inviting the touch, addicted to their naughty play. He took another look around the empty lot and opened his zipper, exposing his cock.

Mickey didn't hesitate, diving down on him and sucking him into his mouth.

"Oh, Stanton…you give the best head." Jeff caressed Mickey's hair and swooned as his lover drew hard suction from the base to the tip. Mickey's hips shifted to get closer, and Jeff reached for the back of his trousers, dipping his fingers into Mickey's pants to his ass crack.

Mickey moaned and writhed on the seat, his bulk making him shake the mobile computer and his knees hitting the glove box.

Jeff stared at the powerful build of his man, his masculinity, the uniform, everything that made Mickey his perfect lover. Mickey rubbed underneath Jeff's balls through his uniform pants and Jeff began to rise to a climax. He leaned over Mickey's back to get to his rim and came, feeling Mickey's solid muscles tense and hearing him whimper as he swallowed. Jeff's heart was beating in his throat while he rested on Mickey's back as he recuperated.

Mickey sat up, leaned against the passenger's door, and exposed his dick.

Jeff looked around the deserted area again then crawled closer and put his face between Mickey's thighs. He closed his eyes and engulfed all of Mickey's length as Mickey sighed and combed his fingers through Jeff's hair.

"Suck me, you gorgeous fucking cop."

Jeff ran his palms up Mickey's chest, over his heavy vest. His right hand rested on Mickey's badge, his left he reached for the nape of Mickey's neck, touching skin.

Gripping that badge in his fingers, Jeff sucked his partner and let Mickey orally fuck him, thrusting into his mouth. He heard Mickey grunting and tasted his pre-cum. Then Mickey's cock hardened to stone in his mouth and Jeff sucked deeper. He felt Mickey's cock pulsating and tasted his cum, swallowing him down.

Mickey cupped Jeff's head and held on as he came, and Jeff kept a grip on that badge, that shield of honor that separated the men from the boys.

Mickey's breathing grew softer and Jeff felt his muscles relax. He sucked to the tip of Mickey's cock and then looked up at him.

The expression of exhaustion mixed with pure adoration was bliss to Jeff. "I love you, ya fucking bastard."

Mickey grabbed Jeff by his shoulders and urged him to his mouth. They kissed and there was a revelation in Jeff at that moment. Suddenly he didn't care who knew, who found them, or if they were ambushed by mad assailants. For the last three years of his life, and career, he had the most amazing partner on the planet. Heaven. It was at times, pure heaven.

He tasted the mixture of their cum and sweat on his tongue and the scents of their bodies on their mouths. Holding his lover, Jeff opened his lips, and closed his eyes, making out with his partner until the shift came to an end.

~

Changing into their civilian clothing, Mickey kept an eye on Jeff, since seeing him undress from his uniform was just as hot as seeing him in it.

Mickey tossed the heavy gun waist pack over his shoulder and shut his locker door. He spotted Jeff pick up a plastic sack and reached for it.

Jeff reacted strangely and pulled the bag away from Mickey. Mickey held up his T-shirt and socks from their shift. "I thought I'd stuff these in it."

"Oh." Jeff nodded and took the clothing and tucked it into the bag.

Mickey watched Jeff as Jeff made sure he had all his possessions and then shut the locker door. They walked out of the building together and into the cool night air.

"What's going on, Chandler?" Mickey took out his keys as they strolled through the dimly lit lot to the where the officers parked their personal cars.

"Huh?"

"Huh?" Mickey repeated in a mocking tone.

Jeff didn't reply and stood by the passenger's side of the truck. As they climbed into it, Jeff went to drop the plastic bag behind the seat, but Mickey caught it and set it on his lap, looking in.

Jeff exhaled a loud breath of frustration.

Mickey immediately spotted the paperwork for the sergeant's exam and then tossed the bag into the back seat. He dropped his gun-pack on the floor by Jeff's feet, started the truck, and fastened his safety belt.

"Well?" Jeff asked as Mickey backed out of the parking space.

"Fuck you." Mickey was hurt. First from the deception, then from the idea that when Jeff was promoted, they were gone, apart. Done working together.

"Mick."

When Jeff went to reach for him, Mickey jerked back. "Get the fuck away from me."

"I knew you'd react like this."

"Like what? Like you're an ass for not even mentioning to me you wanted to take the exam? Like that?"

"I'm burned out!" Jeff shouted, then lowered his voice. "I'm exhausted chasing 911 calls all day."

Mickey understood. What made the mad dashing all over their district tolerable for him was Jeff. If he didn't have Jeff with him, he too would find the work intolerable.

"Mick…" Jeff tried to touch him again as Mickey slowed for a red traffic light.

Mickey didn't push his hand off but wanted to. He stared into space out of the front windshield.

"You should too. You should get off patrol, test for detective or something."

"Just shut the fuck up." Mickey pushed Jeff's hand off his leg. They were so exhausted, Mickey knew whatever they said tonight was going to be regretted in the morning.

Waiting for the light to change, Mickey slouched in the driver's seat and tried not to think about it. The test wasn't for months, the results wouldn't come back for ages, and Jeff may not even do well enough to place on the list. Jeff had no military background, so he had nothing to help prop up his scores.

But…

The fact that it would happen one day, that Jeff and he would be split up? That upset Mickey on such a deep level, he hadn't been this hurt since the beginning of their relationship. At that time, Jeff had just moved to LA from Seattle, and wouldn't commit to him since he had just broken off another relationship.

After a silent drive home, Mickey parked. Before Jeff gathered his items, Mickey took his gun-pack and got out of the truck. Mickey left Jeff behind and headed to the door of their townhouse. He let himself in, tossed his pack on the coffee table and walked to the fridge for a beer.

He heard Jeff enter, then watched him climb the stairs to their bedroom.

Mickey twisted off the cap and guzzled the beer thirstily staring into space.

~

Jeff dumped their dirty laundry into a hamper and placed the packet for the sergeant's exam on the dresser. He stared at it, knowing he should have discussed it with Mickey, but he knew what his reaction would be. Jeff didn't want to be without him either. They watched over each other. Lovers *and* combat partners, there was never a stronger bond in all of military history.

He heard the television turn on downstairs and knew since they had tomorrow off, they had time to actually unwind before bed.

Jeff stripped and showered, preparing himself for sex with Mickey, figuring Mickey would want revenge sex.

Though he had a heart like a lion, and was faithful to a fault, Mickey Stanton had the temper of a cornered wolf, and the two of them had become violent on several occasions.

Jeff stood under the hot water spray and knew what he had done behind Mickey's back had broken Mickey's heart.

~

Drinking the beer, his feet propped up on the coffee table, the television on, Mickey took his phone out of his pocket and texted his sister, Aura. '*U wake?*'

It was nearing midnight and a weekday. He stared at the phone but nothing returned, so he set it on the side table and used the remote control to flip through TV channels. When nothing was on that interested him, he set up a video game and blew people apart with his macho avatar.

He heard the sound of Jeff coming down the stairs and didn't look back. Behind him Jeff scuffed his feet on the tiled kitchen floor and then sat beside Mickey on the sofa, a beer in his hand, wearing just a pair of briefs.

Mickey glanced over at him and spotted his wet hair, then continued playing the video game.

"I'm sorry." Jeff watched the screen as Mickey sliced through demons and skeletons. "I should have mentioned I was thinking about testing."

Mickey was too tired to discuss this, and wondered why Jeff was baiting him. He ignored him, taking his temper out on the cyber villains.

Silence past, Jeff drank his beer quietly beside him.

Mickey's avatar got blown up, so he put the control down and picked up his own beer, then checked his phone. Aura was obviously asleep, she never answered. He stood up to put the empty bottle into the recycle bin and headed upstairs.

"Mick!" Jeff sounded exasperated.

Mickey kept climbing the stairs and stood by the bed to strip for a shower. He stunk from working twelve hours in the boiling heat.

~

Jeff stared at the screen with the ended game still frozen on it. He switched on the television but quickly shut if off since there was never anything on. He sipped the beer and slouched low, wondering how long the silent treatment was going to last.

He stared at Mickey's gun pouch, which was on the coffee table. Giving up brooding for the night, since he was wiped out, Jeff rinsed the beer bottle and dumped it into a bin, then carried Mickey's gun up to their bedroom.

He heard the shower in the master bathroom and placed both their firearm packs side by side on the dresser, and turned down the bed. He tugged off his briefs, wondering why he had bothered to get ready for sex, since it didn't seem as if he was going to get any.

He spotted the lubrication on the nightstand near Mickey's cell phone, then checked his own phone quickly before he shut it off for the night. They had no plans for tomorrow, but it was Thursday so they could muster something up with the boys since they actually had the next three days off.

The shower stopped and Jeff looked at the closed door as he lay down on their bed. He felt guilty as hell. He was wrong. He never should have kept that information from Mickey, and yes, getting taken off patrol? No longer being an Adam car? The dynamic duo split up?

It broke Jeff's heart as well. But being on the front line day after day was literally killing him. At least as a sergeant he was a half a step back from the kill zone. The only problem was, he wanted to take Mickey with him, not abandon him.

The door to the bathroom opened and when Mickey stepped out naked, Jeff rolled to his side and stared at his big brawny frame. Mickey took his wallet from the shorts he had dropped on the floor. Jeff could see him open it, as if looking at his badge and police ID. Mickey set it with the guns and then spun around.

Jeff's cock perked up at the gaze of those punished blue eyes. Mickey shut off the overhead light, then lay on the bed, face up, his hands behind his head.

Jeff snuggled closer, smelling the musky soap and coconut shampoo fragrance from Mickey's skin. "Ya gonna be pissed at me for the next three days?"

Like a trained killer, Mickey had Jeff pinned to the bed in a split second, his hands braced on Jeff's shoulders. Mickey leaned up, and even in the dimness Jeff could see his snarl.

"Always knew it would be you that would break us up."

Jeff gaped at him. "Break us up? You mean here or at work?"

"It's the same fucking thing!" Mickey shook him violently.

"Stop!" Jeff grabbed Mickey's biceps and tried to prevent the coming fury. "I can't talk to you! You see?"

"*You* can't talk to *me*?" Mickey was breathing fire. "I'm right here!" Mickey roared, "Right fucking next to you in the car! In your goddamn bed at night!"

"Mick, please…" Jeff knew he fucked up.

"Fuck you!" Mickey shoved Jeff and stood off the bed.

Seeing Mickey headed outside the bedroom, Jeff raced after him. "You can't even sleep in the same bed with me? Are you kidding me, Stanton?" Jeff grabbed Mickey's shoulder and Mickey's reaction was immediate. He spun around and attacked Jeff, making them hit the wall of the townhouse and nearly fall down the flight of stairs. Jeff went into full training mode and knew with Mickey's power, a fair fight was going to be useless. He pinned Mickey to the wall by his throat and tried to gain control of his hands.

Mickey growled with so much anger, the hair rose on Jeff's skin. "Calm down." Jeff panted to catch his breath.

Mickey tore Jeff's hand from his throat and shoved him away. It was so powerful it made Jeff stumble up the stairs to land on his rump at the top landing. "Mick!"

Mickey came after Jeff like a bear let out of a trap. He wrestled with Jeff, dragging him by his arm to the bedroom. Jeff fought the pain of the police hold once more and struggled to get to his feet. Mickey threw him face down on the bed, and Jeff clenched his jaw in rage. He spun around and held out both hands. "Calm the fuck down!"

"You don't give a shit about me! You think you could have told me you don't want to work with me anymore, Chandler? Huh?" Mickey's fists clenched and his teeth showed as he spoke.

"What?" Jeff shook his head, still holding up his hands to fend Mickey off. "Don't want to work with you? Are you kidding me? I live for it! To go to the calls by your side!"

"Then why are you leaving me!" Mickey's voice broke.

"I'm not!" Jeff screamed out of frustration, "I'm taking the fucking exam! I won't even pass it!"

Again Mickey turned to leave the room. This time Jeff was on his back, stopping him. Mickey exploded with his powerful force and they stumbled around the bedroom in the dark, knocking into the dresser and toppling picture frames that were set up on it.

Mickey fell back on the bed and Jeff was caught under him. Jeff tried to keep hold of him, but Mickey spun around, grabbed Jeff's knees and forced them against Jeff's chest. Jeff instantly knew his intentions. Domination.

"Use the fucking lube!" Jeff could see it on the nightstand. "Mick!" He tried to reach for it and push Mickey back with his legs. Mickey grabbed the bottle and stuffed the tip inside Jeff again, this time roughly.

Jeff flinched and pulled back as it to punch Mickey in the face at the carelessness of his acts, but ended up just clenching his fist. Mickey saw it. He knew exactly what Jeff wanted to do. Mickey threw the bottle against the wall with a bang and began bending Jeff in two to get at him.

Jeff turned his head side to side, pushing against the pain as Mickey forced him to be much more flexible than he was. Jeff grabbed Mickey by the throat again and roared in fury. Mickey batted his arm away and thrust his cock inside Jeff. The minute Mickey made entry into his body, Jeff leg go. He released his anger, his tense muscles and his emotional pain. And as if Mickey felt him go limp underneath, he too lessened the pressure he was exerting on Jeff to comply. Mickey pumped into Jeff a few times and stopped, hanging his head.

When Jeff heard his sob he held onto Mickey and kissed his hair. "I won't test. I won't. Please. Mickey. Done. I won't."

Mickey dropped down on top of Jeff and Jeff felt him recover his breathing and his cock soften and pull out of his body.

"Love you," Jeff said, rocking him. "Love you so much I am in agony over you."

Mickey hid his face in Jeff's hair and lay still.

Jeff caressed his back and neck lovingly, staring at nothing.

Chapter Five

Jeff woke. He felt something akin to a hangover, although he had nothing to drink but one beer the night before. He looked over at the side of the bed for Mickey but it was empty. Listening, Jeff tried to figure out if Mickey was in the bathroom. He looked at the dresser, and the gun-pack was gone. Jeff sat up instantly and scanned around the room. The lubrication bottle was on the floor, a spatter from its tip stained the wall. The pictures that had been toppled over still lay flat on the dresser top.

Jeff stood up and actually felt sore from the fight, or maybe just the fatigue of a very long week. He headed down the stairs but the bottom floor was vacant. Jeff rubbed his face in agony and looked for his phone. He dialed Mickey's number but it went to voicemail. "Mick. Where are you? Come on. Let's talk." Jeff waited and then disconnected. He headed back up the stairs and crawled into bed, staring at nothing, lost.

~

Mickey sat at a café with his sister, Aura. They sipped lattes and Mickey kept his eyes on the occupants as if the little coffee shop would be robbed.

"Mouse?"

Aura had called Mickey that since he was a child. She was two years older than he was, but they were as close as twins.

"Mouse, don't do this to yourself." She reached out to touch his arm. "Jeff wants to move on at work. Aren't you tired of patrol?"

"Not if I ride with him. No. Never." Mickey sipped his coffee and looked at the line of people that went from the door to the counter.

"Why can't you guys talk?" Aura ran her hand back through her highlighted blonde hair. She had the same colorings as Mickey, was petite and wearing her work clothing, since she had taken a break to have coffee with him.

"He snuck behind my back. Talk?" Mickey finished the coffee and crushed the cup.

"Yeah. Talk." Aura rolled her eyes. "Come on, Mouse. You can talk to me. You should talk to Jeff."

"It ain't the same." Mickey sank down on the chair, the gun-pack weighing on him like an albatross today. He rubbed his face and said, "Fuck," in agony.

"So." Aura crossed her arms. "You figured thirty years, partners, on patrol? Like still be in the car answering 911 calls when you're fifty or something?"

"Shut up."

"No, you shut up!" She pushed his shoulder making Mickey nearly fall from his chair. "You're such a cave-dweller, I don't know how Jeff has put up with you for so long." She checked her phone and stood from the table.

Mickey tossed his cup out and followed her outside into the LA heat.

They headed back to her office building where she worked as a law clerk.

Mickey scanned the area as they did, his tactical training never leaving him. Prior-proper-planning-prevents-piss-poor-performance.

It also prevented him from being unaware of something going down and then being unprepared for it.

Aura was used to him looking at everything but her when they spoke. "So?" she said, "You're going to avoid him for your three days off? Then what? What will you do when you go back to work?"

"I was hoping I can sleep in my old room for the next couple of nights." Mickey finally looked at his sister. They shared an apartment before he moved in with Jeff and since he did not let the department know he moved, his mail went to her home.

"And if I say no?"

"I still have a key."

Aura shook her head in disbelief. "Whatever." She entered the lobby of an office building without saying goodbye.

Mickey felt his phone vibrate and took it out of his pocket to read a text. '*Plz tell me where u r.*'

Mickey ignored it and walked to where he'd parked his truck, headed to the precinct to work out in the gym there. He had packed a small bag and couldn't decide whether to go home or stay at Aura's. Meanwhile, he'd pump weights and try to get his mind off of things. The anger had subsided, but the hurt had not.

~

After three hours of pacing and not getting any reply from Mickey, Jeff called Aura.

She answered. "Hi. Figured you'd be calling me eventually."

"Do you know where he is?"

"We had coffee an hour ago. He's a butthead. Why can't you two talk?"

"I'm the butthead. I fucked up. I should have told him I was thinking about testing." He looked out of the front of the townhouse window, seeing the reserved spot where Mickey usually parked, vacant.

"Well, if he doesn't come home tonight, he did mention he may stay over at my place."

"Are you kidding me?" Jeff ran his hand through his hair. "He told you he's not sleeping here tonight?"

"Jeff! Talk to him!"

"How can I talk to him when he won't pick up the phone and I don't know where he is!"

"Well, you'll know where he will be later on tonight. I have to go. I'm at work."

"Sorry. Thanks, Aura." Jeff disconnected the phone and grew enraged at Mickey's avoidance behavior. Was it that bad? So bad that he couldn't sleep with him in the same bed?

"Fuck this!" Jeff stormed up the stairs, stuffed his workout gear into his rucksack and clipped his gun-pack around his hips. He left the house and headed to the station to work out at the precinct gym.

~

Mickey lay back on the bench, a bar over his head with nearly two hundred and fifty pounds of metal plates on it. A few other cops were working out. The music inside the room was extremely loud. It wasn't a big space, but it had all the basics and was free to all the officers to use. Since he had his own locker with his uniform and duty equipment in it, he secured his gun, wallet and phone inside it while he worked out. He didn't know the other three cops that were in the gym. But it seemed two knew each other and were laughing loudly, over the hard classic rock.

Mickey pumped a few repetitions of the heavy weight, not able to do more than two, or three if he pushed, which he did. One of the other cops stepped behind him. "Need a spot?"

"Yeah. Sure. On the next round."

The cop nodded and went on with his own workout routine while Mickey rubbed his chest and arms and recuperated. The door opened and closed but he didn't bother looking up, hoping everyone would leave and he could have the small space to himself. He ran his palms over the bar and raised his head to get the cop over to spot him. When he did, Jeff was standing there, staring at him.

Mickey lay back down and heard Jeff tell the other cop, "I got it." Then Jeff stood behind the bar and stared down at Mickey. "How many are you going for?"

Mickey ignored him, arched his back, and hefted the bulky weight up off the mounts. Jeff kept his hands under the bar but did not touch it as Mickey did two again without help, but the third repetition stopped midway.

"Push, you fucker!" Jeff didn't help, but his hands were there in case.

Mickey roared and struggled as his arms shook.

"Do it!" Jeff shouted like a drill sergeant as the other men in the room stood still to watch.

"Come on, ya fucking pussy!" Jeff taunted.

Mickey sneered at him in fury and used every ounce of strength he possessed to get the bar back on the mounts. The moment he did he jumped off the bench and shook out his arms, his back towards Jeff.

"Good job, man!" one of the cops said. "Fuck! How much weight is that?"

When Mickey did not answer, Jeff yelled over the noise, "Two forty-five!"

"Fuck. You're a bull!" The cop laughed and shook his head.

Mickey threw open the door and stormed out, headed to the locker room.

He could hear someone behind him, catching up, and knew who it was. He didn't look back and entered the men's locker room, dripping in sweat and aching from the weightlifting.

He was thrown against the wall of lockers with a shattering bang, and after the heavy lifting he was too weak to fight.

Jeff cupped his right palm under Mickey's jaw and spoke as close to Mickey's face as he could without brushing lips. "Ya wanna end this, Stanton?" Jeff's top lip curled. "'cause you're headed that way."

Mickey looked around the locker room. Though it wasn't shift change, there were officers coming and going to use the restroom.

Mickey couldn't look Jeff in the eye and also could not battle him. His arms were shaking and he was spent.

"You go sleep at Aura's," Jeff said with so much sarcasm Mickey's skin crawled. "Go on. I don't give a shit." Jeff shoved away from Mickey and left the locker room.

Mickey caught a few odd stares from the men that had spied it but he looked away. He sat down on a bench and tried to recover from both the physical exhaustion and the emotional turmoil.

~

Jeff returned to the workout room, taking the weights off the bar Mickey had used and replacing them on the rack. When it was at a weight he could easily do repetitions with, he lay on the bench, on Mickey's sweat, and pumped the lighter bar into the air. He did sets of twenty and rested between, staring at the stained-worn out ceiling and letting the loud beat of the rock and roll distract him from his thoughts.

After an hour of working out, hammering punches on the kick-bag, training, using the technique he had been taught at the academy, Jeff was worn out. He stripped in the locker room for his shower, knowing Mickey had left at least an hour earlier. Fine. What was he supposed to do?

He and Mickey had been through rough patches before. They would manage to figure this out.

Jeff stood in the shower and washed the sweat off himself as men came and went. It was now shift change and he hadn't even thought of the timing. It didn't matter. He wasn't afraid to be naked in front of other men. He finished washing up and wrapped a towel around his hips after he dried off.

Headed to his locker, he tried to focus on the combination when he overheard two cops talking together in a row behind him, out of his view.

"Don't know…someone said they were going to be separated."

"Why?"

"Heard they were fooling around on duty."

Jeff tensed up and tried to keep dressing, putting on his briefs and shorts.

"Uh oh. That's a big no-no. Stupid shits. How did they get caught?"

"I think someone found out they had moved in together."

Jeff began to feel sick to his stomach. He tugged his T-shirt over his head and checked his phone. Still nothing from Mickey.

"Well, that's the way it goes. Fucking morons to even tell the department they moved."

"Yeah. If I worked with my wife? All she would do was nag me." He laughed and Jeff heard a locker door shut.

He stayed still, his wet hair dripping down his neck.

The locker room cleared out for roll call and he clipped his gun belt around his hips and ran a brush through his hair quickly. Once he was done, he shut the locker door and held his keys in his fingers.

He hit the hot sunshine outdoors and put on his sunglasses, walking to his car. If he and Mickey were found out to be lovers? If Mickey didn't still use the same address as his sister's apartment? They'd not only have been split up ages ago, they'd have been outted.

Out.

Out as a gay man on the LAPD.

Jeff knew even coming from a liberal minded city like Seattle, you did not COME OUT. No way. *No way!*

You may be forced out, but none of the men did it voluntarily. For the women? It was slightly easier. He knew gay women cops in Seattle who had come out. No big deal. He figured being a macho lesbian was a bonus in blue, but to the guys? The men would not only tease you, your back-up would vanish.

Jeff's heart weighed heavily from his worry. And being a police officer in LA? Wasn't that hard enough?

The pressure on him was literally making him feel physically ill. They had counseling available to them if they needed it, but Jeff was too proud. Besides, he'd rather the cops knew he came out than went to a shrink!

He climbed into his boiling hot car and started the engine, cooling off with the A/C.

~

Mickey sat in the living room of his sister's apartment in Cerritos. A beer to his mouth, his bare feet on the coffee table, staring at the blank television while listening to blues on the stereo.

He had a number of friends he could call. All the boys. Blake, Hunter, Josh, Tanner…but if he showed up without Jeff? The twenty questions would begin, and he didn't need to hear it.

He scanned his phone and looked at the listings of numbers. Who would he call to talk to if he wanted to?

Seeing Mark Richfield and Steve Miller's number, Mickey was flattered to be able to call the Nation's Top Model and the ex LAPD cop his friends, but would be embarrassed to let them know he and Jeff were fighting.

He tossed the phone on the coffee table and tipped the beer up to drink.

Once the beer was finished he set it near the phone and rested his head on the sofa, closing his eyes. He and Jeff had been together day and night for years, so when they weren't, Mickey felt the vacuum like half of him was missing.

He stood off the sofa and began searching Aura's cabinets for booze. It was nearing four and she would be home by six. He located a bottle of tequila and brought it to the sofa with him. With the bottle on his lap, he pointed the remote control at the television and surfed channels. As usual, nothing was on. He located a rerunning of *Brokeback Mountain,* set the remote control beside him on the sofa, cracked open the bottle and began drinking from it.

It was bound to happen. Sooner or later, something would have broken their partnership up. But Mickey always assumed it would be an outside force, not one of them initiating it, especially behind the other's back.

That was the cruelest part of it all.

He tipped the tequila bottle up and gulped the strong liquor, wiping at his mouth roughly with the back of his hand.

~

Jeff felt like he was going to lose his mind.

He paced the townhouse like a rabid animal and was about to begin punching holes in the walls or toppling his furniture.

The workout did nothing to alleviate the stress; all it did was make his muscles fatigued.

He had enough. Picking up his gun-pack, Jeff grabbed his keys and phone, stormed out of the townhouse, and slammed the door as he did.

Head to the beach. Head to a movie, walk around a mall…

Yes, there were things he could do. Alone.

Call someone. Talk to Mark. Talk to Steve.

Sure. Tell them what he did? Tell them he fucked up?

He idolized Mark and Steve and would never imagine saying anything to ruin that relationship.

Jeff sat in his car and turned the volume up so loudly on the music CD that his doors rattled. He tried not to be careless, to drive like he was in a patrol car, speed, dart around slow moving cars. But the rush hour on a Thursday in LA had begun and he was about to make his own road rage a top news story.

~

Mickey was wasted. He sat with a half empty bottle of tequila on his lap and stared at the television. The end of *Brokeback Mountain*. He hated the end of that movie.

Dead gay men. Why did all the films about gay men end in death?

He uncapped the bottle and swigged it.

There was a banging noise at the door. Mickey tried to read the time off his watch but couldn't focus his eyes he was so drunk.

"Mick! I know you're in there! Your fucking truck is parked out here!"

Mickey capped the bottle and it slid to the floor and landed on its side with a slosh. He stared at the door as Jeff hammered on it.

"I'll break it the fuck down!" Jeff warned, "You know I can!"

Mickey staggered to his feet and held the wall as he made it to the front door. "Fuck off!"

"Open it, now!" Jeff jiggled the handle.

"Don't use your fucking cop-voice on me, Chandler." Mickey leaned his head on the door and closed his eyes. He jumped when he felt a heavy thud from the other side. Jeff was ramming it with his shoulder.

"Don't break it, ya cunt!" Mickey tried to open the lock and Jeff slammed against it again, making it creak.

Mickey turned the knob and Jeff was about to hit it again and came barreling through the entry. He stumbled and spun around, breathing fire.

Mickey shut the door and tried to walk casually to the kitchen, but he had to hold the counter to not stagger or tip over.

When he made it to the stove he leaned on it and ran his hand back through his hair. Jeff held up the half empty bottle and approached him.

"This is your answer?" Jeff shook it at him.

"Go away." Mickey looked at the wall and tried to sober up.

Jeff slammed the bottle on the counter and grabbed Mickey by his shirt, shaking him. "I want to be your partner! But patrol is killing me!"

"Killing you?" Mickey tried to think. "How can it kill you? We fucking suck each other all day!"

"No! The call volume, the pressure!" Jeff began to break down and Mickey had no idea Jeff felt so much stress from the streets.

"Dealing with fucking needles!" Jeff yelled and he sounded like he was about to cry. "Fucking crackheads! Filthy dopers and whores!" Jeff gripped Mickey's shirt tighter. "How many years do you think I can do this? Huh?"

"With me? Forever?" Mickey felt his eyes burn from his emotions.

Jeff released his hold and turned around, hands on hips, head down.

Mickey touched Jeff's back with his fingertips.

Shaking his head, Jeff said, "Don't ask me to stay on patrol forever. Don't ask me to do that. It's too much."

"Too much?" Mickey became emotional. "Nothing is too much for me!" He pounded his own chest. "I would die for you!" Mickey started sobbing. "I would take a fucking bullet for you!"

Jeff faced him and Mickey had never seen him so conflicted, in so much agony.

Mickey held his own heart. "Who else out there, huh? Who else out there are warriors and lovers?"

"Seems a lot of cops are." Jeff rubbed his face and hair as if he were exhausted.

"No!" Mickey shoved him using two hands to Jeff's chest, making Jeff fall back into the wall. "Seems there aren't!"

Jeff regained his balance and pointed a warning finger at Mickey. "I'd say something, Stanton, but I want you to sober up first so you remember it!"

"Fuck you!" Mickey couldn't see through his tears.

"Don't ya get it?" Jeff threw up his hands. "I don't want us to take that fucking bullet!"

In fury, Mickey reached for Jeff's gun-pack, going for the drawstring pull which immediately opened the zipper for quick access.

Jeff grabbed at Mickey's wrists and the fight was on. "What are you doing, huh? What are you going to do with the gun!"

"Kill me! Just fucking kill me, Chandler! Ya already stuck a knife in my heart!"

"Mouse?"

Mickey backed away and covered his face.

Chapter Six

Jeff heard Mickey's sister enter the apartment. He contained the gun and backed up, trying to appear normal, which was absurd. "…hi."

"Hi." Aura put her purse down and took a peek around a wall to see Mickey standing still, looking miserable. "Um," she obviously knew something was very wrong and worked on defusing it. "You, uh, eat dinner yet?"

Jeff glanced at her work clothing, her smart skirt and blazer, her black pumps. "I'm not hungry."

"Mouse?" She rubbed Mickey's back and he started crying.

Jeff felt sick to his stomach and didn't know what to do.

"Wow. How much did you drink?" She hugged Mickey, and he hid over her shoulder as if he were having a complete mental breakdown. "Don't light a match. The booze coming from you will blow this place up." Aura tried her best to lighten the atmosphere and Jeff appreciated her so much.

"Ya want me to go, Mick?" Jeff asked as he stared at Aura.

"I don't care what you do," Mickey said, not looking at him.

Aura shook her head and mouthed, '*stay*'.

Jeff took off the gun-pack and placed it on the top of the entertainment wall unit, where Mickey couldn't see it, but he had no clue where Mickey had left his. He trotted to the bedroom Mickey once occupied and spotted it, on top of a highboy dresser, near his backpack of clothing. Jeff looked at the doorway and then stuck the gun into a drawer.

When he returned to the kitchen, Mickey shot him a look that could kill and Aura walked Mickey to the bathroom. "Splash your face and calm down," she said as she shut the door, allowing him privacy.

She crossed her arms and shook her head at Jeff. "You two…"

"I know. Ain't love grand?" He picked up the tequila bottle off the counter and asked, "He drank how much?"

"That was a new bottle." She put it back into the cupboard.

"Jesus." Jeff glanced back at the closed bathroom door. "I should have told him I was considering testing for sergeant."

"Yeah, probably." She poked her head into the refrigerator.

"But I won't. I won't test." He rubbed his eyes and they felt gritty from being perpetually exhausted.

"Can't you guys go someplace else in the department together?" She shut the refrigerator and flipped through a yellow pages directory.

"I don't know. And if we did? How gay would that look?"

"Shut up."

"No, you shut up." He nudged her and smiled.

As Aura scanned the directory pages for a pizza place that delivered, Jeff asked, "How can you still be single?"

"I'm picky."

"Christ, you are so amazing."

Aura glanced up at him, appearing surprised.

"If I had a brother, I'd introduce you."

"You have a cousin?"

"Yes. In Seattle." He smiled.

"Does he look like you?"

"No."

She shrugged. "Urmph. Not interested." She picked up the phone.

The bathroom door opened and Mickey stepped out, appearing ragged and tired. Jeff approached him while Aura gave her address to the pizzeria.

"I do love you." Jeff used his finger to touch Mickey's cheek.

"Yeah," Mickey's voice sounded hoarse. "Unfortunately…I love you more."

"Bullshit."

"Wish it was." Mickey sat on the sofa and propped up his feet on the coffee table, pointing the remote at the television. As the news report aired, Jeff sat beside Mickey and leaned on him, pressing his lips to Mickey's neck, then he whispered, "I'd die for you. I'd take a bullet for you."

Mickey glanced at him.

"You know I would. In a heartbeat."

Mickey cupped Jeff's jaw and kissed him. When he heard Aura moan, "Mmmm…" Jeff broke the kiss. He laughed and said to her, "You are so horny."

"Don't even go there." She flipped her wrist and said, "Let me change into comfy clothing. Two pizzas on the way."

"Thanks." Jeff watched as she headed to her bedroom, and his smile fell when he saw Mickey dazed off at the television set, as if he wasn't even seeing it.

~

The tequila buzz was slow to leave, even after eating a few slices of pizza. Mickey was left with exhaustion and a slight headache. As Aura and Jeff talked about politics and the weather, Mickey sank low on the chair at the kitchen table and didn't know what to do. Jeff certainly had the right to advance himself in the department, and at times Mickey felt like a controlling bitch, stopping Jeff from doing what he had in his heart. It was selfish to try and keep Jeff with him on patrol, but Mickey knew how it would be without Jeff beside him. He'd work alone. There was no way Mickey would ever work with another partner again if Jeff moved on.

The anger in him, the sensation of betrayal was simply something he could not shake.

He stood from the table and dumped the crust he had not eaten into the trash, then placed the dish into the dishwasher. As he did, both Aura and Jeff stopped talking.

"There's ice cream in the freezer if you want it," Aura said.

"No. Thanks." Mickey walked to his old bedroom and immediately noticed his gun-pack was not on the highboy where he had left it. He stopped short and rubbed his face, then yelled, "Chandler!"

"What?" was called back.

"Where'd ya hide my fucking gun?" Mickey looked around the room but couldn't see it. He sat on the bed and wondered where they were in this relationship if Jeff felt the need to hide their weapons from him. Jeff didn't answer but he could hear him speaking to Aura, the tone, but not the words. Mickey lay flat on the bed and stared at the ceiling. Was he really going to sleep at his sister's apartment tonight? He checked the time. It was nearing eight. A whole day wasted. And they still needed to do normal-domestic chores. Food shop, laundry, clean the house, rituals he and Jeff did together on a regular basis during days off.

Were they together too much? Mickey didn't think so. Obviously Jeff did.

Without speaking a word, Jeff entered the room, opened a drawer and placed the gun-pack on the top of the highboy. He turned around and stared at Mickey. "What are we doing?"

Mickey leaned on his elbows. "You tell me."

"Are you spending the night here?"

Mickey looked around the room and stood up, packing his pockets with his keys and cell phone.

"Can you drive?" Jeff asked as Mickey fastened the gun-pack around his hips.

"Been worse."

"You know how many cops end up with DUIs?"

"Don't start on me." Mickey rubbed his head. "You want me to stay here or what?"

"I want you to come home."

Mickey nodded and shouldered his backpack.

"I'll tail you. Don't do anything stupid."

"Fuck you," Mickey muttered as he brushed by Jeff to get to the hall.

Aura was standing, as if waiting for them to come to a decision.

"Thanks, sis." Mickey leaned down to kiss her cheek.

"Okay, Mouse. Just talk to each other. Ya think you can do that? Without breaking furniture or putting holes in walls?"

Mickey gave Jeff a glare at what he may have told Aura, and opened the front door. He heard Jeff saying goodnight to Aura and Mickey walked to his truck, tossing the backpack behind the seat. He didn't even glance back as he started it up, pulling out of the parking space and headed to their townhouse in Anaheim.

Mickey spotted Jeff's car behind him. It was still light outside, but the heat had let up in favor of a cool breeze. He didn't speed, didn't do anything reckless. He was simply tired. Tired of the battles, the work, and the sense of inadequacy that he felt at times like this.

After driving from Cerritos to Anaheim, Mickey pulled into his reserved space as Jeff did the same beside him. Mickey climbed out of his truck, slung the backpack over his shoulder and searched his key ring for the front door key. He opened it, walking straight up the stairs to their bedroom. He needed to lie down, close his eyes, and try to figure out who the hell he was in this life and where he was going.

~

Jeff shut the front door behind him and tossed his keys, wallet, and gun on the kitchen counter. He glanced at his phone and noticed several missed text messages from their friends. Jeff looked up at the second floor and had no idea if Mickey and he were up to a day at the beach with the boys or not. Normally, yes.

He didn't respond to the messages, placing his phone near his keys, and walked up the stairs to the bedroom. Mickey was lying on the bed, wearing only his briefs, his back towards the doorway.

Jeff took off his shoes and shirt and washed his face in the bathroom. He caught his own gaze in the mirror and hoped he'd be off patrol by the time he was thirty. It didn't look like that was going to happen. It was only two years away. After washing his face and brushing his teeth, he returned to the bedroom.

He pulled the drapes closed, darkening the room, and spooned Mickey, kissing his hair and running his hand up his arm to his shoulder.

Closing his eyes, Jeff reached one arm around Mickey's chest and drew him near so they were sealed skin to skin. Mickey shifted gently, and held Jeff's arm against his own chest.

The exhaustion and stress finally caught up to both of them, and they fell asleep.

~

Mickey woke abruptly to the sensation of bullets hitting him and bolted upright. He looked around the dark bedroom, drenched in sweat and touched his chest, feeling his heart racing.

Jeff said tiredly, "Nightmare?"

Mickey looked over at him.

Jeff stirred on the bed beside him.

"Fuck. Hate that shit." Mickey wiped the sweat off his face.

"I get weird dreams like that all the time. I think it's like PTSD." Jeff grabbed Mickey's arm and drew him back beside him on the bed.

Mickey rolled to face him and propped his head on a pillow. "I swear, Jeff, in these dreams it feels like real bullets are nailing me."

"I know. Been there. I can't imagine what the real deal must be like if the dreams are that terrifying."

"I think about Billy, ya know? Taking so many rounds in the chest."

"Fuck. At least the vest works." Jeff lay face up and rubbed his face. "Hate naps."

"Sleep when ya can, that's my motto." Mickey thought about their good friend, an LAPD lieutenant who had recently been involved in an on-duty shooting.

A crazy man held his ex-wife, her new boyfriend and a child hostage. No, LT Billy Sharpe was no longer the SWAT commander, but…somehow managed to get himself hit acting like he was one.

Mickey slowly calmed down, as the fleeting dream evaporated. He reached for Jeff's hip and touched him. "I'm sorry I freaked on you."

"I'm sorry I tried to hide it."

"You want to take the exam, take it."

Jeff curled around Mickey, massaging his chest. "No."

"I can't hold you back, Jeff." Mickey placed his hand on top of Jeff's, holding it to his heart. "I just had no idea you were that burned out on patrol."

"How can you not be?"

"Because I have you."

Jeff scooted over so they could interlock legs. "I don't want to be apart. I love working with you. I do."

"Lovers and comrades in arms. Like I always say, there is no stronger bond." Mickey ran his hand back through Jeff's soft hair.

"No. None stronger. Why do you think so many of these Iraq and Afghanistan young vets go back again and again?"

"To protect their boys. Be with their team." Mickey knew that. Knew that feeling well.

"Yeah. So? They love each other. They die for each other."

"Like us. Only we fuck each other too." Mickey slipped his hand into Jeff's briefs, holding his cock and stretching it, wanting it hard.

Jeff climbed on top of Mickey and cupped the back of Mickey's head as he kissed him. Mickey spread his own legs, urging Jeff to be the aggressor. He wanted to lay back and submit.

They were so in tune sexually, Jeff took over, making Mickey remove his hand so they could grind their crotches together while they kissed.

"Want me to fuck you, Stanton?" Jeff purred against his lips.

"Yeah."

"Then get ready for me." Jeff jammed his hips hard against Mickey.

Mickey grabbed a handful of Jeff's hair and gave him a kiss that set both of them on fire. Then he hopped off the bed and entered the bathroom, closing the door behind him.

~

Jeff stared at a framed picture on the wall. Mickey's academy graduation photo. His hand inside his briefs, Jeff played with himself, keeping hard as Mickey prepared for their sex.

Working on patrol…

He tried not to let it get him angry. He had time to discuss this with Mickey, for them to figure out a way to get the hell off the front lines. He had to. Jeff was going crazy.

The bathroom door opened, the light shut and Mickey walked over to the bed naked. "How do you want me, Chandler?"

Seeing Mickey in a very rare compliant mood, Jeff leapt off the bed, spun Mickey to face the wall and said, "Spread 'em."

Mickey spread eagle, facing the wall, his palms pressed flat against the painted surface.

Jeff kicked Mickey's legs farther apart and ran his hands down Mickey's arms to the tufts of hair under his armpits. Next, into Mickey's ear, Jeff whispered, "Don't fucking move."

Mickey didn't reply, but Jeff could hear his breathing deepen.

Jeff back-stepped to the nightstand, stripped off his briefs and peered into the drawer they kept their 'toys' in. He loaded up his hands with items and set them down on the floor. Jeff immediately grabbed hold of Mickey's wrist and ratcheted a handcuff around it, taking his second arm to meet it, cuffing

Mickey behind his back. Jeff pushed Mickey hard against the wall, and snarled in his ear, "Scumbag. Gonna fuck ya good."

Mickey let out a low moan and pressed the side of his face to the wall.

Jeff dropped to his knees and spread Mickey's ass cheeks, running long laps up his skin and nuzzling between. Mickey shifted his wide stance and Jeff heard the cuffs ratchet tighter.

He picked up a dildo and coated it with lubrication. Once he had, Jeff tugged Mickey backwards by the hips and said, "Bend over, slut."

"Fucking pig."

Jeff smiled. Mickey appeared to be himself again. He was hoping to get a battle out of him. That always made the sex hotter. Jeff stood beside him and put pressure on Mickey's upper back. "I said bend over, asshole!"

Mickey snarled and showed his teeth, his fists clenching, but his cock was stiff and bobbing between his legs. He did not obey Jeff's command.

"I said, bend the fuck over!" Jeff pushed so hard on Mickey's upper body, Mickey had no choice. He balanced with his head on the wall and kept snarling like a wildcat. "I'll kill you, pig. You'd better hope I never get out of these cuffs."

Jeff made sure Mickey's balance was completely compromised and said, "Cavity search time."

"Fuck you!"

"No. Actually. Fuck you." He pushed the slick tip of the dildo into Mickey's ass.

Mickey's body jolted and then he groaned so sensually, Jeff pulled on his own cock a few times in reaction. He fucked Mickey with the dildo, going deeper with each push. "My, what have we got here? Hiding dope?"

"I'll kill you! Get your filthy hands off me, ya pig!" Mickey spread his legs as wide as he could and his ass was in a perfect position for fucking.

Jeff reached under him and tugged on his balls. He sat on the carpet, scooted back, and sucked Mickey's balls into his mouth as he held the dildo inside him.

"Oh, fuck! Fuck!" Mickey's body quivered and his legs began to shake.

With his free hand Jeff pointed Mickey's cock downward and drew it into his mouth. A low agonizing whimper came from Mickey and Jeff peeked up at him. Mickey's eyes were closed and he was someplace deep in his mind where he could be the bad guy, the target of Jeff's abuse.

Jeff turned on the vibration button and kept the dildo still in Mickey's ass. Mickey went crazy fucking Jeff's mouth and the handcuffs rattled and creaked as Mickey tugged on them to get free.

Rolling his head on the wall he was resting on, Mickey almost sobbed as he shivered. "Oh, God…"

Jeff felt Mickey's cock go completely rigid in his mouth. He knew he was right on the verge of a climax. Jeff growled and pushed the dildo in deeper.

Mickey's body nearly convulsed and Jeff's mouth filled with Mickey's cum. A low guttural, "*Aurgh…*" sound came from Mickey and his cock throbbed as he climaxed.

Jeff held the base of Mickey's length with both hands and made sure it was a damn good orgasm. Mickey whimpered and moaned and his muscles kept tensing and releasing.

Jeff withdrew from the contact and stood up, roughly moving Mickey to lay over the bed, still straddled. While Mickey recuperated and gasped for air, Jeff tossed the dildo on the floor and drove in. "Like this, ya prick?" Jeff hammered into him, slapping Mickey's ass with hard whacks.

"God! I hate you! Fuck you!"

"Sure ya do. As much as I hate you." Jeff held Mickey's hips and watched his cock penetrating Mickey's ass. Jeff closed his eyes and threw his head back as the intensity hit its peak, the orgasm rich and delicious. He stayed deep inside his man until the throbbing of his cock subsided, then pulled out and took the cuffs off of Mickey. Jeff tossed the handcuffs and the bottle of lube into the drawer, and picked up the dildo, taking it with him to the bathroom.

He looked at himself in the mirror and began washing up.

Behind him a beautiful man's reflection appeared. Jeff felt Mickey's arms surround his waist and Mickey's head rested on Jeff's shoulder.

Jeff nuzzled him and smiled.

Chapter Seven

Jeff woke to see the clock read eleven-forty-one. They had slept for over twelve hours. There was no questioning their utter exhaustion, when on their days off, they did nothing but sleep.

Mickey was still out, sleeping deeply beside him.

Jeff scrubbed his rough jaw and gritty eyes, and stretched his back, knowing they had a day of errands and other time wasting chores before them. He wanted them to at least do something fun, since they'd be back in uniform working their twelve hours shift in no time.

He picked up his phone from the nightstand and turned it on. It hummed with missed text messages. One from his lifeguard buddy, Josh Elliot read, *'where the hell have you guys been?'*

Jeff texted back while Mickey slumbered. '*work, work...sleep'*.

He got a message from Josh immediately. '*come play.*'

Jeff glanced over at Mickey. He wrote, '*cud do dinner.*'

'*BBQ here. Blake n Hunt off?*'

'*Dunno.*'

While he text, Mickey moved closer to him and Jeff noticed his eyes open, as if his police radar had picked up something was going on and, *poof!*, Mickey was awake.

'*6 good?*'

"Who are you texting?" Mickey asked in a low gravelly voice.

"Josh. He wants to know if we're free for dinner. Barbeque at his and Tanner's place."

"Sure." Mickey rested his head on Jeff's shoulder to read the text messages with him.

Jeff wrote back, '*6 is good. Wat shud we bring?*'

'*booze?*'

'*k*'. Jeff set the phone on the nightstand and rolled to his side to face Mickey. "I can't believe how long the gap is between seeing our buddies."

"Shifts. All of ours are different." Mickey yawned and stretched his arms over his head, arching his back.

"We slept for nearly twelve hours."

"I can sleep all day." Mickey propped himself up to his side and tugged the sheet down, exposing Jeff's body.

"Was gonna piss and brush my teeth." Jeff watched Mickey as Mickey pulled on Jeff's soft cock.

"Okay." Mickey released his hold and Jeff climbed off the bed, walking to the bathroom. Mickey followed him and they took care of both tasks, swapping spots from the sink to the toilet.

Jeff spit out the toothpaste and rinsed his mouth, then ran a brush through his hair. "Hate food shopping."

"Me too. Fuck it. Gotta get food." Mickey flushed the toilet and washed his hands. Once he dried them he urged Jeff against the wall. "Wanna shower?"

Jeff smiled and kissed him. "I do."

Mickey started the water and ran his hand through his hair. As Jeff finished up, he spotted all of Mickey's back muscles flex and stared at his tight white bottom below the tan line. Jeff held him from behind, kissing his neck and shoulder. "Looking forward to seeing the boys?"

"Sure. After we get all the shit done."

Jeff chewed Mickey's deltoid muscle teasingly. "You taste good."

Mickey reached back for him and pulled his lips close to kiss.

Jeff stepped into the tub with him, still kissing, as Mickey embraced him under the shower's spray.

As they began to get heated and moan against each other's lips, Jeff knew he never wanted to do anything to hurt Mickey. But sometimes you had to let go of something, to keep it close.

~

Mickey drove with Jeff to Josh and Tanner's place. It was nearing six pm and the day was shot doing errands. After picking up extra food and beer at the grocery store it seemed they were both either tired or deep in thought since neither was speaking at the moment.

The two LA lifeguards fell in love and lived together in Tanner's home in Hawthorne. There was a small age gap between them, but in Mickey's mind, Josh acted like a sixteen year old sex fiend, while Tanner, only four years his senior, was much more stoic and mature. But that's probably what the wild young man needed in his life. A leash!

They also had a built-in swimming pool, so bathing suits and towels were stowed in the truck as well.

Mickey glanced over at Jeff, as Jeff, his sunglasses on, stared out of the window. Jeff looked like a cop, even out of uniform. Mickey assumed he did as well, since they always carried their gun and badges with them.

Jeff seemed to wake out of his daydream as Mickey parked in front of the modest home, seeing Blake and Hunter were already there, recognizing Hunter's pickup truck.

"Think Mark will show?" Jeff asked as he reached for the grocery bag of food from behind the seat.

"That would make your day." Mickey laughed.

"My week." Jeff winked at him.

They climbed out of the truck, carrying the items they brought with them and walked down the paved front path to the front door. Jeff knocked and then turned the knob. It opened so he stepped in, saying, "Hello?"

Mickey shut the door behind him, and simply because he was a cop, locked it. If they were playing out in the backyard at the pool, none of them would hear an intruder. But of course, normal people weren't that paranoid.

"Hey!" Josh came barreling over, wearing just a tiny black Speedo and jumped on top of Jeff for a kiss.

Jeff nearly toppled over, since his hands were full and Mickey shook his head at gorgeous, wild, Joshua Elliot's antics.

"Mmm. Mmm!" Josh was giving Jeff a good wet kiss and Jeff was helpless at the moment to do a thing but enjoy it. "Is that a gun in your pocket, Officer, or are you just glad to see me?"

Jeff laughed. "It's a gun. You're sitting on my Glock."

"Oh!" Josh blinked.

"Uh hum?" Mickey set the bag with their towels down, and then two six-packs of beer on the counter.

"You're next, hot stuff." Josh panted in excitement, jumped off of Jeff and landed in Mickey's arms.

Mickey held him around the waist as Josh locked his ankles around Mickey's back.

"Holy crap, Josh." Jeff placed the food on the counter and the other items they had brought, on the tile floor as he recovered. "Don't you get enough?"

"Mm. Yes." Josh pecked Mickey's lips again and slid down him like a fire pole. "Now I need to come."

Mickey didn't give Josh's actions a thought, since that type of behavior was simply 'Josh'. He could see the other three men outside by the pool, already in bathing suits, drinking beer.

"Is Mark coming?" Jeff asked.

"Don't I wish!" Josh peeked inside the bags to see what they had brought.

"We should have worn the suits. I have to go change." Mickey dug his out of the bag.

"Go? Go where?" Josh gestured for him to stay. "Nothing I haven't seen, is it?"

Jeff laughed, placed his gun-pack on the counter, took his shirt over his head, stepping out of his tennis shoes and stripped.

He slipped his trunks on as Josh stared, moaned, and licked his lips.

Mickey expected Josh to drop to his knees and suck Jeff. It wouldn't be that unusual for the 'wild child'. Since Jeff was being brave, Mickey did as well. He placed his gun beside Jeff's and began changing.

"Wow!"

Mickey looked up as he stepped out of his shorts and briefs to see Hunter entering the kitchen through the back slider.

"If I knew there was going to be a strip act, I'd have let the other guys know."

"Hi, babe." Jeff kissed Hunter on the cheek, then tucked his clothing into the bag after he took out a towel.

"Glad we all finally got a day off that overlapped." Hunter waited for Mickey to put on his bathing suit before he approached and kissed him. "It sucks having all of us on different shift patterns." He picked up two beers from the counter.

"I know." Mickey also tucked his clothing away and noticed Josh leaning on the counter on his elbow, staring at him. Mickey smiled and tapped his nose playfully. "You already drunk, bad boy?"

"Possibly, Officer Dreamy."

Jeff laughed and grabbed a beer, twisting the cap. "Mick's driving. I'm getting drunk." He followed Hunter out of the kitchen to the back patio to join the others.

Josh grinned at Mickey impishly.

"Okay to leave our guns here?" Mickey pointed to the two packs.

"You bring your cuffs?"

"No." Mickey smiled and picked up a beer, opening it.

"I want another orgy. Why do we have to wait for Mark to invite us to his place to have one?"

"We didn't have an orgy." Mickey sipped the beer, looking outside to see Blake and Jeff laughing together.

Tanner entered the house and smiled at Mickey. "I thought maybe you were being held hostage."

"He's behaving," Mickey said, indicating Josh, "Sort of."

Tanner crossed the room and kissed Mickey's cheek. "How are you? We seriously don't see enough of each other." Tanner cupped Mickey's jaw and Mickey gazed into his handsome face and sky blue eyes. Tanner was much bigger than Josh and solid muscle.

Mickey replied, "All right. Trying to keep going, ya know."

Tanner opened the refrigerator and took out a bowl of marinated chicken.

"We brought some chips and salsa." Mickey pointed to a bag.

Josh opened a cabinet and removed two bowls.

"Can I help?" Mickey asked.

"Just open the door for me." Tanner carried the chicken and foil-wrapped potatoes to the back sliding door.

Mickey looked back at Josh as he filled a bowl with the chips, and then opened the glass door for Tanner.

When he stepped out into the hot sun, Blake stood and greeted him. They pecked lips and Blake said, "So good to see you guys away from work."

"Last week was brutal." Jeff swigged his beer. They were all in the shade of two large umbrellas, seated around the tables that were on the patio.

The pool sparkled in the background and the tall palm trees swayed in the hot breeze.

Tanner began laying the chicken on the grill and Josh emerged with the chips and salsa, placing them on a table with other snacks.

"Sit." Hunter tilted his head to a lounge chair beside him.

Mickey tossed his towel on it and sat down with a loud sigh.

Jeff asked, "Did you even try to call Mark and Steve?"

Blake laughed. "Go ahead."

Josh said, "I left a message letting them know we're here." He ate a tortilla chip and then sat on the same chair as Jeff, sitting at the foot of the lounge. Jeff put his feet on the patio so Josh could have room, then Jeff caressed Josh's long brown hair affectionately.

Mickey smelled the grilled chicken and was already hungry. He stood and filled a plate with the snacks and then sat down again to eat them and drink his beer.

"So, what's new on the department?" Tanner asked, placing the foil-wrapped potatoes on the coals.

Mickey licked the salt off his finger and stared at Jeff, wondering if he would mention the sergeant's exam.

Josh leaned back on Jeff, relaxing in his arms and said to Tanner, "If you go back inside, can you get my phone?"

"If Mark got your message, then he'll come if he can." Tanner wiped his hands on a towel and sat down, picking up a beer.

Mickey noticed Josh pout. "Ya got it bad for Richfield, don't ya, Josh?"

"Yeah." Josh shielded his eyes in the glare.

Blake said, "Your boyfriend is right there," pointing at Tanner.

Tanner laughed. "Don't worry, Blake. I'm afraid Josh is destined to admire Mark from afar."

Josh made puckering kissing noises at Tanner. "My baby knows I love him."

"And you're lying on mine!" Mickey smiled.

"And he's getting me sweaty." Jeff nudged him.

"Mm." Josh slid around on Jeff's chest. "Cop sweat."

"Joshua," Tanner said in admonishment.

In harmony, Blake and Hunter said, "Behave!" then laughed because it was what Tanner always said.

Mickey chuckled and shook his head. He set the beer aside and stood. "It's hot, and that pool looks too good to not get in." He stood on the edge and dove in.

He swam underwater to the opposite side and heard a loud splash when he surfaced. Josh was making his way over and Mickey loved the look in Josh's bright eyes. Always full of mischief. So, they began to roughhouse, dunking each other.

~

Jeff smiled as he watched Mickey and Josh play.

Blake said, "You two make such a good partnership. It's hard, isn't it? Working so close and living together?"

"No it's not." Hunter shook his head. "All three of us couples work and live together."

"We don't sit in the same car all day." Blake looked back at the pool as Josh was tossed into the air and splash landed.

Jeff noticed Tanner stand up and tend the food as Hunter became tempted with the playtime in the pool. Hunter dove in and immediately it was two against Josh. Josh appeared to love it and his laughter was echoing in the fenced yard.

Jeff moved to sit closer to Blake. Making sure Blake and he could talk quietly, he said, "I want to test for sergeant."

"Good for you!" Blake smiled brightly.

Tanner obviously overheard. "You'd be great."

"Yeah, um." Jeff made sure Mickey wasn't looking his way. "Mick freaked."

Both Blake and Tanner spun around to look at Jeff in surprise.

"What?" Blake asked.

"Because it will split you up?" Tanner asked.

"Yeah." Jeff rubbed his unshaven jaw. "I love being in the car with him. But I can't do patrol for my entire career."

Tanner let the food cook unattended and crouched by Jeff. "He actually said, no, you can't?"

"Well, no. But he got crazy." Jeff set his empty beer bottle on the patio near his chair. "I don't know what to do."

"Test!" Blake splayed out his hands. "Jeff, come on. You can't not go for a promotion if you want it."

"Hang on," Tanner replied, making a slow-down motion to Blake. "He has to take Mick's feelings into account. I think about how it would be without my Joshua on the job, and…"

All three men looked over at the pool. Josh was on Mickey's shoulders and Hunter was hitting them both with a Styrofoam noodle.

Tanner said to Blake, "Would you want Hunt to leave the fire station? Huh? Go to a different firehouse?"

"I would never stop him." Blake appeared defensive. "If Hunt wanted to advance his career I'd help him study." He looked at Jeff, dead serious. "No way would I hold him back. Not with guilt or any other bullshit." Blake addressed Tanner, "Would you? Really, Tanner? You'd stop Josh from advancing his career?"

Tanner's expression darkened. "No." He stood and began turning the chicken on the grill.

Blake leaned closer to Jeff. "It's up to you. You can't just get stagnant on patrol and do something you hate. It's dead wrong."

"Don't tell him we've discussed this. Either of you," Jeff said to both men, looking over his shoulder at Tanner.

"We won't." Tanner used a pastry brush to marinate the meat.

Blake reached for Jeff's knee and shook it. "If you don't test, you'll resent him. And every day you'll start to hate him for it."

"Blake!" Tanner gave Blake a look of annoyance.

Jeff slid lower in the chair as his emotions sank. "No, Tanner. He's right. I am so fucking torn between being with him, having us watch out for each other, and testing and getting the fuck off the front lines."

"Our job isn't like yours," Blake said, "We don't have to carry guns and get into armed combat. I get why he wants you there. Who better to protect him from harm than you?"

Jeff felt his eyes burn from his upset. "I know. It's like being in the military. He's my brother in war."

"He's your everything." Tanner began removing the cooked chicken from the grill. "Don't kid yourself, Jeff. If you left? Got promoted? And something happened to Mick?"

Jeff looked at Mickey enjoying the pool. Hunter and Mickey were playing tug of war with a hysterical Josh, who seemed to love every minute of it.

"I'd die." Jeff felt his emotions rise and stood up, going into the house to try and calm down before Mickey noticed. As he closed the slider behind him, he could see Blake and Tanner staring at each other, as if they were helpless to do anything about it.

~

Mickey released Josh as Josh climbed on top of Hunter's shoulders. Josh picked up the noodle and began hitting Mickey with it.

Mickey held the end and dragged the two men around the pool by it. He looked back at the others and noticed Tanner busy setting food on the table while Blake cleared empty bottles from the area. Jeff was not there. Figuring he headed in for a beer or bathroom break, Mickey turned his attention back to the other two and used the short end of the foam noodle to bat Josh who was batting him.

"Hey!" Hunter complained, "I'm the horse that's getting hit from both sides!"

Josh let go of his end of the noodle and hung his arms around Hunter's neck as he piggybacked him. "Aww…my hero fireman." Josh made kissing noises against Hunter's neck.

Mickey chuckled and bobbed in the water, looking back occasionally for Jeff.

"I feel your hard cock on my back, Mr Elliot," Hunter said, giving Josh a wicked smirk from over his shoulder.

"You're lucky it isn't in your butt, Mr Rasmussen."

Mickey teased, "Like that would happen. Not to Josh the bottom boy." He looked back at Blake and Tanner again and cupped his mouth to shout, "Jeff taking a piss break?"

Blake and Tanner exchanged looks first, then Blake said, "Yes," but Mickey got a sense he was lying.

"Food's ready, guys." Tanner waved them over.

Hunter carried Josh on his back to the end of the pool closest to the men, and Mickey used the underwater steps to climb out, wiping down with his towel.

"Mm. Looks great, Tanner." Hunter dried off as he investigated the food selection.

Mickey waited, then entered the house, the towel wrapped around his hips. "Jeff?"

"Coming." Jeff emerged from a hallway and looked like hell.

Mickey tilted his head curiously. "You okay?"

"Just tired. Is the food ready?" Jeff brushed passed Mickey.

Mickey stopped him, grabbing his arm. "Chandler?"

Jeff exhaled and met Mickey's eyes.

"Were you crying?" Mickey felt his stomach flip.

"No…I wasn't." Jeff turned away, then his mouth formed a grim line. "Mick."

Mickey embraced him, holding him. "What? What did I miss? Are you upset I played around with the boys?"

"Oh, hell no." Jeff narrowed his eyes in disbelief.

Then it occurred to Mickey. He held Jeff's shoulders and said, "Were you discussed testing for the sergeant's exam with Blake and Tanner?"

"Yeah. But I'm not. I'm not, Mick. Never." Jeff rubbed his nose as if it may be running.

Mickey didn't want to deal with it. Not now. Not tonight. "Let's eat." As he walked by the kitchen counter, he picked up another beer and handed it to Jeff.

"Thanks." Jeff took it and followed Mickey out of the house.

When Mickey and Jeff stepped out onto the patio, the other four men went dead silent. It was so obvious they had been discussing them, Mickey felt sick. Jeff picked up a paper plate and began filling it with food, not making eye contact with anyone.

Mickey caught a strange stare from Blake and said in defense, "I am not stopping him!"

"From?" Josh, seated at one of the shady tables, wiped his mouth with a napkin. "Stopping who?"

Mickey suddenly felt as if he had been mistaken…and paranoid. He used a fork to put a piece of chicken on his plate and took one of the baked potatoes before he sat down.

Josh looked around at the rest of the men. "What the hell? Am I suddenly the kid in the family who can't know what's going on?"

No one answered Josh and Mickey could not only see the frustration on Josh's face, he knew the rest of the men did indeed know, and were being silent.

Jeff ate his food, his focus on his plate.

Mickey tried not to take offense, but it wasn't easy.

"You guys suck," Josh said, resuming eating when no one would explain the comment.

Tanner caressed Josh's hair before he sat down next to him, and suddenly six men, who were usually boisterous and laughing together, were acting as if they were in a library.

Mickey's temper was rising quickly. He stopped eating and wiped his hands, staring out at the pool, the trees swaying, the homes of the neighbors surrounding them…anything to calm down.

Blake, obviously trying to change the mood, said, "Good chicken, Tanner. The guys at the station would love it."

"It's a simple marinade. Just soy sauce, brown sugar, tomato paste…"

Mickey caught Jeff's eye. Neither smiled. They stared at each other and Mickey hated the fact that Jeff had aired their dirty laundry behind his back.

His impulse was to leave. Leave in his truck. Let Jeff find his way home with one of the boys.

Josh perked up to the sound of a ringtone. He hopped out of the chair and raced into the house and then stood by the open sliding door. "Hey! Are you and Steve coming?"

Hunter smiled. "Mark the magnificent."

"Aww. No! Come on," Josh turned his back to the others as he spoke.

Blake said, "Looks like the top model won't be making an appearance."

Mickey picked up his plate and tossed it into a trash bag that was near the grill. He walked passed Josh who was giving Mark the hard sell, and entered the house. Seeing his clothing, Mickey took it with him to a spare bathroom where he could rinse off the chlorine. He wanted to leave. He didn't want to deal with this topic any longer.

~

Jeff wiped his hands on a napkin and sighed.

"Babe." Blake caressed his cheek. "Go. Go work it out with him."

"I thought we did. I can't test." Jeff ran his hands through his hair, then stood and threw out the scraps of his meal and placed his empty bottle into a recycle bin.

"When?" Josh was still battling for a moment with the famous model, one hand on his hip, walking away from the others as he debated.

Jeff smiled as he thought about Josh's infatuation with Mark. It was adorable, really. And Josh acted like a fan-girl every time Mark Antonious was in the room.

Letting go of his thoughts, Jeff turned to the rest of the men and said, "Thanks, guys."

"You're leaving?" Hunter asked, his beer in his hand.

"I have a feeling Mick is."

Tanner said, "I can drive you home."

Jeff made the rounds kissing each of the men on the lips and then glanced at Josh who walked back, pouting like a spoiled child who has been denied his candy.

Jeff cupped his jaw and gave him a sympathetic frown. "He busy?"

"Yeah. Modeling."

"Sorry, baby. He'll fine time for you soon." Jeff kissed him.

"You're not staying?" Josh blinked, his long dark lashes, which surrounded his light eyes.

"No. Gotta go. We'll get together again soon."

"You guys just got here!" Josh followed Jeff to the back sliding door. "Come on. What am I not getting?"

"Josh," Tanner said, reaching out to him.

Josh hugged Jeff and rocked him. "Love you."

Jeff felt his eyes tear up. "Love you too, Mr Elliot."

Josh reached for another kiss, and Jeff gave him one, caressing his hair.

"Be careful out there. You two have the scariest job of the bunch." Josh held Jeff's hips. "Watch out for each other."

"We will." Jeff broke the embrace and waved. "Thanks, guys. Thanks, Tanner, for dinner." They waved back at him and Jeff entered the house.

Mickey was dressed, his hair wet; squatting while he packed the small bag with his bathing suit and towel.

Jeff, since he did not swim, dropped his swimsuit to his feet and dressed, staring at Mickey who clipped the gun-pack around his hips.

"So? Mad at me again?" Jeff tucked in his shirt and picked up his gun-pack to fasten around his waist. "Every time I turn around you're pissed at me?"

Mickey didn't answer, walking to the front door with his keys in his hand.

Jeff didn't know how much more he could take of this shit, but it was wearing on his nerves.

The drive home was silent. But at least Mickey didn't just drop him off and head to Aura's place. They walked into the townhouse together, and Jeff stopped just inside the door to see what Mickey was going to do. Mickey walked up to the second floor and vanished.

Jeff unhooked the gun-pack from his hips and placed it on the kitchen counter, then dropped down on the sofa and stared into space. He used to look forward to their weekends. Not this one. This weekend was turning into hell.

He closed his eyes and tried to decompress. He was in a lose-lose position at the moment. And no matter what he chose, he would make someone unhappy.

Chapter Eight

On Sunday they were back at work, changing into their uniforms, not ignoring each other, but Jeff could feel the friction between them.

They hadn't discussed work. The sex had ceased. It was so unlike their usual behavior, Jeff was at a loss. But he tried to let it go. Maybe once Mickey realized they would be together, permanently, in the car as partners, things would get back to normal.

Jeff closed his locker and made sure his Kevlar vest, gun belt, and uniform were feeling comfortable, considering it was another scorcher outside. There was a slight chance of a passing thunderstorm, which for LA was not common in August.

Carrying a small canvas kit with items he'd need on duty, he glanced at Mickey and spotted him talking to Chris, another member of their squad. Jeff said to Mickey, "Meet you in the roll call room."

Mickey nodded in acknowledgement and Jeff walked by the mirrors before leaving the locker room and brushed his hair back from his forehead. Yeah, regulation said 'above the collar'. He knew he needed to cut it. He blamed Mark's influence for wanting it long, but there were no ponytails or shaggy mops allowed for men on the department. And the women had to keep their hair tied up.

He figured he'd wait until a supervisor said something. Screw it. He wasn't going anywhere in his career now, so he didn't give a shit.

Jeff left the locker room, dropping his kit near the exit and put a fresh battery onto his portable radio. He was about to stop and read the latest information tacked to a bulletin board from their days off when Sgt Adkins tapped him on the shoulder. "Got a minute?"

"Sure." Jeff walked with the sergeant to his desk and stood waiting.

Sgt Adkins pointed to a calendar he had on the wall above his desk. "I'm going to take next Thursday off. I'm going to assign you as acting sergeant."

Jeff was about to refuse, but thought about it first before speaking.

"I want you to see how it feels before you test, and besides, it's great experience for you."

"Thank you, sir." Jeff figured it would be a mini trial separation from Mickey, and he could see how he felt without him for a day.

Sgt Adkins patted his shoulder and when the sergeant picked up paperwork from his desk, Jeff assumed the conversation was over. He left the sergeants' area and met Mickey just entering the roll call room. "Mick," Jeff craned his finger as he called to him.

Mickey backed up and Jeff and he stood close by a bulletin board, which was wallpapered with wanted suspects' posters pinned to it. "The sarge asked me to be his acting next Thursday."

"Cool." Mickey's expression didn't change.

"Just letting you know."

Mickey nodded and continued walking into the roll call room, taking his normal seat.

The reaction was not what he expected, but Jeff wasn't going to complain. He took a few information bulletins to read while he and the rest of the officers waited for roll call to begin. It was Jeff's turn to write, and Mickey's turn to drive.

Jeff sat beside him, leafing through the latest photos of bad guys. He nudged Mickey. "Why are criminals so ugly?"

Mickey actually laughed.

Jeff slid one bulletin over to him on the desk. "Gawd. I can smell him from here."

Mickey looked at the picture. "Charlie Manson eyes."

"I know, right? Christ, you'd have to shoot him. He'd claw you up in a fight." Jeff looked up when the sergeants entered the room and it settled down as they began calling out car assignments, which inevitably was like taking attendance at school.

Jeff took his pen out of his pocket and began adding horns to the picture of the wanted suspect, turning him into a devil. He could see Mickey being distracted by it as the sergeants went over a quick briefing before sending them all out on the street.

"Just keep alert," Sgt Adkins said, "There've been a lot of weapons calls recently, so remember your tactical training."

Jeff drew pointy ears and a wart on the nose of the wanted man. He slid it over to Mickey who took it to look at. Mickey removed his pen from his pocket and wrote, 'Chandler', under the demonic face.

Jeff covered his laugh and went for a grope of Mickey under the table.

"Okay, unless anyone has any questions, head out." The sergeants stood up from the desk.

Jeff and Mickey rose from their chairs and Jeff glanced behind him. A young officer with a buzz cut and pimples on his chin was sneering at him. Jeff didn't know him, and looked at his name tag. 'P. Cochran.'

"What the hell are you looking at?" Jeff asked.

"A fag?" the new guy said.

Mickey spun around immediately as the room became slightly chaotic with cops leaving to go on duty, chatting or laughing in the bad acoustics.

Mickey puffed up and snarled. He tapped the cop's nametag and said, "I'd watch your mouth- 'P-Cock'."

When Mickey's hand was swiped at, Jeff lunged at the skinhead cop. Mickey held him back and signaled to Jeff to leave the room with a tilt of his head.

Jeff kept looking over his shoulder at the young new recruit. On their way out the door, Jeff picked up his bag. "Fucking pencil-neck freak."

Mickey just nudged Jeff with his elbow and they walked into the parking lot together. It was windy and dark clouds were gathering in the distance.

"Who the hell is he?" Jeff looked over his shoulder.

"Never saw him before. He's assigned to a Lincoln car, so he's on his own."

"Douche." Jeff kept glancing back.

"Well, ya grabbed my nuts, Chandler." Mickey opened the patrol car's driver's door and leaned in.

Jeff tossed his kit in the trunk and made sure they had everything they needed for duty. When he sat in the passenger's side and began typing their information into the computer, he noticed Mickey checking the shotgun before he joined him and turned on the car, and A/C.

"I shouldn't have grabbed you like that." Jeff usually behaved in front of other cops.

"I'm irresistible." Mickey shut off his shoulder microphone since the car radio was now on and it sounded as if the dispatcher was sending cops all over the city the minute they logged into service.

"Wonder if he's been sent to our squad since he fucked up in another." Jeff sat correctly in the seat and put the seatbelt on over his bulky Kevlar vest.

"Probably. He's got a homophobic chip on his shoulder." Mickey adjusted the seat for his long legs and said, "Okay, baby. Let's rock and roll."

Jeff hit the computer button that logged them into service.

They both waited for the inevitable dispatch call of Eight-Adam-One.

"Huh." Jeff tapped keys on the computer to see what was holding. After all, it was Sunday mid-day and maybe the city wasn't going to pot just yet. "Nothing holding." He read the computer.

"Son of a bitch. Cool." Mickey drove out of the parking lot and began cruising the high visibility areas to be seen as a deterrent, and enjoy the scantily clad pretty boys of summer in WeHo.

Jeff put his hand on Mickey's thigh and looked at the brightly clothed tourists who were most likely not expecting a rain shower, if indeed it did materialize.

"Coffee?" Jeff pointed to a drive through coffee shop.

"Sounds good." Mickey drove the patrol car behind the small line of cars and rolled the window down, still blowing the air conditioning to keep the interior cool.

"Frap," Jeff said, taking out his wallet.

"Your turn to buy."

"I know." He handed Mickey a ten.

"Ya want a doughnut?" Mickey teased.

"Nah, but ask for one and see what they do." Jeff laughed.

A few radio transmissions came over the air; traffic stops, someone flagged down for an old woman who had fallen…

Mickey pulled up to the window. Jeff leaned down to see a young man with a bright smile greet him.

"Hi." Mickey grinned mischievously.

"Hi. What can I get you?" The young man appeared shy.

Another gay boy with a cop fetish in West Hollywood? Jeff laughed to himself.

"A tall frap for my partner here, and I'll take a mocha frap…and…"

Jeff made sure he looked at the young man.

"Ya got doughnuts?" Mickey said it in such a way that the young man cracked up and turned bright red.

"No doughnuts," the man replied, laughing.

"Don't you know it's all we cops eat?" Mickey held out the ten in the breeze.

"We have cinnamon rolls, croissants..."

"Nah," Mickey teased, "If it ain't glazed with a big hole, we don't want it."

Jeff cracked up as the young man roared with laughter. He took the ten and couldn't stop giggling.

Mickey looked back at Jeff and winked.

Jeff felt so much affection for Mickey at that moment he wondered how he could ever survive without him on the job.

They were handed the cold drinks one by one and Mickey said, "Keep the change."

"Thanks!"

As they drove off, Jeff said, "Wow, you were generous with my cash." He stuffed the straw into the plastic cover.

"He was a gay twink working at a drive-through window."

"Aww. Okay, ya old softie."

"Ain't soft now." Mickey brought Jeff's hand to his crotch.

"Get one hand on the wheel, Stanton." Jeff grabbed it while Mickey sucked on the drink with one hand and used his second one to move Jeff's fingers against his hard cock.

Mickey stuck the drink into the holder and took over steering while Jeff also let his drink sit, since it was so cold it was giving him brain-freeze and he could barely get it through the straw.

"You just want me 'cause I'm a cop." Jeff batted his lashes, flirting with Mickey.

"Yeah. Guilty." Mickey reached to run his hand from Jeff's knee to his groin.

"So many people have cop fetishes," Jeff said, looking at where Mickey was driving, out of the crowded parking lot to the main street.

"I know. Christ, Richfield is the worst."

"Followed by his son." Jeff thought about Alexander. "Wonder why?"

"Dunno. Maybe some people think we're powerful, protectors, heroes…"

"Ha!" Jeff smiled. "Stupid motherfuckers."

"Half the world love us and want to have sex with us, the other half want us dead." Mickey kept his hand between Jeff's legs as he drove.

"Crazy fucking job. Why do we do it?"

"Because *we're* crazy."

Jeff checked the computer to see if anything was holding from dispatch, and to figure out where the other cops were in their area. "Fuck. Everyone's available except for two on a traffic stop."

"Don't complain. Beats running, call to call, to call." Mickey picked up his drink and sipped it.

Jeff perked up and rolled down his window. "Is that thunder?"

Mickey set his drink down and lowered the radio. A loud rumble and a flash of lightning on the horizon gave them the answer.

"We should park someplace and watch it." Jeff slurped his drink.

"Gonna be traffic accidents everywhere. No one knows how to drive in the rain."

"Is it actually raining?" Jeff leaned closer to the windshield.

"Yeah. Can't you see it sheeting in the distance? Look closer."

Jeff pushed his sunglasses to the top of his head. "Oh, yes. I see it. It's over Burbank maybe?"

Another rolling boom came after a white zap of lightning.

"Aww, a rainbow…" Jeff pointed to it.

"I need to fuck you." Mickey took Jeff's hand and began rubbing himself with it.

"Dirty cop...dirty, dirty." Jeff smiled and sucked his drink through the straw. Mickey drove towards the darkness in the sky and used Jeff's hand to practically jerk off.

"Eight-Adam-One."

"Ahh, here we go." Jeff set his empty cup into the holder and picked up the microphone. "Eight-Adam-One."

"Possible ten-seventy-four at the location I sent to your screen."

"Roger." Jeff read the details. "It's someone hanging out at the abandoned place on West Sunset."

"Any description?"

"Two males, twenties. That's it. Anonymous complainant."

"Okay." Mickey made a U-turn and headed in the other direction. "That area needs to be revived. You'd think its prime real estate."

"Well, that's why it's taking so long to come back. Between the lousy market and what they're probably asking for it, no one wants to pay."

After a few minutes in traffic Jeff picked up the microphone to tell dispatch, "Eight-Adam-One, ten-ninety-seven."

Dispatch echoed Jeff's announcement that they had arrived.

Mickey slowly drove down an alley and crept between the graffiti-covered walls as litter blew in the breeze and thunder rumbled. Mickey cruised around the back of the building and stopped the car. Jeff climbed out and they had a look around the area. Fresh 'artwork' had been painted on a brick wall as well as abandoned spray paint canisters dropped on the ground near it.

Jeff said, "What the hell. It's slow. Let me take some pictures of it for the gang unit." He walked to his kit in the back of the patrol car.

"You're such a good cop." Mickey made a face of sarcasm at him.

Jeff chuckled and opened the trunk, taking out his camera.

Mickey picked up the paint canister with a gloved hand. "Wanna fingerprint it, Columbo?"

"Shut up." Jeff laughed and took a few shots of the fresh tags. "I could. Got the fingerprint kit."

"Shut up. Christ, do all you SPD transplants do everything no one else wants to do?"

"Nope. Just me." Jeff took a few digital pictures and put the camera back in his bag.

"Shit."

"What?" Jeff looked up.

Mickey gestured to a steel door that had been pried open.

"Damn it." Jeff keyed his shoulder microphone. "Eight-Adam-One."

"Eight-Adam-One."

"Open premise."

"Eight-Adam-One has an open premise."

Mickey took his gun out of his holster and peered in. Jeff was behind him, gun in hand.

"Would you like the air held, Eight-Adam-One?" the dispatcher asked.

"Negative." Jeff walked behind Mickey into an abandoned retail shop. It was dim but not pitch black since the front was glass pane windows, and sunlight was filtering in. A loud crack of thunder made Jeff jump but he was behind Mickey, glad Mickey didn't see him or he'd be teased about it. Broken glass crackled under their boots and Mickey scanned the area as they walked, slowly into the open space.

Other radio transmissions began to hit the airwaves, so Jeff and Mickey both, in reflex, turned their volume down. Jeff stood to listen to their surroundings. "Don't hear a thing."

"Me neither. Going left."

"Going right." Jeff raised his gun to eye level and walked the perimeter seeing loose wires hanging, holes in the walls where fixtures were tugged out, exposed pipes… It was abandoned, probably in a foreclosure of some kind since it was stripped. Jeff came to a door, tugged it, and it was locked. He had seen all he could see and yelled, "Clear!"

Hearing Mickey still walking on the debris, Jeff lowered his gun and made his way towards him.

"Clear." Mickey holstered his gun and scanned around. "Looks like the transients haven't found it yet."

"No. Doesn't smell like piss." Jeff clipped his gun into his holster and looked up at the torn out ceiling. "Wonder what this was?"

Jeff was slammed hard against a wall and Mickey pressed his mouth over Jeff's. Jeff grunted at the surprise attack, though he should have been used to them by now.

While they kissed, Mickey went for Jeff's belt. Jeff peeked back at the open door but knew they had done this kind of thing before…a lot, and so far had been very lucky not to get caught.

Jeff's cock was exposed and Mickey stroked it while he sucked on Jeff's tongue. Just as Jeff expected Mickey to crouch down in front of him, Mickey spun Jeff to face the wall, and Jeff's heavy gun belt went to his knees.

"Mick! Are you crazy?" Jeff pressed his palms against the dirty wall and looked down as his utility belt hung in a heap over his boots.

He heard rustling and then felt Mickey pushing his cock into his ass. "Fuck!" Jeff closed his eyes and remembered Mickey showing him the packets of lubrication. Mickey held Jeff's cock and pulled on it as he made his way inside.

"Don't get spunk on my uniform!" Jeff gulped from nerves and tried to listen -to make sure no one spotted them- as the rumble of thunder shook the building. The daylight vanished as dark clouds closed in and they were in shadow.

Mickey hammered inside him and jerked Jeff's cock just as quickly. "Come you fucker! Come!" Mickey urged.

It wasn't like they had all day. Jeff struggled under the circumstances to climax but hearing Mickey gaining momentum, he felt the origins of a climax hit his groin.

"Oh, fuck me...fuck me..." Jeff moaned. This was a first. Sucking, yeah, kissing, all the time. Fucking?

A deep sexual grunt came from Mickey and Jeff felt his cock pulsate.

"Jeff, oh, God...Jesus, what a rush." Mickey jerked Jeff's cock harder.

Thinking of what they were doing, and where...Jeff came from the taboo act. The adrenalin jolt was beyond his comprehension. Mickey aimed Jeff's dick at the wall and it splattered his cum and ran down the ripped plasterboard.

"Oh, Christ, oh, holy Christ," Mickey said as he whimpered, milking Jeff's cock.

"Eight-Adam-One, status?"

Jeff panicked and Mickey pulled out quickly, keying his microphone, trying not to pant into it and said, "Eight-Adam-One, under control. Premise checks clear."

Jeff yanked up his pants and felt Mickey's cum running down his inner thigh. He opened up a sterile wipe packet, which they had with their rubber gloves in their pockets, and tried to clean up.

"Eight-Adam-One, under control." The dispatcher's reply echoed in the empty space.

"Oh, Jeff..." Mickey laughed as he fastened his belt. "That was wild as hell."

Jeff tossed the disinfectant wipe to the floor and tugged his clothing up, getting himself together. "If someone checked on us? Spotted the patrol car? Came for a back up? We'd be dead. Out of a job."

"It is so worth it." Mickey purred, grinning like the crazy rogue cop he was.

Finally put back together again, Jeff ran his hand through his hair and heard the rain hitting the front window. It pelted it like hail. He walked to it instinctively and both he and Mickey peered out. People were scattering like cockroaches in the light, none with umbrellas, holding newspapers up or just dodging the downpour. The building rattled as the thunder hit directly overhead.

Jeff looked over at his lover, his partner, his best friend, seeing him watching the white pellets gather on the sidewalk and the sky turn black.

"What am I going to do with you, Stanton?"

Mickey turned to look at him, the affection in Mickey's blue eyes was like a drug to Jeff. "You're doing it."

Jeff cupped the back of Mickey's head and kissed him.

Chapter Nine

Mickey sat across from Jeff at a Mexican restaurant they frequented on duty. While wearing a uniform, you had to be careful where you ate, or something nasty would end up in your food.

Jeff munched on the burrito, eating quickly.

Outside the rain was still moving through the area, starting and stopping like a temperamental dog on a leash. One second the sun would shine through the window they were seated beside, the next moment the wind would whip the rain sideways and it would appear as dark as dusk.

Both Mickey and Jeff perked up when a call came over the radio. Jeff swallowed his mouthful of food and asked Mickey, "Did they just say a ten-twenty-nine victor?"

"Yeah." Mickey turned up the volume. "Fuck! That's right outside the restaurant!"

Jeff pressed his ear to the microphone. "They're bailing out of the car!" He and Mickey left their food and took off, racing out of the restaurant and immediately Mickey could see the stolen car had crashed into a wire fence surrounding a parking lot.

Sirens were blasting from every direction and cops were chasing suspects as they scattered. Mickey scaled the fence with a leap and sprinted after one, a kid, no older than sixteen, who looked back at Mickey as he ran, terrified. Mickey tackled him into the mud and handcuffed him, a knee on the kid's back, and a knee on the back of the kid's neck.

He looked up and spotted Jeff helping another cop cuff a second man who was fighting. Mickey said, "Get up," to the kid and hauled him to his feet.

A member of the squad who had been on the stolen car's track, raced over to Mickey, catching his breath. "Where the fuck did you and Chandler come from?" he asked.

"We were eating. There." Mickey pointed across the street.

"Thanks, dude!" The cop swapped his handcuffs with Mickey's.

"Ya got him?" Mickey asked as the suspect was led away.

"Yeah."

He clipped his cuffs back to his holder on his belt and noticed mud all over his boots. Mickey waited as Jeff walked over to him. Jeff was wiping his hands on his uniform pants and he too had mud on his shoes and one knee.

"Nice leap, Mick! Holy shit, you hurdled a fucking six foot fence like it was a curb."

"How'd you get over it?" Mickey and he walked back to the fence.

"Like this." With less flair, Jeff climbed it and jumped over it.

Mickey did the same and they crossed the street as the madness died down and the scene became controlled. They entered the restaurant and Conchita, their usual waitress said, "I have them warming. I hoped you'd be able to finish eating."

"Thank you, Conchita." Jeff held up his hands. "Need to wash them now."

Jeff followed Mickey to the men's room and scrubbed his hands up, then relieved himself while he had the chance. Jeff did the same.

They returned to their table and Conchita brought out the two half-eaten plates of food.

"What happened outside?" The pretty dark-haired woman put her hands on her hips.

"A stolen car was spotted," Jeff said, picking up his glass of water to sip. "The occupants bailed out and took off."

"Did you catch them?"

"Of course!" Mickey smiled at her, eating his food.

"Of course!" she repeated and gave him a playful whack on the shoulder. Then she set their bill down before she left.

"I love her." Jeff grinned happily.

"She's a gem." Mickey looked at the amount. "Your turn?"

"I paid for the coffee."

"True." Mickey took out his wallet and tossed cash on the table.

"Well, that took up our lunch break." Jeff finished wolfing down his food and gulped the water.

"I know. But what were we gonna do? Sit here when it was going down right there?" Mickey pointed to the door. He held up the cash. "Here ya go, sweetheart."

Conchita approached the table and took the money and the tab.

"No change." Mickey gave her a sweet smile. "And thanks."

"You know I love you two." She batted her eyelashes and walked to the cash register.

"She thinks we're straight." Jeff stood and checked the time.

"Yup." They both waved to her and she threw them a kiss as they left. "Keeps her sweet and helpful."

"You'd think after all this time she'd wonder why we never asked her out for a date." Jeff looked up at the break in the clouds and put his sunglasses on.

Mickey did the same, walking to their patrol car. As they did Jeff keyed his radio microphone, "Eight-Adam-One, ten-eight."

"Eight-Adam-One is ten-eight, ten-four. Call on your screen, Eight-Adam-One."

"Roger." Jeff climbed into the black and white patrol car and as Mickey turned on the engine, the computer began to make noises alerting them a call was on the screen. They pressed their shoulders together so they could both read the information.

"Check the welfare?" Mickey made a face of disgust. "Oh no. Not right after we ate. That's just not fair."

"And its summer. Fuck!" Jeff rubbed his face and hoped for the best. "Why are they sending an Adam car? Come on. Let that newbie take it." Jeff shut off his shoulder microphone and buckled his seatbelt.

Mickey backed out of the spot and began heading to the location. "Says the complainant is an out-of-state family member."

"Fuck!" Jeff shifted uncomfortably in the seat. "Fuck, fuck, fuck." He heard Mickey sigh and they stayed quiet as they drove. The clouds had vanished and the water dried like misty vapor from the hot tarmac. Jeff hated patrol. He had to get off of it. He glanced over at Mickey as he drove through the traffic, which in LA seemed to be the norm.

In fifteen minutes they pulled in front of an older, not well kept home. The paint was peeling, dried weeds swayed on the front lawn. The roof sagged and the driveway cement was cracked and stained with oil or mud.

Jeff made sure he had rubber gloves in his pocket. He looked at the notes on the computer screen again. "We're looking for Clara Brown, age seventy-five."

Mickey nodded and exited the car.

Jeff could already see newspapers piling up outside the home. He picked one up to read the date. "Four days. Fuck!"

Mickey pointed to the window. "Flies."

Jeff and he walked closer and the glass was buzzing with black flies. Thousands.

"We need masks. And petroleum vapor rub." Mickey crossed his arms over his chest.

"Got it in my kit." Jeff walked back to the trunk. He removed two cotton surgical masks and as Mickey stood beside him, Jeff poked some of the strong minty gel around his nose and looped the face mask to hang around his neck. Mickey did the same. Jeff shut the trunk and they walked around the home looking for an easy entrance. As they did they banged on the doors and windows, calling, “Clara!” but they already knew no one would answer.

Mickey tried the back door. “It’s not locked.”

Jeff put the mask on, since he could already smell rot, and gloved up. Mickey pushed open the door. The stench was unbearable, and unmistakable.

Jeff winced and even through the strong vapor rub scent, he could not avoid the reek of death.

“A fucking hoarder.” Mickey took one step into the kitchen and stopped. It was piled with trash and the flies were like a moving black cloud. Both men used their sunglasses to cover their eyes.

“I need a bio suit. You gotta be kidding me!” Jeff stopped short.

“Gotta find her.” Mickey began stepping between the bags of trash and newspaper.

“How do people live like this?” Jeff spotted a sink filled with dirty scraps and crusted plates.

He followed Mickey as Mickey walked slowly, carefully, through the tiny aisles between the trash. The smell grew stronger near a bedroom, or what may have been one, since there was so much clutter in the home, Jeff couldn’t see the floor or furniture. They heard something move and Jeff jumped out of his skin and so did Mickey. “Rats?”

“I wouldn’t be surprised.” Mickey advanced slowly and Jeff tried not to gag.

“Found her.” Mickey stopped at a doorway.

Jeff peered in. A bloated black and dark blue body was on top of a pile of junk on a bed. A snarling noise made Jeff grab Mickey’s arm. “What the hell was that?”

“Oh, fuck no.” Mickey took out his mace from his utility belt.

A mangy dog was nearly invisible in the litter, shaking, and dirty looking. It was growling and showing its teeth. Small, but not happy.

"Gotta let the sarge know." Mickey keyed his radio mike, "Eight-Adam-One."

"Eight-Adam-One," dispatch replied.

"Advise Eight-Lincoln-Twenty we have a ten-forty-five David, and we need animal control."

"Ten-four. Will get you an ETA on animal control and the ten-fifty-five. Eight-Lincoln-Twenty, copy?"

"Copy." Sgt Adkins did not sound happy, but who was when it came to a decomposing corpse.

"Roger," Mickey said into the microphone, letting him know he heard all the information. Then he looked down at the dog.

"Poor thing probably hasn't eaten in days." Jeff scanned around the room. It was so loaded with junk he had no clue if there was dog food around, but he could see feces.

"He ate." Mickey peered at the dead body.

"He ate?"

Mickey nudged Jeff closer and pointed to the body.

"Oh fuck."

"He was hungry. What was he supposed to do?" Mickey looked around the room which was nothing more than a landfill.

"Licking gone awry?"

"Maybe at first. He may have been trying to wake her up." Mickey crouched down, reaching out. "Here, boy."

The dog raised its hackles and snarled.

"Cujo." Jeff didn't even bother, not with the trauma this dog had been through.

"Eight-Adam-One."

Mickey answered dispatch, "Eight-Adam-One."

"ETA for animal control, fifteen, ten for the ten-fifty-five."

"Ten-four." Mickey looked at Jeff. "Well, at least the coroner will be quick."

"He can't go near that body with the dog there." Jeff adjusted his mask and knew the stench was permeating his uniform. It was hot as hell in the house and he was dripping sweat under his uniform vest.

"May as well get out." Mickey started walking towards the back door.

They stepped outside and stood in the shade. Mickey took off the mask and Jeff could see him trying to breathe untainted air. But since the door was open, it was impossible to avoid the stench.

Sgt Adkins called to them over radio, asking them to switch to an alternate frequency.

Jeff lowered his mask and said, "Ten-four." Jeff changed this radio channel. "Ya there, Sarge?"

"Yeah. What do you have?"

"Check the welfare. Appears to be a natural DOA."

"Need me there?"

"Not unless you want to see a bloated corpse with its face eaten by a dog."

"I'll pass. Over."

Jeff turned the radio back to their normal frequency. He walked towards the patrol car, having to write up a DOA report. He heard Mickey following behind him and they both took off the rubber gloves and sat in the car, engine on, air conditioner blasting. Jeff began to fill in the report on the computer.

"So…that's it. One day ya just go?" Mickey looked out of the windshield, his sunglasses still perched on his nose.

Jeff had pushed is to the top of his head so he could read the computer more easily. "Guess so."

"Don't wanna die like that."

"On a pile of trash?" Jeff gave him a look of disbelief. "Ya won't. Believe me."

"No. I mean, old, alone."

"Alone?" Jeff pressed his hand to his own chest. "What am I? Chopped liver? Alone?"

"What if you go before me?"

"I'm younger than you!"

"One year? That's nothing."

Jeff tried to write and talk simultaneously. "Oh, so now I'm going to die."

"Well," Mickey said, splaying out his hands. "We're cops. Cops die."

"Shut the fuck up!" Jeff grew upset. *Why do you think I want to get off the front lines, moron!* "Let me write."

"Alex nearly lost Billy."

Jeff sat back and blew out a breath. "You're killin' me, Stanton."

"Fucker took how many rounds to the chest?"

"Mick!" Jeff glared at him in exasperation. "Why do you think I want to get the hell off patrol?"

Mickey kept quiet and Jeff got back to writing. About forty minutes later, not ten, the coroner's van showed up. Both Jeff and Mickey got out of their car to speak to him.

"There's a dog in there." Jeff pointed to the house. "He won't let you near the body."

"Animal control on the way?"

Mickey looked at his watch. "He was supposed to be here twenty minutes ago. Mickey stepped away and made the enquiry to dispatch again.

Jeff said to the coroner, "She was a hoarder. The place is a pit. Loaded with trash, shit, and flies."

"Perfect summer combination." The older Asian man shook his head and walked to the back of the van, opening the door and pulling out a gurney which was topped with a body-bag.

While Mickey waited for the animal control unit, Jeff walked the coroner to the back of the house.

"Did you guys break in?" he asked.

"No. The back door was unlocked. No sign of forced entry." Jeff put the mask back on as the smell hit. He gloved up.

The coroner took one look inside and said, "Not getting the gurney in there. Jesus."

"Nope. No way."

"Where is she?" He gloved up, but didn't put anything over his face.

"I'll show you." Jeff made his way back to the bedroom, and the dog snarled as they drew close. The pooch was now sitting on the bed beside his…meal.

The coroner waved at the flies and shook his head. "Gotta get that dog out of here."

"Yup."

They both headed back outdoors and just as Jeff looked up, one of the officers from the animal control unit was there with Jeff, holding a pole with a noose on the end.

"Oh fuck." The animal control officer got a whiff. Then he peeked inside. "Goddamn it." He looked at Mickey. "You guys got an extra mask?"

"Yup." Mickey waved him back to the patrol car and the animal officer handed Jeff the pole. "Hold this."

Jeff took it and looked at the coroner. "No mask? Really?"

The small Asian man shrugged.

"Damn." Jeff shook his head. "I never get used to the smell."

"I know. I have, but it still is revolting."

The animal control officer returned, gloved up, his feet covered with white contamination booties and the white mask covering his mouth and nose. He took the pole and said, "Where's the damn dog?"

Jeff entered the house first, followed by the other three. Jeff gestured to the correct room, batting away the flies as they circled his head.

The animal control officer stood still to look in and shook his head. "Sick. Really fucking sick." He reached the pole out to the shaking, mangy mutt and without any trouble, slipped the noose around its neck and began to lead him out. Once collared, the dog went insane, snarling and jerking its head side to side, struggling not to be separated from its owner.

Jeff and Mickey stood by as the officer took the dog away.

"Bye, Cujo." Mickey waved and Jeff heard the control officer chuckle, then he was gone.

The coroner approached the body.

Jeff and Mickey stood at the doorway.

When the coroner rolled the body up slightly, a swarm of black flies took wing and Mickey and Jeff grabbed each other in reaction and backed up. When Jeff heard the coroner gag, he was stunned. The man muttered, "Fucking maggots." How the man could bear the stench without a mask was beyond Jeff.

Mickey said, "I can't take the smell. Christ, he unleashed something when he moved it."

"Gases from the decomposition," the coroner said.

Jeff said through the mask, "We'll be at the back door."

He and Mickey left the house and tried to breathe. A few minutes later the coroner appeared. "I can't see any sign of trauma. It looks like a natural death but I'll know more after I examine it at the morgue."

"Okay." Jeff shrugged.

The coroner picked up the body bag and said, "Give me a hand?"

Mickey and Jeff exchanged horrified glances, but what were they going to do?

"You get the feet," Jeff said to Mickey as he followed the man back into the house.

"No, you do."

"No! You do!" Jeff knew from experience what happened when you were on the wrong end of a rotting corpse. You got slimed.

"I will," the coroner said, "Christ. You two are a regular comedy act." He climbed right over the mess fearlessly and, with little effort, by himself, placed the body into the bag.

Jeff and Mickey waited. Once it was zipped in, he waved them over.

Jeff tried not to gag as the stench, even with the vapor rub up his nose and a mask on, it was unbearable. He and Mickey grabbed the top end of the bag, the coroner, the feet end, and they hauled it out over the piles of trash and dog poop.

Once it was on the gurney, the coroner nodded, “Thanks,” and wheeled it away.

Jeff pointed to the back door of the house. “We have to secure it.”

“Let’s look for a board and nails.”

“Hang on.” Jeff inspected the lock, turned a little knob and closed it. He gave the door a shake and it didn’t open. “Mission accomplished.”

They walked back to the car again, peeled off the rubber gloves and taking off the masks. Jeff inhaled the fresh air a few times but the smell was in his uniform and sinuses. He checked his boots for anything that may have stuck, but he had not stepped in shit. “God! I hate this job!” Jeff sat in the patrol car as Mickey walked around the other side and got in behind the wheel.

“Jeff.” Mickey put his hand on Jeff’s knee. “Chill.”

Jeff threw the gloves and mask on the floor of the passenger’s side and adjusted his sunglasses.

“Let’s hang onto the call a while and decompress. Okay?”

Jeff nodded and Mickey drove them to their favorite hiding place at the church.

~

Mickey backed into the corner of their ‘spot’ of the large parking lot. Since it was Sunday, there were a few cars behind the church, but it was late in the day and most of the functions were over. The parking area was so large, Mickey doubted anyone from the church would even notice them, or care.

He put the car in park and rested his arm behind Jeff, nudging Jeff to relax against him. After slight resistance, Jeff did, his head on Mickey’s shoulder.

“I could sleep.” Jeff yawned.

"Two hours to go. We're almost there." Mickey kissed Jeff's hair, nuzzling in.

"Would you consider any other branch of LAPD, Mick?"

"SWAT."

"Jesus." Jeff shook his head. "That's going the wrong way. More danger, not less."

"Fucking love the rush.

"The adrenalin is toxic."

"I know." Mickey stroked Jeff's hair gently. He held him close and caressed Jeff's leg as well, running his hand up his thigh.

"I can't believe you fucked me on duty."

Mickey smiled. "I know, right? One for the nightly journal."

"We should tell Mark. He'd cream."

"Remember the first day we met him? When we got the alarm call at his house?" He heard Jeff laugh.

"He and Steve walked in on me giving you a BJ."

"No. I was giving you one. Wasn't I?"

"No. I was giving you one."

"Whatever. I thought we were dead after seeing Steve's academy graduation picture hanging on the wall. Imagine if he were some hard-ass lieutenant?" Mickey ran his hand over the bulge between Jeff's legs.

"Seriously, Mick. What were the odds of us getting that call to Mark's house?"

"Now that we know him, we've been to a couple of calls involving him. Remember when Alex disappeared and it ended up being those pathetic frat morons trying to get Alex to join?"

"I remember. Not to mention the night Mark fainted in the parking lot. I can't believe when he does those modeling shoots he starves himself so much he passes out." Jeff touched Mickey's leg.

"Fucker dropped in the parking lot at the photography studio." Mickey massaged Jeff's cock as it hardened under his hand. "He's lucky he wasn't stripped of his wallet and watch in that neighborhood."

"I couldn't handle him." Jeff sat up so he could see Mickey while they spoke. "Seriously. I could not handle having him as my husband."

"I think that's why Steve needs Jack and Adam so much. He can't either." Mickey tilted Jeff's jaw up with the tip of his finger. They kissed.

Jeff shifted on the seat to be able to lean against Mickey's chest, vest to vest, and they made out, digging into each other's hair and cupping each other's jaw.

Twirling his tongue around Jeff's, Mickey knew this is what made patrol bearable for him. Jeff. Jeff's kiss, his touch, his cock… If he didn't have Jeff as his partner, he'd literally go out of his mind.

Jeff parted from Mickey's kiss and smiled wickedly at him. "I'd blow you, but you had your fucking prick up my ass."

"I did indeed." Mickey grinned. "I should make you suck it anyway."

"No. You're not that cruel." Jeff used the tip of his tongue to tease Mickey's mouth.

"I need to come."

"You always need to come." Jeff ran his hand over where Mickey had grown hard. Jeff stopped moving as if listening to the radio. "Is that someone asking for a backup?"

"Yeah. It's that P. Cock prick. Fuck him."

"No one's answering up." Jeff shifted, moving back to his seat.

Mickey stopped him, wanting more kisses. "It's what happens when you're a douchebag."

Jeff gave Mickey another kiss and then dispatch relayed over radio, "Code two- All units. Code two for Eight-Lincoln-Two. Eleven-ninety-nine."

"That asshole!" Mickey threw the car into drive and Jeff picked up the radio microphone as he gripped onto the dashboard for balance. "Eight-Adam-One, responding."

"Eight-Adam-One, ten-four."

Jeff held onto the handle over the passenger's door, trying to fasten his seatbelt with his left hand, as Mickey turned on the lights and sirens and put the pedal to the metal.

"Location?" Mickey asked Jeff as the computer began to beep and give them the details of the call. Other officers finally offered to go as well. 'Help the officer' calls were of the highest priority to all of the cops in every district.

"Santa Monica Boulevard. Keep going." Jeff waved him on and read the details. "Fucker is on a traffic stop. He ran a license plate but I don't see any warrants or names on the call yet."

Since it was a Sunday night, the traffic was light and Mickey flew over the streets, his sirens wailing and yelping as he headed cautiously through red traffic signals.

"There!" Jeff pointed.

Mickey spotted a patrol car and screeched to a halt. They raced over to the marked unit and could see a chopper style motorcycle had been pulled over, but neither the cop nor the rider were there. Jeff got on radio, "What's his twenty, radio?"

Before she replied, a shot rang out. Both Mickey and Jeff ducked and drew their weapons, racing behind the buildings towards an alley. Mickey stopped, gun pointed down, finger off the trigger and looked around the corner first.

An officer shouted over radio, "Shots fired!" To Mickey it sounded like Cochran's voice.

"Eight-Lincoln-Two, ten-twenty?" dispatch tried to get the dipshit to tell someone where he was. "Eight-Lincoln-Two, do you have a suspect description?"

They heard a breathless voice reply, "Foot pursuit!" over the air. "Male…helmet…leather jacket…" was gasped into the microphone.

"Where?" Mickey looked around the wall, throwing up his hands.

"That fucker doesn't know where he is!" Jeff took off down the alley, still holding his gun, while Mickey could hear the sirens of other units begin to flood the area. Another shot was fired and both Jeff and Mickey stopped running, taking cover behind a wall. “Where is that coming from?” Mickey asked.

“It’s gotta be south of us, down the alley.” Jeff took a deep breath and they kept searching. No matter how many times the dispatcher asked for Cochran’s location, he either couldn’t give it, or didn’t know it.

“Is he firing the shots or is someone shooting at him?” Jeff asked as he ran, looking up and down the driveways and between houses.

Finally Mickey spotted Cochran, his gun in his hand, gasping for breath, bent over, hands on knees. They jogged over to him.

“Where’s the suspect?” Jeff asked.

“Lost him.” Cochran could barely talk he was so winded.

“You shooting the rounds or was he?” Mickey spun around, gun up at eye level, scanning.

“Me.”

“Why?” Jeff asked.

“Fucker ran!”

“Ran?” Mickey gaped at him. “Was he armed?”

“Don’t know.”

“You don’t fucking know?” Mickey yelled, “So you were just shooting at a guy who ran from a traffic stop?”

“Fuck you!” Cochran snarled at him.

Jeff spoke on the radio, giving dispatch their exact location.

Sgt Adkins’ voice came over the air. “Eight-Lincoln-Twenty, en route.”

“Roger,” dispatch replied.

Mickey was about to kill someone. “Let me get this straight!” He sneered and gripped his gun. “You pull someone over…”

Jeff asked, “The Harley?”

Cochran nodded, catching his breath finally.

“And the guy runs.” Mickey kept an eye around the area, still trying to figure out if the man they were chasing was armed.

“Yeah.”

"And you blew rounds off at him?" Jeff gaped in shock.

"And the guy wasn't armed?" Mickey echoed his tone.

"He said he was going to kill me! He reached for something!"

"You're a fuckup! You give cops everywhere a bad fucking name!" Mickey kept looking around. "He may go back for his bike. I'm heading back."

Keeping his weapon in his hand, Mickey was breathing fire. Jeff walked behind him and he could hear Cochran following. Mickey spun around and said, "You stay put! Sarge is coming to that location!" Mickey pointed to where they found Cochran.

"Fuck you! Who do you think you are, asshole?" Cochran still held his gun in his hand.

Jeff stepped between them. "Calm down and holster!"

Mickey put his gun into his holster and glared at this fuckhead.

"Holster!" Jeff ordered Cochran.

"You're not wearing stripes on your sleeve, fuck you!"

Jeff touched Mickey's arm and urged him to continue walking back to their car. He could see black and white patrol vehicles still circling the area, looking for? What? Some guy who maybe didn't have insurance?

"Fucking fags!"

Mickey spun around instantly and Jeff grabbed Mickey to stop him.

"Mick. He's out of his head and he is still holding his gun. This asshole fired two rounds already."

"What'd you call me?" Mickey stormed back.

"No, Mick!" Jeff tried to restrain him.

Mickey dragged Jeff with him. When Mickey was looking down at Cochran, he roared with hatred. "I said, *what did you call me*?"

Jeff ordered Cochran, "Holster your weapon, now!" Jeff pointed his pistol at Cochran.

Mickey flexed his arms and said, "Ya wanna shoot me, P-Cock?"

"Hate you scum. Fags like you are ruining this department, this country."

Mickey saw Cochran's finger move to the trigger. Jeff got into a shooting stance. "Drop the weapon, Cochran!"

Cochran jammed his gun into the holster, sneering with disgust at Mickey.

Jeff slowly lowered his gun and didn't holster it.

"Why did we back a pig like you? Huh?" Mickey asked. "Calling us fags?"

"Heard you were." Cochran wiped his face as it dripped with sweat.

"Heard we were?" Jeff choked in shock and then put his gun in his holster.

"*Heard we were*?" Mickey repeated loudly and stepped closer, looking down his nose at the young punk. "What are you doin' in our squad, huh? What did you do to get transferred?"

In the background, one by one the officers who had offered their backup for the search, cleared and left the area. Mickey figured the sergeant was coming from the station, and that was why he was taking so long.

"Fuck you." Cochran spat at Mickey's feet.

Jeff shook his head at Cochran. "Don't provoke Mick. His bite is way worse than his bark. He'll knock you sideways."

Mickey poked Cochran in the chest, hard. "You don't know who the hell I am. You don't know shit about me."

"Only that you take it up the ass, ya cunt."

Mickey went crazy. He grabbed Cochran by the shirt and pinned him to a brick wall so hard Cochran hit with a loud thud.

Jeff shouted, "Mick, he's going for his gun!"

Mickey clamped his hand around Cochran's preventing him from drawing his weapon. With one hand on Cochran's throat, the other trapping his hand on the holster, Mickey completely subdued the man.

Jeff went crazy. He knew people with cameras lurked everywhere, and Mickey did not need to be seen as the aggressor. This call, this shit, had nothing to do with them. "Mick!" Jeff got Mickey in a headlock and physically dragged him off Cochran. "We're done!" He grabbed Mickey by the arm and forced him to walk away. Jeff kept checking behind them, making sure this complete idiot didn't shoot them in the back.

When the sergeant's car pulled up, Jeff breathed a sigh of relief. He kept Mickey heading to their patrol car. "Done. You hear me?" Jeff said. "This incident never happened."

Mickey was silent, which was how Mickey dealt with his fury. Either that or with violence.

Jeff walked him back to their car and pushed Mickey to the driver's side. Cochran's car and the abandoned motorcycle were still there.

"Go. Clear the area." Jeff waved his hand for Mickey to drive away. "We did an area check and that's it. You got it, Stanton!"

"Yeah." Mickey shut down the overhead lights and drove off, looking so angry, Jeff knew this was not the end. Only the beginning.

Jeff followed Mickey as he stormed through the police station corridor. It was finally the end of their shift. The steam cloud of fury coming from Mickey was so intense, Jeff knew this wasn't going to be a good night. Carrying his kit, Jeff watched Mickey vanish around a hall. Jeff stopped, looking for someone; the sergeant, the lieutenant, anyone!

But at the end of shift, no one on their watch was left. Jeff didn't want Mickey to run into Cochran at the moment. Off duty, both armed? It would be worse than on duty.

"Fuck!" Jeff couldn't find anyone that would help and be discreet. He gave up and entered the locker room. Mickey was already hanging his gear and his uniform was in a pile on the floor to be sent for dry cleaning.

Jeff tucked his kit into his locker and began undressing. He tried to keep alert for Cochran but was so exhausted he didn't know if he could prevent an inevitable conflict.

"I have to get off patrol," Jeff muttered to himself as he hung his heavy gun belt up, taking his pistol out and putting it into his waist pack and pinning his badge into his wallet. He changed into his shorts and T-shirt, sniffing his pits and hating summer. The vest was a heat trap.

A loud metallic bang sounded and Jeff turned to look over his shoulder. Mickey, appearing homicidal, stood still after he had slammed the locker door.

Jeff finished changing and he too had his uniform in a ball to be sent to the cleaners. "Come on, Mick." He tilted his head to the door.

As they were leaving, Cochran entered the locker room, still in uniform, obviously intending on changing and going home. Jeff immediately body-blocked Mickey, forcing Mickey to hit the wall of sinks, allowing Cochran to walk by. The two sneered at each other, but no words were exchanged. Jeff grabbed Mickey's shirt and gave him a good shove to the doorway out.

He heard Mickey say, "I will kill him."

"Let him hang himself." Jeff kept nudging Mickey, first to drop off their uniforms for cleaning and next to the exit.

Once they were outside, Jeff blew out a breath of frustration and they walked to the lot where Jeff's car was parked. "You'd make a lousy supervisor."

"Don't wanna be one."

"He's provoking you. If you let him, he'll get you to do something you'll regret." Jeff opened the door locks and sat behind the wheel.

Mickey dropped heavily on the seat beside him, tossing the bag with their dirty T-shirts on the floor by his feet. "If he goes around telling everyone we're fags, how long you think it's going to be before someone believes it and separates us?"

"Come on. Everyone knows we're best friends. All partners end up being close comrades. Shut up, will you? I have a fucking headache."

Mickey exhaled loudly and rubbed the back of Jeff's neck as Jeff pulled out of the parking lot.

"Ow. Right there." Mickey hit a sore spot. "I swear its tension. I'm gonna have a stroke one day, and with you and that asshole pointing guns at each other. Jesus Christ!"

"I didn't point it, you did." Mickey dropped his hand to his lap and slouched low.

"What is his deal? We have to find someone who knows why he was transferred and why he's still a cop. He's mental."

"I know someone who'll know."

Jeff looked at Mickey while he slowed the car for a traffic signal.

"Our guy in IAG." Mickey smiled wickedly.

"Billy! That's right. He's in internal affairs now. Get him on the goddamn phone."

"It's late." Mickey looked at his cell phone. "He works nine to five now."

"Text him." Jeff glanced over as Mickey did. "What are you writing?"

"Just asking if he's there."

Mickey set the phone on his lap as Jeff continued driving to Anaheim in the light traffic. "We need a kick-bag or punching bag at home, Mick."

"I know. I could use to pound something right now."

"No way it's gonna be my ass."

Mickey gave him an evil grin.

Jeff laughed and shook his head. "Oh, Stanton, you are a wicked, wicked cop."

"Grrr." Mickey grabbed Jeff's inner thigh.

"And I love ya." Jeff gave him a playful jab to the jaw.

Mickey glanced at the phone. "Nope. Nuthin'."

"Probably fucking Alexander."

"Probably." Mickey stared out of the window, turning the music louder.

"Wonder what fucking Alex is like?"

"Rumor is he likes it rough."

"Damn." Jeff squirmed in the seat.

"I'm so glad I'm not jealous." Mickey waggled an eyebrow at him sarcastically.

"Oh, hun, we'd fuck him together. Believe me."

"He'd love it. Billy? Not so much."

"Billy would never let anyone near him. Do you blame him?" Jeff lowered the music since they were talking.

"He's very protective over that imp." Mickey rubbed his jaw.

"Twenty year age gap. Boggles the mind."

"Nah. Not really. Alex needs someone like Billy. It's a good match."

"I suppose." Jeff slowed for a stop sign as they drew closer to their home. "Did we remember to record Alex's TV show?"

"I think it's programmed to record the whole series now. So, yeah. Should be."

"Not keen on vampire shit, but love watching Alex nude."

Mickey whacked his shoulder, hard.

"Ouch!" Jeff rubbed his arm. "Jerk."

"Asshole."

"Bitch."

"Ya better watch it, Chandler, or you won't make it inside the front door."

Jeff laughed and smiled at Mickey. "Ahh, the good ole days."

"They ain't gone. I'll fuck you anywhere."

"You made that fucking obvious!" Jeff blew out a breath in disbelief.

At their approach to the townhouse, Jeff slowed down to park in his assigned spot. "Do I have to race you to the door? Or will you let me walk in like a normal human being?" He shut off the engine.

Mickey didn't answer, climbing out, taking the bag with their T-shirts with him.

Jeff was wary. He exited the car and armed it, keeping back from Mickey as Mickey walked to the front door.

Though Mickey appeared casual, putting the key in the lock, turning it, Jeff knew him. Oh, yes. He knew him. He tried to be ready.

Mickey entered the townhouse, threw the plastic bag with their T-shirts on the sofa, and when Jeff stepped in, he was attacked. Even though he expected it, Jeff was slammed against a wall and Mickey used his foot to shut the front door. Between hot kisses, Jeff said, "We both…need…a shower…"

Mickey took off his gun-pack and tossed it on the couch, then did the same with Jeff's.

"You didn't fuck me." Mickey dropped to his knees and opened Jeff's shorts.

"Mick. Oh, Christ." Jeff leaned back against the wall as Mickey drew his entire length into his mouth. Holding Mickey's shoulders, Jeff closed his eyes and braced himself.

Mickey held his cock and sucked long hard suction from the base to the tip.

Jeff's skin began to tingle and his groin swirled with pleasure. Mickey released the suction and nuzzled into Jeff's balls.

"You love my sweat." Jeff tried to catch his breath.

"I love everything about you, you bastard."

When Mickey stood up, walking to the kitchen, Jeff stared at his hard dick. "Hey. Uh, you forget something?"

"Nope." Mickey took a bottle of tequila out of the cupboard and swigged it.

Jeff made his way over making his dick sway side to side. "Share?"

Mickey handed it to him. Jeff drank a gulp as Mickey used his hands to keep Jeff hard. "Let's get wasted."

"Mm." Mickey took the bottle and drank it.

They both had empty stomachs since they hadn't eaten since the Mexican restaurant. Mickey passed the bottle to him and Jeff took a long chug, feeling it burn its way down his throat.

He wiped his mouth and closed his eyes. "Only you."

"Hm?" Mickey took the bottle and drank more.

"There is only one man for me. You."

Mickey put his arm around Jeff's waist and hugged him close. He held the bottle to Jeff's lips and poured.

Jeff gulped it down and Mickey drank the rest. Between them, they finished half a bottle. Mickey slammed the empty bottle on the counter, dropped to his knees and continued sucking.

Jeff swooned and felt lightheaded. "Suck me, you dirty cocksucker." He thrust his length into Mickey's mouth, holding the back of his head. Mickey moaned in pleasure.

"Fucking-cock-sucking pig!" Jeff fucked his mouth. He went into a climax and held Mickey close, making him take him deep. Mickey ran his hands down Jeff's legs and sucked hard and strong.

The climax nearly knocked Jeff off his feet.

Mickey stood, lunged at him, and kissed him, making Jeff fall back against the refrigerator with a bang. His scent and taste was on Mickey's lips along with the tequila.

Mickey's vocalizations began to get wild and he tugged his own shorts down.

"I ain't sucking your cock until you wash it, bitch!" Jeff said, huffing for air.

Mickey turned to the kitchen sink and used the dish soap and water, scrubbing himself up. Jeff opened the fridge and twisted the cap off a beer, beginning to get very heady from the booze.

Mickey dried his cock on a dishtowel and then took the beer from Jeff, guzzling it. He grabbed Jeff's hair with his free hand and forced Jeff to his knees.

Jeff took one look at Mickey's fabulous cut cock and devoured it, grabbing his balls and pushing his finger up his wet ass.

"Fuck! Yeah!" Mickey yelled and the beer bottle was dropped into the sink. "Yeah! Chandler! Yes!"

Jeff closed his eyes sucked hard, allowing Mickey to orally fuck him the way he had done to Mickey. Literally in seconds, Mickey was coming, filling Jeff's mouth. Jeff moaned and swallowed, drunk on sex, drunk on booze, and out of his mind in love.

Chapter Ten

The alarm buzzed.

Mickey moaned in agony and whacked it to shut up. He pulled Jeff close and grabbed at Jeff's crotch, holding his morning wood. Ten minutes later, the alarm went off again.

"Oh, God…*nooo…*" Jeff moaned and covered his head with a pillow.

Another twelve hour shift awaited them. It was Monday.

Mickey shut off the alarm and lay on his back, staring at the ceiling. His cock tented the sheet. With every ounce of energy he had, Mickey sat up, putting his feet on the floor, looking down at his stiff dick. After he ran his hand over it, he glanced back at Jeff who was hiding under a pillow.

"Let's go."

"No." Jeff curled into a ball.

Mickey leaned on his elbow and ran his finger down Jeff's ass crack. "Shower."

Jeff took the pillow off his head and groaned. "I'm either hung over or exhausted."

"You're not hung over. Get up." Mickey stood from the bed and made his way to the bathroom. With both hands leaning on the sink he stared at his blue eyes and sighed. Since he had an erection, he took out his shaving kit and began spreading cream on his jaw, waiting for it to go down so he could piss. Looking in the mirror's reflection, Mickey spotted Jeff stagger in, his hair wild from his sleep, and his jaw dark with his new beard growth.

Mickey watched Jeff try to point his stiff cock at the toilet to pee. He became distracted, then looked back in the mirror to finish shaving.

Jeff managed to relieve himself and started the shower running.

Mickey rinsed his face and stood at the toilet as Jeff took his turn at the sink and spread the shaving gel on his jaw.

"You need a haircut, ya hippie." Mickey released his stream into the toilet as the room began to steam up from the shower.

"No. Gonna do a Mark Richfield. Fuck 'em." Jeff shaved his face.

Mickey chuckled. "See how long you can go before someone writes you up."

"Exactly."

"You can't be a sergeant." Mickey opened the shower door. "*You* don't even obey the rules."

"No one obeys them all." Jeff splashed his face and joined Mickey in the tub.

They took turns washing each other's hair and backs, which was what they had done since they met.

"No. I suppose not. Just who gets caught and who doesn't." Mickey massaged Jeff's scalp. Jeff moaned sensually and Mickey's cock responded. "I wanna fuck you."

"You always wanna fuck me." Jeff rinsed his hair and they swapped spots.

Mickey propped himself up on the tiled wall as Jeff washed his hair, returning the favor. The scalp massage was wonderful. Jeff patted Mickey's bottom, indicating he was done. Mickey rinsed off and soaped up his hand, pressing both his and Jeff's cocks together to jerk off.

Jeff spread his legs and watched.

Mickey righted their erections and jerked them, loving the feel of Jeff's cock against his. Jeff began kissing Mickey's neck, pinching Mickey's nipples.

"Oh, Chandler…why can't I get enough of you?" Mickey already felt the climax beginning to hit. He jerked their cocks faster and Jeff held onto Mickey's biceps and came. Mickey did as well, and they grunted in the wet space, hearing it echo.

Mickey turned to rinse off and allowed Jeff to do the same, then reached for a towel.

Jeff shut off the water and they dried themselves and stepped out of the tub. Mickey tossed the towel over the rack and dressed in light camouflage pattern shorts and a white tank top, checking his phone for missed messages.

Jeff slipped on a pair of beige shorts and a black sleeveless tee, and they headed to the kitchen for breakfast before they took off.

"Anything from Billy?" Jeff asked as he started the coffee pot.

"No." Mickey put four slices of bread in the toaster.

"Huh." Jeff tossed the empty alcohol bottles from the night before into the recycle bin and put butter, peanut butter, and knives on the table.

Mickey set out the milk and their two favorite ceramic mugs as well as travel mugs.

The toast popped up and Jeff spread butter on his, handing off two slices to Mickey, who used peanut butter.

They sat at the kitchen table and ate, both quiet, either tired or thinking. Mickey was thinking. Thinking of what he was going to do if he heard one more gay slur from Cochran.

He and Jeff had been partners for years. There was no doubt people knew they were tight. There was nothing unusual about partners becoming inseparable. It happened to all of the close working pairs. Not only them. And of course being attached to your partner did not necessarily mean sexually.

Cochran assuming he and Jeff were gay was not only irritating Mickey on a deep level, it was a rumor he was not going to allow to flourish. That would mean an instant transfer for one of them and certainly the end of their partnership in the patrol car. And he had just convinced Jeff not to test for sergeant. This was the last thing he needed.

"Stop."

Mickey looked up at Jeff, interrupted from his thoughts.

Jeff said, "Stop obsessing."

"I have to put an end to his insinuations. I know the difference between the guys teasing us for a laugh and someone who is going to be a threat."

"Mick." Jeff shook his head in warning.

"I'm going to fix this...problem," Mickey said with a sneer, "Before it goes viral. People may assume he has proof."

"Babe." Jeff touched Mickey's hand. "He's a little shit who is already disliked. No one offered to back the prick until we answered up. And that was a code two call from dispatch."

"Fucking douche, shooting off rounds like that? He already needs his badge removed." Mickey stood and poured coffee into his travel mug.

"You're right. If either one of us did that, we'd be on instant admin leave and then handed our walking papers." Jeff cleared the table and washed the knives and mugs.

"Let's go. The traffic will be shit." Mickey prepared two travel mugs with coffee and made sure he had his badge with his wallet.

They grabbed their gun-packs, two fresh white T-shirts, and their coffee mugs, and left the house. Mickey walked to his truck. They alternated that too. Whoever had to drive at work, didn't have to drive the commute. So, Jeff was due to drive the patrol car, and Mickey used his truck to get them to the station.

They climbed into the high pickup and Jeff put his mug in a cup holder and fastened his seatbelt. Mickey did the same. It was another bright blue July summer's day in LA, and Mickey never knew what would happen once they were in uniform. It was a crapshoot. You either survived to go home another day or you didn't.

~

Jeff put on a new CD into the music system. Mickey was already amped up too high for hard rock. He liked a few female vocalists, so he put a Lucinda Williams CD into the player.

Mickey didn't speak during their commute, and Jeff wanted to figure out a way to keep an inevitable confrontation between Mickey and Cochran from occurring. He just didn't know how. Not without backup from the brass.

Jeff took out his phone and called Billy's phone number. It went to voicemail. "Sharpe, it's Jeff. Look, I know you're busy, but, could you call me back sometime today? Thanks." He disconnected it and stared at it.

Mickey let out a loud exhale.

"What the fuck?" Jeff felt frustrated. "No one's that busy."

"He just got shot. What do you want from the guy?"

"He got shot, but he got shot in the vest. He's just bruised up."

"Oh?" Mickey looked over at him as he slowed for the highway ramp, headed to the commuter lanes. "So, now you know what it feels like to get hit at close range with 9mm ammo?"

"Shut up."

"No. You shut up." Mickey punched his shoulder.

"Ass." Jeff rubbed his arm.

"Prick."

"Do not, I repeat, *do not* confront Cochran. Do you hear me?"

"I'm not saying a word." Mickey held up his hand and then merged into the HOV lane which was moving a little more quickly than the rest of the highway.

"I know you. You won't say a word, but you'll bust his teeth out." Jeff ran his hand over his hair, feeling its length and tugging at the ends.

"Maybe."

"Look. I want to kick his ass too. You know how much I want to kill the little pecker? But we can't. Let's be the better men, okay? And if we make our battle with him public? Who do you think will be out, him or us?"

Mickey's mouth formed a tight line.

"Let it go, Mick. Just let his shit go right through you, or there will be an inquisition into our lives, our living together, the works. Don't let him bait you."

"Hate it when you're right."

Jeff ran his hand inside Mickey's leg to the edge of his shorts. "I know." Jeff cupped Mickey's cock. "But I always am."

He heard Mickey chuckle and smiled, but Jeff's smile soon faded from his thoughts.

~

Mickey held the door of the station open for Jeff and allowed him to walk inside first. He stared at Jeff's ass in his shorts but resisted grabbing it. The interior of the building was cooler than outside, and already bustling with cops coming on shift, sergeants exchanging information, and the computers and common areas filled with officers writing reports or stuffing evidence envelopes.

He noticed Jeff stop at the bulletin board and stood behind him, seeing if anything new had been posted. The dates for the sergeant's exam were still listed. In annoyance, Mickey turned away from it and continued walking to the locker room. A few cops he knew said hello to him as he passed. He unhooked his waist pack and stood at his locker, spinning the combination.

When he glanced up at someone close behind him, he saw Jeff holding two uniforms, both back from the cleaners.

"Oh. Thanks." Mickey took his and hung it inside his locker, tearing off the thin plastic wrap on it.

As Mickey changed, Chris walked over to speak to them, looking back as if paranoid. "Hey. Guys."

"What's up?" Jeff asked, toeing off his shoes and dropping his shorts and putting on his uniform trousers.

"What's with that new guy?" Chris kept looking behind them.

"Cochran?" Mickey asked.

"Yeah. You guys showed up at the foot pursuit. I never heard anything about it. Was he being shot at?"

Jeff let out a sarcastic laugh. "No."

After putting on the white T-shirt, Mickey Velcro'd his vest in place and put on his uniform shirt. "That ass shot off rounds at a fleeing suspect."

"Armed suspect?" Chris asked.

"Not sure." Jeff gave Mickey a warning glance, not to say too much.

"You gotta be kidding me." Chris shook his head in disbelief. "I think he's got a screw loose. No one offered to back his stop."

Mickey zipped up his uniform shirt and made sure his badge was pinned on, then wrapped his gun belt around his hips.

"He…" Chris whispered softly, "He's telling everyone you two are gay lovers."

Mickey froze and his muscles went tense. He didn't react verbally, but wanted to scream.

Jeff laughed. "Yeah, right. You thought that once too, asshole. So? Two guys in a car together? That means every set of same sex partners on the department is gay?" Jeff made a noise in his throat. "Gee, Chris, maybe the K-9 officers are fucking their dogs."

Chris laughed and Mickey finally turned around to look at him. Mickey slid his gun into his duty holster and snapped it in, staring at Chris. "You think we're gay?" Mickey's top lip curled.

Chris' smile dropped and he backed up. "No way, Mick."

Jeff kept trying to make a joke out of it. Mickey knew he was downplaying it so it didn't become an issue.

Jeff said, "Chris, the guy came from someplace in the department, and they stuck him with us. Why? That's what I'm going to find out."

"When you do, tell me. I think he should be taken off the streets. There's something not right about the guy."

Mickey watched Chris walk away and continued to get ready, snapping the leather 'keepers' around both the gun belt and the belt on his pants, holding the heavy utility belt in place.

"Fuck." Jeff shook his head and closed the locker. "What an ass."

"You let me take care of Cochran." Mickey started walking out of the locker room.

Jeff grabbed his arm. "No! You hear me, Mick? No!"

Mickey jerked out of Jeff's grip and stormed out of the men's locker room. Once he was in the main area of the station, Mickey had a look over the room dividers and didn't see Cochran. Knowing how close it was to roll call, Mickey walked over to Sgt Adkins' desk, seeing him sorting through paperwork.

"Sarge?"

Sgt Adkins looked up. "Hey, Mick, what's up?"

"How's it looking for a half shift?" Mickey pretended to want half the day off so he could see the schedule.

Sgt Adkins took a book out of his tray shelving and flipped pages. Mickey leaned on the desk next to him so he could read it. He immediately noticed Cochran had taken a furlough; a day off today.

Before his sergeant could reply, Mickey said, "Never mind, Sarge. You look short-handed. Maybe some other time."

"I could squeeze you out a few hours early." He held up his pencil. "Jeff too?"

"You sure?"

"Sure." He erased the pencil marks by Jeff and Mickey's names and wrote in two hours off. "Are you going to test for sergeant, Mick?"

"Doubt it."

"Why not?" Sgt Adkins put the schedule book aside and shifted in his chair to look up at Mickey.

Mickey shrugged. "I hate paperwork, desks…I'd go nuts."

Sgt Adkins smiled. "So detective work is out too."

"Oh, fuck yeah. No way."

"Where do you want to go in your career? I can't see an intelligent guy like you doing thirty on patrol."

"SWAT. Special Ops."

"Tough fucker." Sgt Adkins smiled at him, standing with his clipboard as it came close to roll call time.

"Love the rush." Mickey walked with him to the roll call room.

"Your partner is moving in the opposite direction. I think Jeff wants off the street."

"I know." Mickey tried not to wince.

Sgt Adkins patted Mickey's back and entered the room. Mickey spotted Jeff at their usual table and joined him. He leaned on Jeff and said, "We got two hours off at the end of shift."

"Oh. Good. Why?"

"Sarge offered."

Jeff held up his hand and Mickey gave him a high-five.

"The prick is furloughed." Mickey looked around the room. Everyone was quieting down as the sergeants began their briefing.

"Good." Jeff leaned his elbows on the table and paid attention to their commanding officers as they went through car assignments and information bulletins.

Mickey glanced at Jeff, wondering how long they had left to be together on patrol. Sgt Adkins was right, both he and Jeff were headed in opposite directions.

~

An hour later, Jeff was behind the wheel of the patrol car while Mickey sat beside him, looking around the area, running license plates and hunting for wanted suspects associated with them.

Mickey's mobile phone rang. Jeff glanced over as he answered it.

"Bout time, Sharpe."

Jeff smiled and kept driving.

"We wondered how long it takes to fuck Alex." Mickey laughed and then asked, "How're you doing?"

Jeff tried to listen and Mickey noticed he was, so he put his phone on speaker.

"Good. Better. Thanks for asking, Mick."

"Hey, Billy," Jeff said as he slowed for a stop light.

"Officer Chandler, hello. Are you two on duty?"

"Yup." Mickey held the phone up between them so they could both talk into it.

"So?" Billy asked, "The call social or official?"

"Both!" Jeff said before Mickey answered. Mickey gave Jeff a wry look. Jeff shrugged. "Wouldn't mind seeing Alex."

"Hello?" Billy said over the phone.

"Look, Sharpe," Mickey said, "A new guy got transferred into our squad. P. Cochran…"

"Oh."

Mickey and Jeff exchanged looks. Jeff pulled the patrol car into a parking lot so he could pay attention.

"Oh?" Mickey asked. "You know him?"

"Unfortunately."

Jeff asked, "What's his deal, Billy?"

"He's a fuck up. Already been to AIG and I recommended termination."

"Shit." Jeff rubbed his face tiredly.

Mickey asked, "What was he in for?"

"Excessive force. Get this…" Billy said over the phone, "It was against a gay couple. He was on a domestic call and he ended up macing one of the guys. They filed a complaint."

Jeff groaned and ran his hand back through his hair.

"He's already slinging shit at me and Jeff." Mickey looked around the parking lot as shoppers came and went, giving them little regard.

"Are you kidding me?" Billy asked, "What kind of shit?"

Jeff said, "You know. Do we have to repeat it? He was involved in a foot chase yesterday and fired rounds at the fleeing motorcyclist. He wasn't even sure the guy was armed."

"Shit." Billy sounded frustrated.

"If it was one of us, Sharpe," Mickey said, "We'd be out on our ass. Blowing off rounds at a fleeing suspect?"

"He's…"

Jeff and Mickey leaned closer as they waited for Billy's comment.

"He's a councilman's son."

Jeff sat up in the seat and made a face at Mickey as if he got it, got why the fucker was being treated so differently.

"Billy," Mickey said into the phone, "If he calls me a cocksucker again or fag, I will kill him."

"Calm down, Mickey. Stop talking shit," Billy said.

Jeff leaned towards the phone again. "He's not kidding, Billy. He and Cochran almost exchanged rounds yesterday. And I don't mean in the ring."

"Goddamn it," Billy said.

"You back on duty?" Mickey asked.

"Light duty. I am still working in AIG but they make me go home early most days…you want to file a formal complaint?"

"No!" Mickey yelled into the phone, "Beef another cop? Get it around me and Jeff are fuck buddies?"

"All right, Stanton, calm down," Billy said.

Jeff added, "Been trying to get him to calm down, Billy. But it will explode. You know Mick."

Mickey elbowed Jeff in annoyance.

"Where are you guys now?" Billy asked.

Jeff looked up. "Sunset Boulevard."

Mickey said, "We're off a couple hours early at the end of shift. Can you meet us for dinner?"

"With Alex?" Jeff asked and Mickey nudged him again.

"I think so. Let me check with Alex first and get back to you."

"Thanks, Sharpe." Mickey sat correctly in the seat.

"No problem. And Mick- Keep a cool head. Will ya?"

"Ha!" Jeff said then held up his hands to prevent another nudge.

"Bye." Mickey shut off the phone and stared into space.

"Already on file for homophobic behavior." Jeff drove out of the lot. "Let him hang himself, Mick. I'm not going to tell you again."

Mickey heard the dispatcher call them and picked up the microphone to answer. "Eight-Adam-One."

"Eight-Adam-One, ten-thirty-three, location on your screen."

"Eight-Adam-One, ten-four." Mickey hung the microphone on the clip and looked at the computer as it displayed the details. "Someone is reporting what sounds like a house or commercial property alarm." Mickey read the screen to Jeff as Jeff drove. "Looks like it's not monitored since it's an area check."

"Okay." Jeff looked at the address and made the first U-turn he could, headed back from where they came.

Mickey thought about what Billy had said about Cochran macing a gay man on a call. *Son of a councilman? So? That meant the ass could do as he pleased?*

Mickey looked down at Jeff's hand as Jeff held his thigh.

"Stop stewing," Jeff said.

"He maced a gay man?"

"Maybe he had to. Gay men fight cops too, ya know."

"Sure, Chandler. Sure." Mickey rubbed his chin as he thought about it. He was not going to take any abuse from this piece of shit, no way.

~

The area check done, nothing audible heard in the vicinity, Mickey searched the computer screen to see what calls were holding in their district as they were about to clear the alarm call.

"Flo is on a traffic stop. Wanna drive by and make sure she's good?" Mickey asked.

"Yes." Jeff looked at the address on the screen. "She's running all those names? And she's on her own?"

"Looks like it. Unless she's got backup that didn't log onto the call." Mickey kept an eye on the information Flo was getting via her computer.

Then dispatch called her over the airwaves. "Eight-Lincoln-Two, ten-twenty-nine-frank."

"She's got a felony warrant hit," Mickey said, "Go!"

Jeff turned on the lights and sirens and sped up.

Mickey picked up the radio microphone and said, "Eight-Adam-One, clear the ten-thirty-three, headed to back Eight-Lincoln-Two."

"Eight-Adam-One, ten-four, backing Eight-Lincoln-Two."

Mickey waited for Flo to acknowledge she had a hit on one of her suspects. Flo did not answer dispatch.

Mickey picked up the microphone again. "Eight-Adam-One, Eight-Lincoln-Two's status?"

The dispatcher called Flo again, asking her status.

There was a gap in the air waves.

"Eight-Adam-One, no answer," the dispatcher said.

"Eight-Adam-One, roger, code two." Mickey heard the heavy engine of the patrol car rev as Jeff sped through side streets. Mickey's heart was beating hard in his chest in panic as he expected to see Flo being beaten by a gang of thugs. Jeff pulled up to her patrol car and Mickey spotted her talking to three individuals, who were all outside of a car she had stopped.

They shut the siren down and walked over to her. Flo appeared surprised at their abrupt arrival and the suspects, nervous.

Jeff stood on one side of the men, and Mickey on the other as the three men leaned back on the driver's side of their car.

"Hello," Flo said.

"Did you not catch the ten-twenty-nine frank?" Mickey had no idea which man had the felony warrant.

"No. Shit." Flo checked on her radio volume and then her pad. "Stand by, let me look at my computer."

Mickey knew she was checking to see which man had the warrant for his arrest.

Jeff peered into the suspect's car, which was a beat up sedan with expired registration tabs, most likely the reason Flo stopped them.

One man out of the three appeared extremely nervous.

Jeff asked, "Who owns the car?"

"I do," the smallest of the men raised his hand.

"Do you have a valid license and insurance?"

"Yes. I showed the lady cop." He nodded, reaching for his back pocket.

Mickey held up his hand. "Don't move. If she has your info, you're good." Mickey looked at the second man, one standing in the middle of the other two. He was pouring with sweat. He had to be the one. "You." Mickey pointed at him. "Come here."

The man appeared paranoid. "Me? Why?"

"I want to have a chat with you." Mickey beckoned him closer.

Mickey glanced at Jeff and of course Jeff got it. Jeff kept his eyes on the other two while Mickey singled the man out.

Mickey walked the man over to his patrol car. "You have any weapons on you, buddy?"

"Huh? Weapons? No." He began to pant audibly.

"No rockets, no grenades, no AKs?" Mickey tried to make it sound like a joke.

"No." The man gave a nervous chuckle.

"Mind if I check?" Before the man answered, Mickey spun him around to face his car. "Palms of the hood, spread your legs."

Flo stepped out of the car. "Right one, Mick."

Mickey knew it. He went for the man's wrist to cuff him, and the fight was on.

Flo pounced on the guy as he flailed his arms and foamed at the mouth, possibly high on something.

Jeff yelled, “Stay put!” to the other two, since neither Mickey nor Jeff knew if Flo needed them for anything else.

Mickey dropped the suspect to the ground, face down, and managed to get one cuff around one wrist.

Flo said calmly to Mickey, “Turn your face away, sweetie.”

Mickey noticed a can of mace in her hand. He looked away, back at the other two suspects and Jeff, who was trying to maintain them and not allow them to go.

A hissing sound came next, and a loud cry of pain from the suspect, then the smell of chemicals. Mickey tried to avoid inhaling it or getting it near his face.

The suspect whined and Flo brought his wrist up to cuff easily. One of them holding each arm, he and Flo got the guy to his feet.

“My eyes! My eyes!” he cried as he kept them shut.

Flo said, “That’s why you never mess with a cop, buddy.”

Mickey asked Flo, “Can we turn these other guys loose?”

“Yeah. Let me just have the driver sign a ticket. You got it, Officer Stanton?” She grinned and put her mace back into her utility belt.

“I do.” He winked.

Mickey stared at the guy who was whimpering from pain, and leaned him over the hood of his car again. “Ya got needles on you?” he asked as he gloved up.

“My eyes! Ow! My eyes are burning.”

“I know, dude.” Mickey patted him down carefully. He glanced at Jeff who was watching everything and standing like a guard over Flo. She had the driver sign the ticket and sent the other two off. Once they left, Jeff opened the trunk of his patrol car and held a gallon bottle of water as he walked closer.

“Dope.” Mickey tossed a plastic bag of what appeared to be crack cocaine onto the hood. “Pipe.” He set a glass tube down. It was covered in tar and well used.

"Watch for needles." Flo stood by as Mickey turned the suspect's pockets inside out carefully. No needles.

"I'm dyin', come on, man!" The suspect moaned.

"His warrant was for drugs and possession of a firearm." Flo bagged the crack and pipe into evidence envelopes she had in her trunk.

"You done, Mick?" Jeff asked.

"Yup." Mickey walked the suspect away from the patrol car and said, "Bend over and tilt your head."

Jeff waited and when the suspect did, Jeff poured water onto the guy's face and eyes. "Try to open them."

The man did. "Thanks. Fuck, that sucks."

Jeff used a little more water, then stopped. "It'll wear off."

Mickey asked Flo, "Want us to transport?"

"Yes, please!" She grinned.

"See ya at the station." Mickey walked the man to his car while Jeff put the water back in the trunk. Jeff raised the divider to cage the man in the back before Mickey put him in.

"Watch your head." Mickey made sure the suspect didn't whack his skull on the car, since the man could not see.

He shut the door and tugged off his gloves, climbing into the passenger's side and pointing the air conditioner vent at himself as he dripped sweat.

Jeff said, "Great police radar, dude." They bumped fists.

"He was sweating the most. It was a no brainer."

"I felt like it was a game. I was trying to see who had the pea under his shell." Jeff shut down his overhead lights.

Mickey laughed and picked up the car microphone as he turned off his personal radio. "Eight-Adam-One."

"Eight-Adam-One," dispatch replied.

"Ten-fifteen, transporting to the station for Eight-Lincoln-Two."

"Roger, Eight-Adam-One."

They heard the suspect groan and Mickey could see he still had his eyes shut and his skin was red from the chemical spray.

He knew what it felt like. All the cops did. They were sprayed during training. It sucked.

After driving through LA traffic, Jeff pulled into the sally port at the station. As Jeff shut off the car, Mickey climbed out. He opened the back door and reached for the man in the back seat, smelling both his BO and the chemical spray. The man was able to see finally as the mace wore off. He waited as Jeff opened a secure door and brought the man into a holding cell. Mickey gloved up once more and had the man spread his legs as he again made sure everything the suspect owned was out of his pockets and into an envelope as Jeff added the man's name to a clipboard.

Once the man was checked, his shoes removed and inspected, he was uncuffed and Jeff locked him into one of the holding cells. "I'll move the car."

"Okay." Mickey sealed an envelope containing the man's personal items, wrote his name on it, and locked it up, then took off his rubber gloves, tossing them out. He entered the station, feeling the air conditioning with relief. Exhaustion beginning to creep up on him, he headed to the men's locker room and washed his hands and face, then stood at a urinal. He could still smell the mace and sniffed his uniform shoulder. He sighed tiredly and emptied a very full bladder.

~

Jeff met Flo as she carried the drugs into the station. They walked into the write-up area together and she said, "Thanks, Jeff. I can always count on you guys."

"Keep your radio turned up, young lady." He wagged his finger at her.

"My bad." She laughed. "Let me go screen the arrest with the sarge."

She walked off and Jeff wondered how on earth more cops didn't die or get hurt on the street. It was simply one of the most dangerous jobs on the planet.

He headed to the men's locker to wash up and take a much needed pit-stop, when he spotted Mickey at the urinal. Jeff washed his hands, checked his appearance in the mirror behind the sink and then stood beside his man. Jeff sighed as he released his stream. "Been holding that all day."

Mickey glanced over the divider at Jeff's cock. "Been craving that all day."

Jeff chuckled and they both heard the locker room door swing open. Mickey flushed his urinal and walked back to the sink.

"Hey," a cop from another squad said to Mickey in greeting and kept walking.

Mickey acknowledged him and waited for Jeff.

Jeff flushed, tucked himself in and rinsed his hands. He checked his watch. "With our two hours off maybe we should sit on this a while, then take one more call and we're done?"

"Yup." Mickey headed to the exit.

Jeff stared at his ass in the dark uniform and licked his lips at how gorgeous Mickey was.

They found Flo at the computer with a stack of paperwork to complete, processing a prisoner, putting drugs into evidence…

Jeff leaned beside her at the computer. "Want help?"

"Nah. Just a statement. Sarge says since I hosed the guy we have to document it as a use of force."

"Got it."

Mickey and Jeff sat side by side at available computers and began logging on and tapping keys. Jeff said, "I didn't do shit. You were the one who fought him."

"Yeah. About that," Mickey gave him a narrowing of the eyes in admonishment, "Nice backup, dork."

"I had two other guys to watch. You wanted them to pile on?"

"Excuses, excuses." Mickey typed quickly.

"And you needed little Flo to help?" Jeff made a playful pouty face at him.

"Shut up." Mickey punched his shoulder.

"You shut up!" Jeff punched him back.

Over the divider Flo said, "Children, behave."

Mickey laughed and Jeff typed up a very quick statement, since all he did was watch the two of them fight and watered the guy after.

They finished at the same time and printed out copies for Flo's felony paperwork.

Flo asked Mickey, "Where'd you find the dope?"

"Crack in his front right pocket, pipe in his left. It's in my statement." He handed it to her. "You want us to help out?"

"Nope. I found my shift killer." She smirked.

"We're off two hours early, so we need one more to kill this one," Jeff said, leaning on the divider.

"Don't get in over your head or you'll be in for OT instead of two hours off!" She sealed up an envelope.

"True." Mickey met Jeff's gaze. "Ready?"

"Sure." Jeff headed out to the parking lot and immediately felt the hot breeze. "Sweating under this vest. I swear I'm going to grow mushrooms." He tugged at it.

Mickey said, "You told me after you left Seattle you'd never complain about the weather here."

"I lied." Jeff pointed to where he'd parked the patrol car.

They sat down on the bench seat together and then Jeff lowered the divider once more, opening the back of the car. "Stinks."

"Keep it up." Mickey pointed the blowing fan vent at himself.

"Gotta air it out for the next shift."

"Aw, you're too nice." Mickey read the computer. "Crap. There's a ton of shit holding now."

"It's Monday night. Why don't people just chill for a day?"

"Because its summer in LA. Duh."

"I don't want to do anything else. I've had enough for today." Jeff pulled out of the parking lot.

Mickey's cell phone rang. He took it out of his pocket and said, "It's Sharpe."

Jeff headed to their hiding spot at the church.

"Hello, L-T," Mickey said with a teasing lilt to his voice.

Jeff gazed at the cars ahead of him, wondering if a traffic stop would help them finish the shift. It was a crap shoot. If they got a cluster-fuck like Flo did, they'd be doing hours of overtime.

"Sounds good. Okay. See ya there." Mickey disconnected the call.

"Alex coming?" Jeff asked as he pulled into the church lot.

Mickey raised an eyebrow at him. "You really want to fuck him?"

"No!" Jeff lowered his voice. "Maybe. But only with you."

"Déjà vu." Mickey unhooked his seatbelt and sank in the seat as Jeff backed up. "Why are we discussing this again?"

Jeff put the car in park and checked the time. "We have an hour. We can't milk Flo's call the whole time."

"Yeah, we can. But let's just sit for a minute and rest, okay?" Mickey lowered the police radio.

"Where do they want to meet us to eat?"

"Their place. Billy said the paparazzi have been after Alex again and the fans go nuts when they are seen together in public."

"Oh. Okay." Jeff couldn't imagine not being able to dine out without a mob scene. But Alex was not only the star of *Being Screwed*, he was also now modeling with his dad, Mark. And ever since their private wedding in New York, the two love-birds had been highlighted on all the celebrity gossip rags. Most saying the age gap was going to be their doom.

Jeff rubbed his face and yawned. "I swear I am so exhausted."

"Want to get coffee?"

"No. No more caffeine. I hate the shit after a while. And we need to be drinking more water."

"Makes me pee. I can't stand having to piss and being on a call."

"Hate patrol." Jeff yawned again.

"I know. Okay?" Mickey yelled.

"Okay! Don't get defensive!" Jeff held up his hands.

"Just take the fucking exam! I swear, Chandler, I am not dealing with your whining about being on patrol every fucking day!"

"Fuck you!" Jeff was too tired to argue. He knew he was going to be 'acting' sergeant tomorrow, so a trial separation for a day was upon them soon.

Mickey spun around and grabbed Jeff by his uniform collar roughly. "Test! Okay? Stop whining, moaning, and giving me a headache!"

"What are you going to do if I get promoted? Huh? How am I supposed to watch over you?"

"I don't need watching over." Mickey released him and sat back, staring out into space.

"You do! I know you! You'll 'check and advise' on everything. You'll play Mr Macho and won't wait for back up!"

"Shut. The. Fuck. Up!" Mickey balled his fists.

Jeff lunged at Mickey, pinning him to the passenger's door. "I know you," he said, breathing fire, "You'll get yourself hurt or killed to spite me!"

Mickey tensed up and then they met gazes. Jeff got lost in the light blue ring around the black pupils in Mickey's eyes. He pressed his mouth against Mickey's and Mickey dug his hand into Jeff's hair and grabbed it in his fist. They both groaned and opened their mouths deepening the kiss and passion.

Jeff cupped Mickey's jaw and held him so tightly he knew he was hurting Mickey, but…if anything ever happened to this man, he'd lose his mind, literally- rubber room- go postal- or blow his own brains out.

A sob came from Mickey and Jeff broke the kiss and held him, pressing his cheek against Mickey's, catching his breath. "Don't be stupid without me. Please."

Mickey didn't reply but Jeff felt Mickey's grip tighten around his vest like boa constrictor.

Chapter Eleven

Mickey drove them home after an uneventful hour of work. They had been dispatched to an area check of suspicious people that had been holding for an hour, so nothing was there when they arrived. Thankfully they were able to leave work early.

Back in their civilian clothing, Mickey thought about tomorrow, not having Jeff in the car with him for the first time since they became partners, nearly three years ago.

It made the pit of his stomach ache. But…this is what was bound to happen. Jeff would no doubt get very high marks on the sergeant's exam, be selected quickly, and off he would go. Where? Anywhere the LAPD needed him.

He pulled into their space at the townhouse and climbed out, taking his empty travel mug inside, as Jeff did the same.

Mickey tossed the mug into the sink, took his gun-pack off and left it on the kitchen table, then trotted up the stairs to strip for a shower.

Jeff entered the bathroom when he too had removed his clothing and as he stood urinating beside Mickey, Mickey watched, keeping one hand under the running water as it warmed.

Jeff spun around when he was done and the two of them locked gazes. Why did it feel to Mickey as if he were going to lose Jeff?

Lose him how? Jeff would never walk out of his life completely. That much he was sure of.

Mickey gestured for Jeff to step into the tub first. Jeff did, and wet down. Mickey stared at him, his hair touching his shoulders when it was soaked, his muscular arms flexing as he rubbed the water over his face, and Jeff's cock was beginning to swell.

Mickey filled his palm with shampoo and Jeff backed up towards him, getting his hair washed for him. "God, I love this. I feel so spoiled after such a long day." Jeff made a humming noise.

Mickey massaged his scalp, lathering up Jeff's thick brown hair and pulling it back, but it wasn't long enough for a ponytail. There would be no way Jeff would get away with hair that long on the LAPD.

Mickey soaped up Jeff's shoulders, rubbing his sore muscles, working his way down Jeff's back to his perfect ass. He cupped it and then ran his finger down the crack.

Jeff spread his legs and rested his hands on the wall, the water rinsing his hair as he did.

Mickey soaped up his cock and pushed the tip inside Jeff.

Jeff moaned and reached for his own dick.

Mickey said, "Don't jack off. I'll suck you after."

Without a verbal response, Jeff placed both his hands on the wall again.

Mickey pulled out and used more soap, keeping his cock slick. He placed just the head of himself inside Jeff and jerked off into him. Watching the act, seeing Jeff's bottom muscles tighten up around his dick, Mickey began to get the rush of a climax. He pushed in slightly deeper but since Jeff hadn't prepared for their coupling he did most of the work with his hand. He came, clenching his teeth and pulled out to spray Jeff's ass and thighs with his cum. In the running water it washed off quickly.

Jeff spun around and pointed his stiff cock at Mickey.

Mickey dropped to the floor of the tub and held the base of Jeff's dick, sucking and moaning as he did.

"Oh, Mick…son-of-a-bitch…love your fucking mouth."

Mickey peeked up at Jeff, seeing his eyes closed, his chest and abdomen muscles showing through his tanned skin. When Jeff opened his eyes and looked down, Mickey caught the green color and that sensuous leer. He closed his own eyes and cupped Jeff's balls as he drew him deep and sucked hard suction.

Jeff panted and then grunted in a low masculine rumble. Mickey swallowed the mouthful of cum and sat on his heels, staring at Jeff's cock. Jeff put shampoo into his hand and nudged Mickey to get his hair wet.

Mickey stood and rinsed under the hot water, then let Jeff baby him. He was dreading tomorrow without him. Dreading it.

~

Jeff checked his appearance in the full length mirror in his walk-in closet. He wore a pair of his favorite soft faded, blue jeans and a sleeveless black T-shirt. He clipped his gun and badge on his belt, and sat down to put on his socks and shoes.

Mickey sat on the bed beside him and smiled. "You look hot. Alex will be all over you."

Jeff chuckled. "Jeans? Come on."

"Just saying."

"He likes the uniform. He's not into us in civilian clothing."

Mickey tapped Jeff's holster. "That and your badge is enough."

"True." Jeff looked at Mickey. He had on a pair of black jeans and a white T-shirt. Jeff leaned over and pecked his lips. "Should we bring anything?"

"I guess. We should stop for wine or beer, something." Mickey stood and took his gun from the pack and also used a holster, clipping it to his belt, along with his LAPD badge.

Standing, Jeff patted Mickey's bottom and asked, "Ready?"

"You driving or am I?" Mickey followed him out.

"I will. You already drove…up my ass." Jeff made a face of ecstasy at him to tease him.

"Don't get me started." Mickey wagged his finger.

"Everything sets you on fire, Stanton." Jeff pocketed his phone and grabbed his keys. "You're the horniest man I know."

Mickey shut the lights and locked the door behind him, as Jeff used the remote to disarm the car and sat behind the wheel. "So? Should we hit the grocery store or the 'stop and rob'?"

Mickey leaned over to look at Jeff's dash gauges. "May as well fill it up at the stop and rob."

"Okay." Jeff backed out and headed to Bel Air, to the ritzy part of town, where not only Billy and Alex lived, where Mark and Steve owned a home as well.

On the way he pulled into a service station and up to a pump. Mickey climbed out to head to the mini mart as Jeff filled it up. Jeff called to him, "Don't start a shoot out!"

"Ha. Ha." Mickey gave him a weary look and walked to the main entrance.

Jeff stuck the nozzle into the gas tank and used his credit card, looking at the people coming and going, always on the alert. He wore his gun and badge off duty for a reason. He had to. And if something went down and he didn't have it? He'd never forgive himself.

He leaned against his car and watched the numbers fly by on the pump, filling it up and seeing the cash amount climb quickly. He noticed a group of young kids outside the front of the small market, laughing and behaving obnoxiously. Someone else gassing up had their car radio blasting loud as they pumped. Jeff tried not to get distracted. A small television monitor was on the gas pump, airing commercials. There was simply nothing more obnoxious to Jeff than that. *Only in LA*. He shook his head.

The nozzle clicked and Jeff topped the tank and hung the hose back up, replacing the plastic cap. He looked into the market and spotted a line. Jeff climbed into the car and parked right in front of the group of young kids, some with skateboards, a few smoking.

None looked over sixteen.

Jeff got out of the car and leaned on it, folding his arms, watching them as he waited for Mickey.

One by one the kids noticed his gun and badge. He overheard one say, 'Po-po'.

The cigarettes were put out, neatly placed into a trash can and they walked or rolled off, pouting as if Jeff had crashed their party.

He shook his head and said, "That's another reason never to have kids."

Mickey stepped out of the store with a bag and looked to where Jeff was staring. He said, "What'd ya do now, Chandler?"

"Po-po came and made them leave." Jeff climbed back into his car.

Mickey sat down, the six-pack of beer at his feet and put on his seatbelt. "Yeah. I got some looks inside as well. Christ, when did cops become public enemy number one?"

"Don't know." Jeff backed out and as they left they drove by the little group of young men. Mickey leaned down to look out of Jeff's window and the whole little gang stared at Mickey and Jeff as if they were doomed and going to be arrested for possessing cigarettes underage. Jeff laughed and drove off, covering his chuckle. "Probably all of fourteen years old."

"When the day comes that I write up a kid for having smokes, I'll know I'll need to retire." Mickey straddled his legs and held onto Jeff's thigh.

"No kidding. I don't even want drugs to be illegal. What a waste of time."

"Don't get me started."

Jeff held Mickey's hand and drove them to Bel Air, wondering how men and women chose the police profession as a career in the first place. It certainly was a labor of love and not high paying or fun…anymore.

Since it was after the evening rush hour, the drive was an hour on the freeway, and clear of heavy traffic. Jeff pulled up in front of a two-car garage and said to Mickey, "This is the first time we've been invited here."

"I know. Christ. You believe Sharpe lives in a house like this?" Mickey picked up the bag with the beer.

Jeff met him on the walkway up to the front door. Before they knocked, Jeff stopped Mickey and had a look around the house first. "Shit, Mick. How much you think they paid for this place?"

"Gotta be upward of a mill. Come on. Don't get all fan-girl on Alex."

"Shut up." Jeff shoved him as they approached the front door.

"No, you shut up!" Mickey pushed him back.

The door opened and Billy looked out, smiling. "Do I have to call the cops?"

"Billy." Jeff reached for him and gave him a hug.

"Ow. Easy." Billy flinched and smiled through what appeared to be pain.

"Shit. Sorry." Jeff backed off and looked at Billy's chest. "Still sore? Fuck."

Mickey whacked Jeff on the arm. "He got shot! You dork."

"Come in." Billy stepped back and Jeff got his first look at the enormous interior, all open plan, white, high ceilings, a large sectional sofa, a flat screen TV on the wall, and a panoramic view from the back of the Getty Museum beyond a pool.

"Holy shit, Billy." Jeff spun around and admired the décor. "You son of a bitch."

"I know. Right? I'm the kept boy now." He took the beer from Mickey. "You both want one, right?"

"Yeah." Mickey walked to the sliding doors and looked out, whistling. "Wow."

"Where's—" Just as Jeff was about to ask, Alexander came barreling at him from another room and jumped on him, ankles locked around Jeff's hips and gave him a smirk of wickedness.

"Hello, Officer." Alex held Jeff around the neck.

Jeff stared into Alex's gorgeous features, his long dark hair and feline green eyes. "You are trouble."

Alex went for a sniff of Jeff's neck. "Is that dad's cologne?"

Knowing Alex meant his father's trademark scent, *Dangereux,* Mickey said, "Yeah, he wants to smell like your dad all day. It makes him horny."

Billy laughed and said, "Alex, get off Jeff, will ya?"

Jeff rocked Alex side to side, not wanting Alex to get off him. Wanting to get off on Alex. But he never would.

Alex pecked Jeff's lips, jumped to his feet, and went for a hug and kiss from Mickey.

"So? How big is this monstrosity?" Mickey asked, taking the beer from Billy.

"Twenty-two hundred square feet," Billy said, handing another beer to Jeff, "three bedrooms, two and a half baths."

Alex said smugly, "Nine double oh-four-nine!"

"Ooh," Mickey teased, "Zip code snob!"

Alex stood in front of Jeff and when he reached down, Jeff thought Alex was going to grope him. He held his breath as Alex touched his holstered gun. "Jesus, Alex! You gave me a heart attack. I thought you were going to touch my cock."

"Ha!" Alex ran his finger along Jeff's badge next.

"Alex!" Billy said in exasperation and held a glass of something amber in his hand. "Go set the table or something. Check on dinner."

"Billy-the-Bully." Alex pouted and began taking dishes out of the cabinets.

"Sit." Billy gestured to the couch. Jeff and Mickey sat together while Billy was opposite them on a loveseat. "What did Cochran do?"

"Called me a fag, called us fags…" Mickey tipped up the beer to drink.

"What?" Alex asked, gasping. "Who did that?"

"Some schmuck we're stuck with." Jeff couldn't believe from the back Alex's hair reached between his shoulder blades. The young twenty-three year old was slightly androgynous, and looked exactly like his top model dad.

"Stuck with?" Alex asked, placing silverware around the table.

"Alex, let them talk." Billy said to Mickey, "Go ahead."

Mickey swigged his beer and replied, "He got real aggressive at that call we had with him yesterday. Jeff had to order him to holster his weapon."

Billy sat up, listening carefully.

Jeff kept being distracted by Alex acting domestic. Placing bowls on the table, taking things out of the fridge… it was making Jeff horny as hell.

"We backed him on a call," Mickey said, "No one else would. So, he's already got a reputation following him. I don't know who knows about him and who doesn't."

Jeff sipped his beer and caught Alex's eyes. Alex smiled sweetly at him. Jeff smiled back.

"He was hyped up from a foot pursuit and blowing rounds off at the fleeing motorcyclist," Mickey said, "Then out of nowhere he turns on us- the two fuckers who backed him up."

"I told you. File a complaint."

"Fuck no." Mickey shook his head. "Beef another cop? Let it get out he's claiming we're sexual partners?"

Billy said, "I got news for you, Mick, we got a written anonymous letter about you two as well."

Jeff quickly focused on Billy. "No."

"I downplayed it. Tossed it into a file." Billy looked up when Alex walked closer. He reached for him and Alex sat on his lap. "Did you take the lasagna out of the oven for it to set up?"

"Yes."

"Thank you," Billy said and kissed Alex's cheek.

The aroma of baked food suddenly hit Jeff and his stomach growled.

"When did you get this letter?" Mickey asked, holding the empty bottle in his hands.

"Last Friday. You two were furloughed so I didn't even try to contact you. We've had bullshit like that before, and if its anonymous we don't do anything with it. I wanted to burn it."

Jeff gave Mickey a nervous look.

Billy said, "I checked your records. Mick, you still have your old address listed, so I don't know how they can assume you two live together."

"Fuck it." Mickey threw up his hand in frustration. "He's going to test for sergeant anyway. Fuck it!"

Jeff noticed Alex pout as he leaned his head against Billy's shoulder.

"You're testing?" Billy asked Jeff.

"I don't know. We don't want to be pulled apart." He set the bottle down on a coaster on the coffee table.

"Billy," Alex said, "Don't let them break up the dynamic duo."

"How do I get into SWAT?" Mickey asked.

Before Billy answered, Jeff said, "No. No way, Stanton! Billy got shot!"

Alex flinched and Jeff felt badly to be so careless with his words.

"Yeah, right?" Alex said sarcastically, "And he's not even a SWAT lieutenant anymore, he was just 'playing one' for fun." Alex gave Billy a look of annoyance.

"Don't bring that up." Billy held up his hand and sipped his drink.

"How bad was it?" Jeff asked. "Getting hit in the vest?"

Billy shifted Alex aside and raised his shirt.

Jeff leaned forward and Mickey stood to look. The bruising was dark and over a large mass of Billy's chest. "Oh, fuck."

"Like getting hit with a baseball bat, repeatedly." Billy lowered his shirt and Alex gently rubbed his hand over the bruised area. "You don't want to experience it. And I didn't even get hit with a bullet to the flesh, accept for a slight grazing on my thigh."

"Stop." Alex put his hands over his ears.

Mickey returned to sit on the sofa and looked at Jeff.

Jeff said, "You want to do that? Be a target for bullshit?"

"Yeah. That or special ops. I'm not sitting at a desk doing paper." Mickey tipped the last drop of his beer up and set it down on the table.

"I'll get you two more." Alex took the empties and walked to the kitchen.

Jeff said, "I'm sorry, Billy. Sorry you had to go through that."

"I blame myself." He looked over his shoulder at Alex and spoke quietly. "I played the fucking hero."

Jeff glared at Mickey and pointed at him. "Don't you ever do that. You got it? Your coming home is priority. I don't care who fucking dies."

Mickey ran his hand over his hair and didn't reply.

"He's going to get a death wish on me now," Jeff muttered growing angry.

Alex returned and handed each of them another cold beer.

"Thank you, gorgeous," Jeff said, infatuated with Alex like the whole world was.

Billy stood, slowly, holding his chest as if he still had pain from it. "Let me see if the lasagna is ready to cut up."

Jeff watched him walk to the kitchen, noticing Alex also keeping an eye on him.

"You okay, baby?" Jeff asked Alex quietly.

"Almost lost him." Alex's eyes grew glossy.

Mickey stood and reached for Alex. Alex hugged him, closing his eyes.

Jeff teared up at the closeness they all shared and met Mickey's gaze. '*Love you*,' Jeff mouthed to his man.

'*You too,*' Mickey mouthed back, rocking Alex in his arms.

Chapter Twelve

Stuffed on lasagna, garlic bread, and salad, Mickey helped clear the table and spotted Jeff yawning. He checked the time and it was only ten o'clock but the long shift killed them.

Alex asked, "Want to sit out by the pool?"

Mickey met Jeff's gaze. "Too tired, Chandler?"

"You'll just keep me up for hours fucking." Jeff winked at him.

Mickey heard Billy laugh.

"Mm." Alex rubbed between his own legs and expressed ecstasy comically.

"Oh, Christ, Alex," Jeff said, moaning, "Don't turn into a sex siren on me."

Mickey and Billy exchanged knowing glances, and sure enough, that was all it took for Alex to slink over to Jeff like a cat. He hung his arms around Jeff's neck and came close enough to kiss. "Do you ever think of me when Mickey is screwing you?"

"Oh, Christ," Jeff repeated, closing his eyes as if in agony.

Mickey laughed and said to Billy, "I don't know how you do it, Sharpe."

"Believe me. Neither do I."

Jeff ran his fingers through Alex's long hair as they stared into each other's eyes.

Mickey could see they were pressing crotches together, and had no doubt a little throbbing excitement was going on. "Okay, uh, should Billy and I be jealous?"

"How about a four-way, like Dad does with Steve, Jack, and Adam?"

"No." Billy wiped the counter with a cloth, tidying up.

"You can all do me."

Mickey rubbed his eyes in amazement as Jeff whimpered.

"Alex," Billy said, "No."

"Aww." Alex gave Jeff a good grind of his cock and let go. He started laughing as if it was all a joke, and Mickey assumed it was, at Jeff's expense.

"Damn." Jeff stuck his hand into his pants to adjust his cock. "What a tease. Jesus."

"Time to go?" Mickey asked.

"No. Sit by the pool," Alex said, removing his shirt, showing off his hairless chest and a nipple ring.

"Get me the hell out of here." Jeff threw up his hands. "I can't handle it."

Mickey approached Billy and caressed his hair. "Thanks for dinner, and the heads up about the anonymous letter."

Billy kissed Mickey on the lips. "You're welcome. If I hear anything more, I'll let you know. Oh, and stay the hell away from Cochran. With this latest shooting incident, he is seriously hanging himself. And even his councilman father won't be able to help."

"I don't know how to keep away from him when he's in my squad and in my face." Mickey turned to look at Jeff. Jeff was ogling Alex who was now topless and opening the top of his pants seductively, just to tease Jeff.

"Mick," Billy said in warning, "That's what he wants. To bait you. Don't let him."

Mickey was about to comment when he noticed the little dance of love going on between Jeff and Alex, each putting on a display a peacock would envy. Jeff ran his hand down his own chest to his gun, then his hard cock.

Alex was licking his lips and making expressions of fake orgasms.

"You believe these two?" Mickey gestured to Jeff and Alex.

"We're playing," Alex said, trying to appear innocent.

"I'm about to cream my briefs." Jeff groaned.

"I was about to offer to help you study for the exam, Chandler," Billy said with a smile, "But I don't think you can handle being here with Alex. Too much distraction."

"Huh?" Jeff massaged himself from outside his pants, staring at Alex who was creeping closer.

Billy scooped Alex up from behind and held him, kissing Alex's hair and neck with loud smooching sounds.

Alex began laughing and squirming playfully.

"That's our cue." Mickey walked over to Jeff and said, "Say goodnight, Chandler."

Jeff whimpered and bit his lip. "You lucky shit."

"Hey!" Mickey shoved Jeff's shoulder.

"Well?" Jeff gestured to Alex and Billy. "Come on, man, are you blind?"

Mickey glanced back at Alex who was smirking wickedly as Billy nuzzled him and pinched his nipples.

"You are a lucky SOB, Sharpe. In more ways than one." Mickey put Jeff in a headlock and used his knuckles to rub into his scalp. "Now come home so I can fuck you!"

"Do it here! Let me watch!" Alex grew excited.

"Bye." Mickey began dragging Jeff to the door.

"Dad got to watch you for his birthday!" Alex called after them. "No fair!"

"Goodnight, guys." Billy smiled and waved at them.

"See ya, Sharpe." Mickey opened the door and pushed Jeff outside.

"Bye!" Jeff yelled and stumbled out.

Mickey kept grabbing at Jeff's ass as he did his best to tease Mickey and dodge his grasp.

Mickey made a dash for Jeff and tried to pin him against Jeff's car. Jeff scrambled out of his reach and now they had the car between them, giving each other 'the eye' over the top.

"What are ya gonna do, Mick?" Jeff teased, "Attack me on the front lawn of a lieutenant's home in swanky Bel Air?"

"Yeah. If I can get my hands on you." Mickey started moving to the front of the car then faked right and moved left. They made a loop around the vehicle and Jeff started laughing so hard he couldn't stop.

"If you let me get us home, you can do what you want…ya big dumb cop." Jeff kept moving side to side as Mickey did, keeping one step ahead.

Mickey acted as if he had given up, and stood by the passenger's door. "Okay. Open it up."

Jeff tilted his head warily. "Once you have me in the car? What are you going to do to me?"

"Do to you?" Mickey pressed his hand to his chest and batted his lashes in a gesture of innocence. "*Moi*? Nothing. Why would I do anything to the man I love?"

Jeff gave him a look as if he knew Mickey was being a wise-ass and unlocked the doors with his key fob.

Mickey sat down on the passenger's seat and waited, seeing Jeff peer in cautiously.

"Get the fuck in here!" Mickey reached to the driver's door and opened it.

Jeff climbed in and stuck the key into the ignition. He glanced at Mickey, and Mickey knew he was expecting the ambush any second.

But instead, they went for each other, met in the middle and kissed. Jeff reached for Mickey's cock and Mickey for his. Over the console they began to go crazy, swirling tongues and tugging each others' pants open. Mickey had Jeff's cock exposed and pulled on it feeling Jeff reaching into his briefs for his. When both of them had their dicks out, Jeff parted from the kiss, breathless, and dove down on Mickey's lap.

At the pleasure rush, Mickey kicked out his legs and combed his fingers through Jeff's hair as Jeff gave him a blowjob. Mickey looked at the stately house, figuring Alex and Billy were already naked in the bedroom fucking like wild animals.

"Chandler, fuck..." Mickey shivered and raised his ass off the bucket seat as the sensation grew to an explosive level. Jeff moaned and shifted in excitement. Mickey couldn't reach Jeff's cock but imagined he was about to come as well, judging by his vocalizations of bliss. Mickey closed his eyes and came, coughing at the intensity, feeling Jeff slow down his suction and speed, to milk Mickey, prolonging the pleasure.

Jeff sat up, looking dazed.

Mickey pushed him hard against the driver's door and bent down to take his cock into his mouth, the heavy holster and badge flopping to the side as he opened Jeff's pants wider.

~

Jeff glanced around the area, but the property in front of the house was large enough, only Billy and Alex could see them, and that was only if they looked out of the front window.

He relaxed and felt the heat and wetness of Mickey's mouth. He ran his hands over Mickey's short hair, down his neck to his back and groaned. Alex's antics had gotten Jeff so hot he was on the edge quickly. But when he came? He stared at his big beautiful police partner. That's what made him the hottest. Jeff went limp against the seat as he climaxed and let out a low purring moan. "Oh, Stanton...your mouth...damn."

Mickey kept sucking and mouthing Jeff's cock until Jeff began to grow soft, then Mickey sat up. They caught gazes and went for each other's lips once more, tasting cum on their tongues.

Jeff cupped Mickey's jaw and they parted slowly from the kiss as their hunger became sated. Mickey used his thumb to wipe the corner of Jeff's mouth and Jeff melted at his tender side. He looked back at the house and thought of Billy, then said, "Don't you ever get shot."

"I won't. Promise." Mickey sat up and tucked his cock back into his pants, straightening his holster and badge.

Jeff fixed his clothing as well, but he knew...that was one thing Mickey could never promise.

~

Jeff drove them home. It was finally dark outside. The summer nights were short, and although Mickey hated the heat, he preferred the long days to the long dark nights. Especially on duty.

Jeff kept his hand on Mickey's leg as Jeff drove south on the freeway, the music on but not too loud. Exhaustion was creeping up on Mickey and with the long shifts it was a perpetual state for them both. Sleeping for twelve -or more- hours on their days off didn't seem to help them catch up. At work it was the stress that took its toll, and yes, maybe being on patrol for an entire career wasn't what he wanted.

But a desk job? Paperwork? A phone? No way.

He glanced at Jeff's profile and had a strange image flash of Jeff in uniform, sergeant stripes on his sleeve. Jeff Chandler would make an outstanding sergeant, and an even better lieutenant.

Mickey picked up Jeff's hand in both of his and brought it to his lips to kiss.

Jeff perked up from his driving stupor and smiled at him. "Hello, gorgeous."

"What do you have to do to prepare for the exam?"

"Mick. I'm not taking it. Forget it."

"Jeff." Mickey squeezed his hand. "Tell me what you have to do?"

Jeff blew out a loud breath and said, "Just rote memorizing of all the fucking codes, procedures…shit. That's what. A load of studying."

"Let me help."

Jeff glanced at him as he drove. "Why the change of heart?"

"I love you."

Jeff's expression softened to putty. "I won't get on the list anyway. I suck at tests."

Mickey held Jeff's hand on his lap and knew that was bullshit. Jeff was extremely smart and would ace the exams. Mickey wouldn't be surprised if Jeff tested in the top five.

Off the freeway, getting closer to the townhouse, Mickey stifled a yawn and couldn't stop thinking about being on his own tomorrow in the patrol car. He was trying not to let it piss him off and upset him, but it was doing both.

Jeff pulled into his parking spot and shut off the headlights, then the engine. Mickey pushed open the car door and hoisted himself up, dragging suddenly, as if he had the weight of the world on him. Jeff was behind him, and Mickey felt his touch on his back; light, meant to comfort.

The door opened, the lights on, Mickey walked up the flight of stairs to their bedroom. He placed his holstered gun and badge clip on the dresser, and stripped to wash up for bed.

Jeff entered soon after, chugging a bottle of water, and staring at Mickey as he undressed.

Mickey entered the bathroom and looked at his reflection in the mirror as he brushed his teeth.

He heard Jeff moving in the other room, the closet door opening and drawers pulling out. Spitting the toothpaste into the sink, Mickey rinsed his mouth and frowned at himself. *Tomorrow is going to be one long-ass shitty day.*

~

Jeff knew after spending time with Billy and Alex that Mickey was trying to be supportive and open to him testing. But Jeff knew. He knew Mickey was miserable.

He leaned on the doorframe of the bathroom as Mickey finished washing up, getting ready for bed. Once Mickey was standing at the toilet, Jeff moved to the sink, scrubbing his face and brushing his teeth.

He peeked at Mickey and could see his exhaustion and possibly even some upset, expressed on his handsome face.

They had been riding high together for a long time. Partners for three years; playing, battling, working side by side, no issues, a great team… Suddenly? Jeff was suffering burnout, a homophobic prick was in the squad, and anonymous letters were being sent to AIG.

What the hell happened?

Mickey brushed passed Jeff as he left the bathroom, and Jeff didn't even get a swat to the bottom. It was disappointing. He washed up, and shut the light, seeing Mickey set the alarm clock and crawl into bed. Jeff turned off the table lamp and snuggled in beside him. He spooned Mickey, sealing their nakedness together. Mickey reached between his thighs and drew Jeff's soft cock between them gently, then Jeff heard a deep sigh come out of his man, and Mickey lay still.

Jeff caressed Mickey's shoulder and arm, staring at his silhouette in the dark room. Images of Billy's bruised chest flashed through Jeff's brain. And that was with a vest. Billy had come so close to dying on duty, Jeff had to hold back a sob. It was bad enough cops were being executed all over the world, and throughout California. If someone Jeff knew and loved got killed?

He bit his lip to stop it from trembling and wrapped his arm around Mickey's chest, feeling the beat of his heart.

Jeff nestled into the pillow beside Mickey and felt a hot tear roll down his cheek.

If he wasn't with his lover, how would they protect each other?

Jeff simply did not know what to do, and the anxiety was killing him.

Chapter Thirteen

Like a cloud of noxious smoke, Jeff felt the foul mood in the air. After the alarm went off, Mickey didn't hit the snooze button. He just got up and closed the bathroom door behind him.

Laying back, staring at the ceiling, Jeff heard the central air conditioning kick on, and thought about the day ahead. He knew what it was going to be like. Sitting at the desk doing paperwork, screening arrests and DOAs, and going to priority calls on the street. Alone.

Jeff rubbed his face and didn't know what he wanted anymore. But maybe having this day apart would help him decide.

Climbing out of bed, Jeff opened the bathroom door and spotted Mickey shaving at the sink. They caught gazes. Mickey broke the stare first and continued to run the blade over his jaw.

Jeff closed the door to let him continue alone, slipped on a pair of briefs, and headed down the stairs to start the coffee pot.

~

Mickey finished shaving and cleaning up, left the bathroom and dressed in a pair of shorts and a tank top. He put his gun back into the waist pack, removing it from the belt holster, and pinned his badge into his wallet. Seeing his phone needed charging, he plugged it in, then headed downstairs. Jeff had coffee brewing and had placed two bowls on the table along with milk and a box of cereal. Jeff only glanced at Mickey quickly before he headed up the stairs to clean himself up and get ready for his 'acting sergeant' shift.

Mickey tried not to sneer, and sat at the table filling his cereal bowl. In reality, he was feeling sorry for himself. His buddy, his lover, his man, for the first time in three years would not be by his side at work.

Separation anxiety? Call it whatever you want Mickey was going crazy and began wanting the day off.

A few minutes later, Jeff came trotting down the stairs in a pair of white shorts and an old worn out, light blue T-shirt with a Seattle Police crest on the chest. He poured two mugs of coffee and placed them on the table, then sat adjacent to Mickey and shook the cereal into his bowl. They ate quietly and Mickey could see Jeff running his hand back through his hair. A gesture of anxiety Jeff did when his hair became slightly too long and fell over his forehead. So Mickey asked, "Nervous?"

"A little." Jeff raised the bowl to his lips to slurp the last gulp of milk from it.

"You'll do fine."

"Thanks, Mick." Jeff placed his hand over Mickey's and stood, setting the bowl into the sink and drinking his coffee.

Mickey glanced at him and could see him staring off into space, no doubt his mind racing in a million different directions.

They arrived at work like any other day, except this time since Mickey was going to be on his own on patrol, Jeff drove them into work. Mickey had suggested taking separate cars, but Jeff said, "No way. If you have overtime, I'm waiting."

Mickey wasn't going to argue. He was already unhappy with doing both the driving and writing on duty and preferred splitting it with Jeff.

Jeff parked in the civilian lot and they climbed out of his car and walked in the hot breeze to the back entrance to the station. Patrol cars came and went and the officers coming on duty looked tired and preoccupied.

Once they changed into their uniforms, Jeff gave Mickey a long sad stare and said, "See ya in roll call."

"See ya." Mickey watched him leave the locker room and took a moment to compose his emotions before he headed to the roll call room *by himself*, and sitting, *by himself.*

He walked passed the sergeants' area and spotted Jeff being briefed by the sergeant going off duty and standing beside the sector sergeant from the other team they had roll call with. There he was, Acting Sergeant Jeff Chandler, already appearing like a supervisor and leader. He didn't need the chevrons on his sleeve, his presence was already powerful.

Mickey stepped into the roll call room and immediately spotted Cochran. Avoiding him, knowing he would kill the bastard if he opened his homophobic mouth, Mickey sat in his seat, the chair beside him empty, and rested his elbows on the table.

Flo and Chris, who were at the table in front of Mickey immediately turned around towards him. Flo gave Mickey a sad pout. "The A-team are split up for the day."

Chris asked, "Is Jeff testing?"

"Yeah. He is," Mickey told Chris and smiled at Flo to hide his hurt.

"Are you going to fly solo?" Flo asked.

"I'm not working with anyone else." Mickey looked around the room. The officers inside it were still chatting and laughing before the roll call began.

The group suddenly quieted down and took their seats. Mickey tugged at his vest to get it comfortable as Jeff and the other sector sergeant entered the room, clipboards in hand.

As if he realized Mickey was not going to be riding with Jeff, Mickey caught Cochran take notice and look from him to Jeff.

His heart not into today's shift, Mickey stared at Jeff but didn't hear a thing he said. Jeff gave out car assignments, read a bulletin…something…Mickey just kept thinking of how long today was going to be. How unbelievably unbearable.

"Okay, hit the streets. Be safe out there."

The men and women began to disperse, headed to their patrol cars.

Mickey watched Jeff as the other sergeant continued to brief him, train him. Jeff kept being distracted by Mickey, who hadn't gotten up from his chair. The room emptied.

Jeff nodded his head at something the other sergeant said and then both of them looked directly at Mickey.

The second sergeant teased Mickey, "Don't forget your call sign. You've been Eight-Adam-One for so long, you're liable to not hear dispatch call you." He patted Jeff's back and walked out of the room, leaving Jeff holding his clipboard, staring at Mickey.

Mickey asked, "So? How do you like it so far?"

"Not sure." Jeff walked over to him. "It's already a lot of paperwork bullshit."

Standing up, pushing in his chair, Mickey said, "Yup. See ya."

"Mick." Jeff held his arm. "Please. Be safe."

"And you. Don't get a paper cut." Mickey gave him a playful punch in his vest and walked out of the room, picking up his kit and not looking back.

Mickey did all the checks of the car himself, made sure he had his flares, first-aid kit, the shotgun was loaded and ready…

Alone in the car, Mickey logged into the computer as Eight-Lincoln-One and knew he'd forget his call sign the minute he rode onto the streets of LA.

The moment he was available he was dispatched to a car accident via his computer. Mickey blew out a breath of annoyance and prepared to take all the shitty one-man paper calls for twelve hours, trying not to explode in frustration.

~

Jeff tried to keep his ear to the radio as he sat at Sgt Adkins' desk and went over paperwork, reading reports before he signed off on them. It felt as if he were nailed to the damn chair as officers stood next to him to screen arrests, babbling about what they did on the call, why the suspect was in custody, reporting injuries even as minor as a scrape to the elbow.

Mired in reports, Jeff was amazed at how lousy some of the information on the paperwork was. Even done on the computer with spell-checking capabilities, the grammar, punctuation, and use of incorrect words was making him wonder if he was surrounded by morons or cops who simply were past caring.

The old-timers wrote one line reports, didn't give a shit since they were nearly done with their thirty year careers, and the young ones were either illiterate or rushing to get out to the next call. It would come back to haunt them if any of the suspects' cases went to trial.

By the time he had finished the work piled on the desk, Jeff checked his watch. Three hours had gone by and he hadn't heard 'Eight-Lincoln-One' come over radio once. Most of the lower priority calls came through the computer inside the patrol car, but he wondered if Mickey was sitting alone in the church lot, fuming.

He stood from his desk and looked around the area, then picked up a fresh radio battery before he left and grabbed Sgt Adkins' patrol car keys.

Just as he was about to leave and look for Mickey, an officer approached him and said, "You acting today, Chandler?"

"Yeah. Why?"

"Guy in the holding cell won't cooperate. Says he wants to see a supervisor."

Jeff pocketed the car keys and walked with the other officer to the cell area, trying not to mutter profanity under his breath. All he wanted to do was see Mickey.

~

Mickey had parked in the church lot after stopping at the drive-through coffee shop and getting himself an iced coffee. He tapped the computer keys, having just taken a report of several car prowls that had occurred overnight, but hadn't been discovered until a few hours ago. There were four cars hit in one block, so Mickey read his notes on his pad and added the tedious information into the little boxes on the report, ready to lose his mind.

The dispatcher came over the air, "All units, a report of an incident…in progress…at the USB Bank…"

Mickey grabbed the microphone, knowing the dispatcher would not say a 'bank robbery' over the air waves, but it wasn't hard to figure out.

Cochran offered up first, and Mickey got on the air second, "Eight-Lincoln-One, responding code-three." A second after Mickey hung up the microphone, the airwaves were flooded with cops offering to head to the bank.

Mickey turned on his lights and sirens but since it was 'in progress' he hoped the cops were intelligent enough to shut down the noise before they drew too close to the bank.

As he flew down the boulevard, his adrenalin pumping, the updates continued being broadcast by the dispatcher over radio; "An employee describes two suspects; motorcycle helmets, leather jackets, each armed with semi-automatic pistols."

As the incident was being broadcast as it was occurring, Mickey heard an FBI unit responding as well as K-9 and traffic units.

Mickey was so close to the bank, he shut his sirens down and began to roll up cautiously. A patrol car was already parked directly in front of the bank entrance, and a red Honda motorcycle was nearly at its grill.

"What the fuck?" Mickey wondered if the robbers had fled or the cop who pulled up to the front door was out of his mind.

He picked up the microphone about to announce his arrival when he heard popping sounds.

"Fuck!" Mickey gunned the car engine and his tires squealed as the heavy patrol car spun in a half circle in the parking lot, facing the entrance. He jumped out, gun in hand, and used the car door as cover.

Two men, holding backpacks and black handguns, wearing motorcycle helmets and leather jackets, hopped on the motorcycle. The motorcycle did not start, so the suspects got off of it. One stood still, pointing his gun down at something on the ground.

The second suspect began to flee and more popping sounds made Mickey jump out of his skin.

He set his gun sites on the suspect who was shooting off rounds and shouted, “Stop! Drop your weapon!” The suspect aimed his way and opened fire.

Mickey pulled the trigger of his Glock and his hearing and other senses shut down. All he could see was a gun pointed at him and what actually felt like surreal apparitions of two armed men with helmets and face shields moving around him. One of the men fled instantly, dropping his gun and racing towards a high chain-link fence.

Mickey blew off more rounds at the first suspect, and he too turned, ran a few steps, but then suddenly dropped face down on the pavement.

By then, marked and unmarked patrol units were everywhere, flooding the scene. Mickey stared at the downed suspect and didn’t see him move. He stood slowly, his gun still pointing at the man as he lay prone, and then felt a tickling sensation running down his arm. He looked to his left shoulder and blood was soaking through his uniform shirt sleeve.

An officer carrying a shotgun raced towards Mickey, both of them wary of the downed gunman and the suspect at large. The report was of two helmeted armed men, but of course, there was no way to know who or what was going on in the chaos.

Then suddenly the cop with the shotgun beside him, who Mickey realized was Chris, yelled, “Mick! You’re hit!”

Mickey’s senses were so dull and he couldn’t feel pain. He pointed his gun at the downed suspect and walked closer to him. Chris did as well, his shotgun pointed directly at the prone man. The man did not move. He was still as stone, having fallen on top of the backpack he was attempting to race away with.

Over the air someone yelled, "Officer down!"

Mickey touched his shoulder and looked at his hand. His palm was bright red.

"Dude. Sit down!" Chris pulled Mickey back behind his patrol car and set the shotgun beside him. He rolled up Mickey's short sleeve shirt and grimaced. "Oh, fuck, Stanton!"

"What?" Mickey had his gun in his hand, it was hot from firing and since he had blown all the rounds off, the slide had locked back, cutting his the skin between his thumb and index finger.

Chris opened Mickey's trunk and pulled out the first-aid kit, holding a gauze pad to his shoulder. "Need fire! Officer shot!" Chris said over the air, his voice cracking with emotion.

Dispatch asked, "Is the scene secure for fire?"

"Negative!" a commander's voice came over the air. "The scene is not secure."

"I have an officer ten-forty-five-boy!" someone who sounded panicked yelled into the radio. "Send in fire now, north side is secure, north side is secure!"

Chris looked at Mickey. "Who else is hit?"

Mickey looked at his arm. Blood ran down his skin passed his elbow and dripped to the hot tarmac. "Another patrol car is at the front entrance. I heard shots when I approached."

"Who? Who the fuck is down?"

"I don't know." Mickey stopped looking at his shoulder because the sight of his own blood was making him lightheaded.

~

Jeff flew over the city streets like an Indie racer. He used all the siren sound effects to clear intersections, blast passed slow cars, hoping to hell the chaos of this bank robbery and officers down didn't mean…didn't mean…

He stopped his patrol car using the ABS braking system and it slid to the curb between fire trucks and medic units. Hopping out of his car, Jeff raced around the medical crew and looked at another patrol car parked directly in front of the bank doors, a 'crotch-rocket' type motorcycle at the grill. "Mickey, tell me you weren't stupid enough to park here with an in-progress bank robbery!" He ran to the group of medics working on a uniformed cop and had to bite back his vocalizations of relief when he found it was Cochran. Cochran had been hit in the neck and thigh and was being hoisted on a backboard to a gurney. Jeff listened over radio, trying to figure out where the hell Mickey was in the madness. Reporters had arrived, helicopters circled, a perimeter was trying to be maintained for the escaped suspect. No one knew if the scene was secure since there was still a fleeing bank robber at large.

He knew getting over the air to try and find his man would be impossible. Jeff began trotting around the bank, gun in hand, looking everywhere at once.

He spotted his and Mickey's usual patrol car and a few yards in front of it was a man, all in black, face down, with a motorcycle helmet on his head. Jeff aimed his gun at him and walked carefully to the patrol unit. Behind it were two cops, crouching down. He recognized Chris, and then…Mickey.

The patrol car had nearly twenty bullet rounds in it; holes in the windshield, holes in the door, the fender. When Jeff spotted blood on Mickey he bit back a scream and raced to him. "Fuck!"

"I'm trying to get a medic here!" Chris yelled at him. "That suspect is dead! The scene is secure!"

Jeff tried to function as Mickey's arm was running with bright red blood and Chris was a bloody mess trying to stop the flow. "Eight-Lincoln-Twenty- Second officer down! North of the bank. Need a medic unit immediately. The scene is secure!" Jeff dug through the first-aid kit and wadded gauze against Mickey's shoulder. "Mick. Mick, look at me."

Mickey did, slowly.

"You're okay." Jeff asked Chris, "Is he hit anywhere else?"

"Fuck, I don't know. I didn't think to look."

"Hold this." He made Chris press more gauze on Mickey's shoulder. Jeff, sobbing and trying to fight it, checked his lover for any other wounds. He took the Glock out of Mickey's hand and could see he had fired all his rounds and the slide had locked back, cutting his skin. That was it.

"Fuck, Chandler!" Chris said in agony, "The exit wound is where all the blood is coming from." Christ shifted so he was holding the gauze on the back of Mickey's arm.

"Mick." Jeff cupped Mickey's jaw. "You're okay."

Mickey said nothing, staring into space.

The medics finally found them and rushed towards Mickey. They took Mickey's shirt off and when Jeff saw the black bullet hold in his shoulder, he nearly lost it.

A pack of men in suits jogged over and Jeff could see their FBI badges flapping on their belts. Jeff pointed. "One suspect DOA. One fled."

The men walked cautiously to the still body. They waved a fire crew over and the medics rolled the dead man to his back and took off his helmet.

Jeff touched Mickey's hand as he was tended and then took a look at the dead suspect.

He was young. Very young, still clutching a high caliber pistol with a large, extended clip of ammunition. The FBI unit opened the backpack and Jeff could see it was filled with cash.

"Who shot him?" one FBI task force member asked.

"Officer Stanton." Jeff looked back at Mickey.

"Hell of a marksman. He took the front site off this guy's gun. All the rounds hit center mass. Son of a bitch, that was unbelievable shooting."

A lieutenant arrived finally and was assessing the situation. "Still haven't found the second suspect?" he asked Jeff.

"No. At large. Last report was he dropped his weapon and leapt over that fence." Jeff pointed.

The lieutenant noticed Mickey and approached him. "Where are you hit?"

A medic said, "Shoulder, sir. Bullet went in and out."

The lieutenant looked back at Jeff, tilting his head. "Get the fuck up to the hospital with your partner."

"Yes, sir. Thank you, sir." Jeff tried to stop his eyes from overflowing with tears.

He walked with Mickey's gurney to the medic unit and placed his hand on his good arm. "Ya with me, Stanton?"

"Yeah. With ya, Chandler."

"I'm following you up to the hospital."

"You'd better, ya prick."

He watched as Mickey was loaded into the back of the ambulance and tried to function. He felt a pat on his back and spotted Chris.

"You believe this shit went down while you were acting?" Chris said, wiping his bloody hands on disinfectant towels, the shotgun leaning against his leg.

"Yes. Unfortunately I do." Jeff nodded to him and said, "Thanks for taking care of Mick."

"Just doin' my job." Chris held the shotgun and walked back to his car.

Jeff sat in the driver's seat of his sergeant's car and followed the medic unit as it flew to the hospital, his lights and sirens blaring with them.

~

Mickey stared at the ceiling of the ambulance, feeling it slowing and speeding through the city streets, hearing the siren wail. Beside him a young medic tried to clean his wound and stop the bleeding. He had a gauze patch on both the front and back of Mickey's wound and began using wet disinfectant wipes to wash Mickey's arm of the blood.

"How you doin'?"

Wishing it was Blake and Hunter, Mickey glanced at him. "I don't know. You tell me."

"You don't need surgery. That's good, right?"

Sinking mentally, Mickey stared at the cabinets as they rattled and shook with their movements.

"Are you in pain?"

"I don't know." Mickey was numb, trying to recall what had actually happened. He remembered driving up to the scene and seeing a patrol car at the bank's front door. A rookie mistake. One he never would have made.

"I can give you something if you are."

Mickey looked at the young man, so young he must have been in his early twenties. "Why do we do this job?"

"To help people."

"We don't help anyone."

The young man shut up, continuing to clean the blood from Mickey's hand and arm.

He felt the ambulance stop and the sound of the sirens shut down. The back door was opened and the driver of the ambulance helped the young medic pull the gurney out. Jeff was immediately by his side, and Mickey could see a dozen uniformed officers keeping back reporters at the emergency room entrance.

He was wheeled to a room with curtain dividers and a doctor in scrubs, with a mask and gloves on, stood by as nurses began to take off Mickey's gear and clothing. Jeff was there to handle his items, and the gun Mickey used was immediately given to a homicide supervisor who bagged it separately for evidence.

Jeff held open a huge brown bag and Mickey's uniform was taken off and his boots handed to Jeff with the vest.

Mickey was covered with a blanket and the gauze was removed from his wound. He heard the medical staff discussing it and stared at the drop ceiling, pretending this was a bad dream.

"We need to flush it out. The exit needs a stitch."

Someone leaned over Mickey to ask, "Are you in pain?"

"I don't know." Mickey felt disoriented. He raised his head. "Jeff!"

Jeff rushed over, appearing confused, as if he'd been busy doing something else. Mickey noticed he no longer held the brown bag or the gear. "I'm here."

Mickey reached for Jeff with his good hand. Jeff clasped it.

"Are you his partner?" the nurse asked as she prepared to flush the wound.

"Yes." Jeff nodded.

"He wasn't today," Mickey said, feeling woozy. "He was my sergeant today."

"This may sting."

It did. Mickey hissed out a breath of air and shut his eyes, clenching Jeff's hand.

"Mick. Hang on. Mick… you're okay."

"Fuck!" Mickey yelled and tried to jerk his arm away. He was retrained and the stinging continued until Mickey thought he may pass out from the pain.

"He's diaphoretic, Doctor, and his blood pressure is up."

"Hang in there, soldier," the doctor said, continuing to clean out the bullet wound.

"*Fuck!*" Mickey roared and squeezed Jeff's hand so hard he couldn't feel his own.

~

Seeing his beloved in pain was killing Jeff, not to mention the death grip on his hand. He clenched Mickey's fingers and wanted so much to bring them to his lips, but he was not going to do it.

"Okay. The worst is over." The doctor inspected the black hole in Mickey's shoulder. "Roll him over to his side so we can put a stitch in the exit wound."

Mickey was rolled by a group of attendants. Jeff saw how pale and sweaty Mickey was from the pain and held onto his good hand, not letting go.

The doctor shot a needle into the area near the tear in Mickey's skin, to numb it. "Good thing you're a bruiser, Officer Stanton. This bullet never touched bone."

Mickey closed his eyes and withstood what Jeff imagined was unbearable agony.

"You feel this?" a nurse asked as she pricked near the torn skin.

Mickey shook his head.

Jeff couldn't watch as they sewed the hole closed.

A small commotion was heard near the hallway. Murmuring of men's voices. Jeff looked back and spotted the Chief of Police. He didn't see him in person very often but with a high profile shooting like this, here he was.

Jeff released Mickey's hand and backed up, saluting the man. "Sir."

"No need for that…" The chief looked at Jeff's nametag. "Officer Chandler." He smiled and reached for a handshake. "I hear that's your partner."

"It is, sir."

"Stay with him. I have someone else acting sergeant for the rest of the day."

Jeff choked up and swallowed it down so he didn't show his emotion. "Thank you, sir."

"Now. Where's my hero?" The chief walked closer to Mickey. "That was fine shooting you did, Stanton. A true marksmen and fine asset to the department."

Jeff bit his lip as his eyes were ready to overflow.

"Thank you, sir." Mickey opened his eyes but Jeff could see he was still very pale as they sewed his skin.

"You saved an officer's life, Stanton. If you hadn't been there, Officer Cochran was about to be gunned down in cold blood."

Jeff felt his stomach pinch.

"Sir?" Mickey asked as the nurse finished stitching his arm and brushed brown liquid over the wound.

"When the suspects exited the bank, they confronted Cochran. He was shot twice and witnesses said if you hadn't been there, the suspect was standing over him, ready to execute him."

Jeff rubbed his face in agony.

Mickey didn't reply, just stared at the chief.

The nurse rolled Mickey to his back and they tended the entry wound.

"I'm going to recommend you for a commendation for bravery, Officer Stanton."

Jeff sobbed and swallowed it down again, battling with his agony.

"Was the second suspect located?" Mickey asked.

"No. As far as I know, they are still searching the area. But we recovered his gun and the backpack with the money in it. Seems he climbed a nine foot chain-link fence, topped with barbed wire, and left a bloody trail through an apartment building. That was one determined suspect."

Mickey nodded and glanced over at the bandage the nurse was dressing his arm with.

"Good work." The chief patted Mickey's good shoulder and then looked at Jeff. "Take care of him. Take some days off."

Jeff dabbed at his eyes as discreetly as he could. "Thank you, sir."

The chief shook his hand and Jeff heard him ask, "Where's Officer Cochran?"

"In surgery, sir," someone replied.

The noise of men talking in the hall vanished and Jeff felt his phone hum. He knew he couldn't talk in the ER but he removed it from his pocket and looked at it. He had received more than a dozen missed text and voicemail messages from everyone he knew; Blake, Hunter, Tanner, Josh, Alex, Billy, and even Mark and Steve.

No doubt the news report was making them all nervous wrecks.

"There ya go." The nurse stepped back.

The doctor said, "I want you to take antibiotics as well as anti-inflammatory medication. I'll also give you pain medication, just on an as-need basis."

Mickey nodded but Jeff could see he had checked out mentally.

"Doc?" Jeff approached him. "Tell me. He's out of it."

"Okay. Come with me. Let me print out the prescriptions."

Jeff followed the doctor to a computer, looking back at Mickey with worry.

"He should heal fine, but if he has any fever or other strong symptoms just either call us, or take him to his family doctor."

Jeff was handed paperwork.

"There's a pharmacy just down the hall."

"Thank you, sir." Jeff nodded.

The doctor smiled kindly at him and walked away.

Jeff approached Mickey and said, "Let me get these filled and I'll take you home."

Mickey nodded, appearing glossy eyed and exhausted.

Jeff inhaled for strength and left the ER, looking for the pharmacy, seeing many plain-clothed detectives and uniformed cops still there, including guild representatives.

Why wasn't I with him? Why? Jeff knew this day would haunt him forever. And it was a sign that he could not leave patrol or his partner's side. He swore to himself he never would again.

Chapter Fourteen

Mickey was helped by a nurse to put on his uniform pants, socks, and boots. His arm was in a sling and a hospital gown was draped around his shoulders, but open in front. As he was tended, Mickey began to feel his shoulder throb and the injection of the numbing chemical wear off. Jeff appeared at the doorway, holding an armload; Mickey's vest, gun belt, a brown bag with his T-shirt and bloody uniform shirt, and another small white bag with what Mickey suspected was from the pharmacy.

"All set." The nurse gestured to a wheelchair.

Mickey dropped down in it and was rolled out, Jeff walking beside him to the exit. Cops stood guard in a line, keeping photographers back, as they began to jam in the minute Mickey was seen.

Jeff said, "Wait here. Let me get the car."

Mickey nodded, not talking, looking at his hand. The one the slide had skinned. In reflex he tried to move his left arm to touch it but the sling prevented him and then intense pain.

A few tough motorcycle officers, in their black boots and leather jackets pushed back the spectators and press as Jeff pulled up as close as he could to the entrance. Mickey stood, and swayed.

A CHP officer was right there, steadying him. He walked Mickey to the passenger's door as Jeff was about to race out to help.

Mickey sat down and nodded thanks to the officer, and the patrol car door was shut.

"I'm taking you home. Then I'll head to the station and change and get my car."

"Fuck that. That's too far to drive. We're closer to the precinct. Just go there and change."

"Mickey! Don't argue with me."

"Fuck you!" Mickey flinched and held his arm still. In a slow controlled sentence he said, "Go to the station and change."

"Fine." Jeff pulled away from the hospital as cops held back pedestrians and stopped traffic, waving Jeff through.

Mickey spotted a half full plastic cup of what was probably a Frappuccino. "Where are the pills?"

"There." Jeff pointed to the floor near Mickey's feet.

He hadn't even seen the bag when he got into the car. Mickey picked it up and looked in. He checked all three bottles and spotted the painkillers. Shaking two into his hand, he swallowed them with the drink.

Jeff drove in rush hour traffic, tapping his fingers on the steering wheel as if he were impatient or going crazy.

"Fuck it." Jeff flipped on his lights and sirens and forced the traffic to yield.

Mickey was glad he did because he was in agony.

Once he arrived at the division's civilian parking lot, Jeff shut down the emergency equipment and climbed out of the car. He opened Mickey's door and pointed to his car. "Get in. I'll only be a minute."

"Okay." Mickey was hauled by Jeff out of the patrol car and helped to sit in the passenger's seat of the sports car.

"Here." Jeff handed him his cell phone. "Everyone is going out of their mind. Call them and tell them you're okay." Jeff dropped the keys on Mickey's lap and drove the patrol car away.

Mickey started the car, reaching over the console, turning the air conditioner on and the radio off.

He slouched in the seat and with his right hand began scrolling through messages. One by one, he called his best friends.

~

Jeff held Mickey's gear and began to grow enraged. *Why?* For so many reasons Jeff's head was about to explode. As he walked through the halls, other officers shouted, "How's Mick?"

"Okay." Jeff nodded, kept walking, and didn't want to delay his departure. Dropping Mickey's items at his feet, Jeff opened the locker and began undressing quickly, jamming his gun belt into it and changing. Once he was in his shorts, his waist pack on his hips, he spun around to Mickey's locker and took a piece of paper out of his wallet for the combination. He opened it, and hung up Mickey's vest and gun belt, removing his civilian clothing and before he placed them into the bag at his feet, he took out the bloody T-shirt and uniform shirt.

Jeff barely held it together and pressed the clothing to his face, catching Mickey's scent. He wiped his eyes and removed Mickey's badge, putting it into his waist pack with his own gun. He kept the T-shirt to wash at home, bringing the uniform shirt to the dry cleaning section with a bio-hazard bag over it. He left the shirt in the pickup area for uniforms, and on his way out he was again bombarded with questions.

"How's Cochran?"

"Is it true Mickey saved his life?"

"Is Mickey still at the hospital?"

Jeff said, "I gotta go." He pushed through the exit with Mickey's clothing in a plastic bag and jogged to the civilian parking lot to his car.

Climbing in, tossing the bag in the back seat, he sat behind the wheel as Mickey spoke on the phone.

"Alex, stop crying." Mickey rolled his eyes at Jeff.

Jeff bit his lip on his own emotions and headed home.

"Alex, I'm fine. It's just a scratch."

Liar. Jeff wiped his nose as it ran, biting his lip and trying to deal with what was impossible to handle.

"Put Billy on. Alex, please. Stop crying." Mickey took the phone away from his ear and blew out a breath. "I can't do this Jeff."

"Then don't."

Mickey put the phone back to his ear. "Alex, I have to go. Okay? I'm very tired. Bye." He not only disconnected it, he shut off the phone and dropped it in the cup holder.

"How's the pain?" Jeff asked.

Mickey didn't answer, closing his eyes and holding the sling with his right arm.

The guilt was killing Jeff. Killing him.

In an hour, enduring horrible rush hour traffic, Jeff pulled into his parking space for the townhouse. He rushed to the passenger's door and opened it. Mickey looked exhausted, worse than Jeff had ever seen him. He reached out his hand to haul Mickey out of the car. Mickey gripped Jeff's forearm and used him to get up. Mickey immediately held his sling and his body language was of pure pain. Jeff left everything in the car and walked Mickey to the front of the townhouse. The hospital gown had fallen off in the front seat and Mickey wore only his uniform pants and boots. Jeff opened the front door and Mickey stopped inside it and said, "I'm not wearing these filthy boots in our home."

Jeff crouched down and unlaced them, taking them off. "Get in bed."

Mickey jerked away from Jeff and stood in the kitchen, opening a cabinet where Jeff knew they kept the booze.

Jeff left the townhouse, going back to retrieve everything out of the car and wondered how he was going to deal with this, any of it.

~

Mickey opened a bottle of vodka and gulped it. He coughed at the nasty taste and leaned against the counter, his arm throbbing.

The home phone rang and Mickey looked at the answering machine to see the red light flashing and a dozen missed messages.

Once Jeff brought all the bags into the house, he trotted to get the phone. "Hello? Hi, Aura. Yes, he's here." Jeff held up the phone. "It's your sister."

Mickey put the bottle down and took the phone. "Hello."

"Mouse! Oh, God, Mouse! I was watching it on the news! I saw helicopter footage of the incident. When I spotted Jeff running with an ambulance gurney, I knew it had to be you who got hurt!" She cried, and said, "Then they said two cops were shot and I couldn't get either of you on the phone—"

"Aura." Mickey made for the kitchen chair but struggled to move it so he could sit.

Jeff pulled it out for him and then placed the medicine bottles on the counter after inspecting the labels.

"I'm fine." Mickey watched as Jeff set pills on the table in front of him and a bottle of water.

"Oh, God…what happened?" Aura cried.

"I got grazed on my shoulder, okay? I'm fine." Mickey looked up at Jeff and mouthed, '*I cannot deal with this!*'

Jeff reached for the phone. "Aura, hi, look, Mickey is very tired. He's fine. He got one bullet to the left shoulder and all it needed was a stitch."

Standing, Mickey reached for the vodka, sat down, and tipped the bottle to his mouth. Then he stared at his uniform pants and noticed blood on them. He stood, swaying, and then steadied himself, taking them off using one hand, dropping them to the floor and stepping out of them. Mickey took the bottle with him and made his way to the top floor bedroom.

"No, don't come over right now, Aura. Mick's exhausted. He's going to bed…we're both on leave. Yes. Both of us."

Mickey closed the door so he couldn't hear the conversation. He sat on the bed and kept drinking the booze, feeling it burn his throat.

The murmur of Jeff's voice still audible, Mickey took one more gulp of vodka and set the bottle down, lying back on the bed and closing his eyes.

~

"I'll let you know." Jeff looked at the pills Mickey did not take.

"Is he okay? Jeff?"

"He's shocked. We're all stunned. It was a messed up incident."

"Were you with him?"

Jeff felt a stab to his chest. "No. I…The sergeant made me acting sergeant today, in his absence."

"You weren't with my Mouse?"

"Aura, please." Jeff began growing emotional.

"I'm coming by tomorrow after work. You tell him that, ya got it?"

He could hear the fury in her voice.

"I got it." The line disconnected and Jeff put the phone down. He sat on the living room sofa, staring at the uniform pants, the boots, and the bags he had brought from the locker room. Removing Mickey's badge from his pack, Jeff stared at it, rubbing the shield with his thumb, then he covered his face and began sobbing, shaken to the core.

~

Through a blur Mickey could see Jeff moving in the room. The bathroom light turned on, the door closed, the sink ran with the water. A moment later Jeff exited, turning off the light, stripping his shirt and shorts off, and lying beside him on the bed.

Jeff used the back of his knuckles to run down Mickey's bare chest, above the sling.

Mickey parted his lips to speak. Although the painkillers and booze had finally made him pain free, he felt like he was in a deep sleep yet awake. Nothing seemed real. The drugs and booze made him sleepy. He closed his eyes and drifted off to sleep.

Gunshot blasts woke Mickey up. He gasped and blinked. When he went to sit up, his arm and shoulder ripped with pain.

"Mick." Jeff was lying in the dimness of their bedroom beside him. "I'm here."

Mickey was drenched in sweat and breathing hard. He lay back down and tried to catch his breath.

"You need anything? You should take the other meds, not just the painkillers." Jeff ran his hand over Mickey's forehead. "You're drenched. Let me get a cool rag."

Before Jeff climbed off the bed, Mickey snatched Jeff's arm and yanked him back. "That moron parked right in front of the bank entrance."

"I know." Jeff leaned on his elbows as he spoke quietly.

"In progress! What did he not hear about 'in progress'?"

"He's a fucked up douche. Mick, calm down."

"No!" Mickey tensed up and his arm throbbed. "This is because of him! I got shot because that fucked up prick didn't listen to radio! Because he set himself up and all of us up for failure!"

"Mick, please. Calm down." Jeff tried to sit up but Mickey dragged him by his upper arm, closer to him.

"He parked right outside their escape route?" Mickey snarled and breathed fire. "Seeing the fucking bike there? Knowing we were getting reports from an employee watching the whole incident on video camera! Play by play!"

"God, Mick…calm down. Please."

"I'm shot!" Mickey screamed. "I am shot!" He tried to move his arm. "Not in the vest! Not bruised! I have a fucking bullet hole in me!"

Jeff began to fall apart, biting back his sobs.

"I was nearly gunned down for that prick?" Mickey squeezed Jeff's arm tightly. "I killed a guy! Jeff, I fucking killed someone today!"

"Oh, God…" Jeff cried and rocked. "It's my fault. I should have been with you. God, oh God, I will never forgive myself."

Mickey stared at his lover as he convulsed in heaving sobs. "I should have kept driving. I should have let them murder that SOB."

"No. You'd never do that. Never." Jeff wiped at his eyes and coughed as he wept. "I know you. Even to protect a prick like Cochran, you'd do what you could. He's one of us."

"How can you defend him?" Mickey pushed Jeff away.

"I'm not! I'm defending you! Your instincts to help. You're the one. You're the damn hero!"

"A hero?" Mickey gestured to his shoulder. "You think I want to die for bank money that's insured by the fucking federal government? Huh? You think I want to enjoy that lovely long train of patrol cars at my funeral? Have the bagpipes play *Amazing Grace* while I get lowered in the ground…for insured money?"

"Mick. God. Mick. Calm down."

"I. Got. Shot!" Mickey showed his teeth and felt his eyes sting with tears. "You listening to me? For what? Huh?"

"Baby…baby…" Jeff sobbed, rocking where he sat, trying to comfort Mickey.

"Get me another painkiller. Please, Jeff." Mickey wiped his eyes.

Jeff stumbled off the bed, as if he were blind with tears, and used his hands to find his way down the stairs.

Mickey stared at the ceiling as his rage grew. He let loose a roar like a battle cry of frustration and his body became riddled in throbbing pain.

"Fuck! *Fuck you*!" He hated the world, hated the job. "Fuck all of you!"

~

Shaking, miserable, and losing his mind, Jeff couldn't even read the pill bottle labels through his tears. He looked up at the second floor and heard Mickey's anguish as he yelled at life, railed at the universe, and did not blame Jeff. *He did not point his finger at me? Me! I should have been there. I should have.*

Jeff stared at the bottle of vodka and opened it, drinking it down, choking and coughing on it. He looked back up at the second floor and dreaded Mickey's rage.

Helpless, wishing he could go back in time and not allow Mickey to be alone in the car, Jeff sat on the chair in the kitchen, drinking the booze. He spotted his cell phone and sniffled as he picked it up, scrolling the numbers. Dialing, he put the phone to his ear.

"Hello?"

"Help me. I can't deal with it, with Mick. Help me." Jeff started crying.

"On my way."

~

Mickey wondered why it was taking Jeff so long to get a pill. He forced himself to sit up, holding his arm to his chest. With a great effort he stood and walked to the bathroom, turning on a light. When he saw the state of himself in the mirror, the crusty brown blood still on his skin near his neck, his face, his blue sling and the white gauze on his shoulder, the weight of the incident hit him. With his right hand on the sink to steady himself, Mickey cried and rethought his actions again and again. What did he do wrong? Why did he get hit? And why was Jeff not with him?

Turning on the water, Mickey splashed his face, trying to wash off the dried blood. Everything was awkward with one hand, but at least it was not his good arm that was damaged.

He heard soft footsteps on carpeted floor behind him, and Jeff, looking miserable, his eyes red and his expression worn out, held a bottle of water and a handful of pills towards him.

Mickey dried his face and took the pills, popping them into his mouth and guzzled the water. Once he had he said, "I feel like I need a shower."

"I'm sure you shouldn't get that wet." He pointed to the gauze. "I can bathe you."

Mickey at first reacted badly, thinking of being an invalid and needing a nursemaid, but he let go and nodded. "Okay."

Jeff leaned down to the tub and filled it, testing the water.

As he did, Mickey attempted to get the sling off, but every movement made him wince in pain.

Jeff sniffled, as if trying not to get upset, and loosened the strap, taking off the sling.

Mickey held his arm to his chest and looked at the gauze patch, front and back, in the mirror. He was so angry he had to keep his mouth shut or he'd continue to scream expletives.

Jeff swirled his hand in the water and then gestured for Mickey to climb in. Mickey did, Jeff holding him steady, and sat in the hot water. Slouched low, trying to hurry the painkillers to work, Mickey felt Jeff using a soapy washcloth on his back and closed his eyes.

"Do…" Jeff cleared his throat as his words mixed with sobs. "Do you want me to wash your hair?"

"It'll get the gauze wet. No."

"I can tape plastic over it."

"Tomorrow. Just get the fucking blood off me."

Jeff nodded and ran the washcloth against Mickey's neck and arm. Mickey listened to the water running in the tub and tried to unwind. The touch was soothing and it felt good to get clean.

Indicating he was done washing his back, Jeff knelt upright beside the tub. Mickey got to his knees, trying to soap up his crotch near the running water. Immediately Jeff took over, scrubbing Mickey's cock, balls, and ass for him. Mickey hissed out a breath of air in relief, wishing he could fuck Jeff, get his mind off this crap, but his cock was not responding to the touch.

Crawling on his knees Mickey moved closer to the running bath water, and Jeff rinsed him off, splashing the water against Mickey's body in combination with the washcloth. Then Jeff shut the tap.

He hauled Mickey to his feet, helped him step out of the tub, and used a towel to dry him.

Mickey tried to dry himself with his right hand but when he did, he moved his left inadvertently and moaned in pain.

Jeff reached for the sling. "Here. It'll keep it still."

Mickey tried to be patient, but convalescing was not his strong point. After Jeff retied the sling he used the towel to dry Mickey's back and bottom, then knelt down to wipe his legs.

"Thanks."

Jeff nodded, not answering, not meeting Mickey's eyes.

Mickey walked back to the bedroom and looked at the time. It was only seven. He pointed to a drawer. "Can ya help me get my underwear on?"

"Yes. Sure." Jeff took out a clean pair and held them out for Mickey to step into. Once he had, Mickey held onto the wall of the staircase, intending on zoning out in front of the TV. He picked up the bottle of vodka and sat with it on his lap, pointing the remote control at the screen. Flipping through channels of shit, Mickey threw the remote onto the sofa and screamed, "Fuck!" in pure frustration.

Chapter Fifteen

Jeff stood behind him, powerless, lost. He was shaken up from what had happened so badly that when a knock came at their door, he jumped out of his skin.

Mickey reacted as if it were gunshots and flinched. "Who the fuck is that?" Mickey asked, the bottle on his lap, his eyes glazed.

Jeff knew exactly who. He opened the door to the lieutenant.

He and Billy exchanged glances, and without a word, Jeff communicated to Billy, '*not good*' with a shake of his head.

Billy stepped into the living room and Jeff closed the door.

"Sharpe?" Mickey asked, appearing confused.

"Can I sit down?" Billy pointed to the sofa beside Mickey.

"You here on a social or official call?" Mickey asked.

Jeff trotted up the stairs to put on a pair of shorts over his briefs, he paused at the top landing and wondered if he should let Billy and Mickey speak in private, then decided to just stay in the kitchen, out of the way. Slipping on shorts quickly, Jeff headed back to the kitchen.

Before he sat at the table and kept quiet, he asked Billy, "Can I get you anything?"

Billy looked at the vodka bottle Mickey was holding and then said to Jeff, "Ya got a beer?"

"Yeah." Jeff took one out of the fridge and handed it to the lieutenant, seeing Billy's gun holster on his belt, clipped beside his gold lieutenant badge.

Mickey looked numb, staring in the direction of the TV, but not appearing to see it.

Jeff backed up and sat at the kitchen table, planning on being the quiet observer. The guilt in him was so intense, he was about to lose his mind.

Billy drank the beer and then asked, "Can I lower the sound?" pointing at the TV.

Mickey tossed him the remote.

Billy muted the volume and let out a deep sigh as he stared at Mickey. "Who do you want to kill, Stanton?"

Mickey snarled and didn't answer.

Jeff hoped it wasn't him.

After taking another gulp of the beer, Billy set the bottle down on the coffee table. "I wanted to kill myself. I fucked up. I had no goddamn reason to be leading the SWAT team that day. I was there to hostage negotiate."

Jeff thought about Billy's role in the shooting at a hostage crisis a few weeks ago. Billy's old pals on the SWAT team lured the lieutenant in, since they were eager to save the lives of the innocent hostages inside the apartment where they were being held. But Billy was not their commander. He had already been reassigned to internal affairs.

"I fucked up. But you know what, Stanton?" Billy asked.

Mickey didn't even look at him, holding the bottle against his sling.

"No matter how many times you replay that shit in your head, you can't go back. You can't change a fucking thing."

"Fuck!" Mickey yelled and Jeff jumped from the volume. Mickey raised the bottle as if he were going to throw it against the wall. Gently, Billy took it from him and set it on the table.

"You went into tactical mode." Billy leaned his arm on the back of the sofa near Mickey. "You saved a fellow officer, bystanders, medical personnel, and you got one hit to your shoulder. You saved you."

Hot tears ran down Jeff's face and he swiped at them. *When are you going to accuse me, Mick? When?*

"The shooting will of course be ruled 'good'," Billy said, "No question. And I'll make sure you two will be allowed to stay off duty until you return to work. Together."

"I don't want to be off!" Mickey faced Billy finally, his eyes red and his skin ruddy from his pain and most likely the booze and pills. "You think I want to sit here and watch fucking soap operas all day?"

"Nope." Billy actually chuckled. "Did I? Nope."

"Goddamn it, Sharpe! That asshole parked in front of the fucking bank! He practically pushed the suspect bike with his patrol car bumper! How stupid is that?"

Jeff knew. Very stupid. He figured Cochran assumed the suspects had left. *Assumed. An Ass out of 'u' and me.*

"His incompetent act nearly made him commit suicide." Billy picked up his beer to sip. "Word on the division is he's done with police work. So you're rid of him."

"Thank fuck." Mickey picked up the vodka and drank a gulp.

Jeff repeated what Mickey said in his head. *Yes, thank fuck that ass is gone.*

"What about how you feel about your partner?" Billy thumbed over his shoulder at Jeff.

Jeff sat up in alarm and braced himself.

Mickey looked beyond Billy at him.

The lump of regret and guilt in Jeff's throat grew.

"I'm glad he wasn't there. He could have been shot. Or killed."

"You and I both know that's bullshit." Billy set his beer down and looked back at Jeff. "Chandler, how you feel about not being by Mick's side today?"

Jeff suddenly resented calling Billy, but this shit had to come out now or it would fester. "Guilty. Forget the judge and jury. Hang me now."

Billy gestured to Jeff. "Right? Jeff was acting, left you to defend yourself? Hate him, Stanton?"

Jeff winced and nearly covered his ears to avoid the reply.

It took a while for Mickey to answer, as if he were thinking long and hard. "I can't hate him. He's my lover."

"Calling bullshit on you again." Billy waved Jeff over.

Jeff didn't budge.

"Get the fuck over here, Chandler. That's an order."

With great reluctance Jeff stood, clenching his fists and battling back so much anger he didn't know how to express it.

Billy continued to beckon him closer until he could grasp Jeff's hand. Then he looked at Mickey. "You know how guilty this man feels right now?"

Jeff struggled not to shake out of Billy's grip and hide.

"I'm talking to you, Mickey," Billy spoke with more force. "Get this shit out in the open now!" He tugged on Jeff's hand. "I know you guys too well! Let it the hell out!"

Mickey's eyes filled with tears and he glared at Jeff. "Still wanna test, Chandler? Huh?"

"No!" Jeff broke the hold Billy had on him. "It's all my fault, okay?" Jeff folded his arms over his chest. He pointed to Billy's gun. "Just shoot me now and we'll be even."

Billy removed his gun and handed it to Mickey. "Here. Is that what you want?"

Mickey stared at the gun and Jeff began to shake where he stood. The gun was ignored and Mickey gulped more vodka.

Billy slid his gun back into his holster. "No, eye for an eye?"

"He didn't do it," Mickey said. "That asshole who is dead on the ground today did it."

"*There we go.*" Billy smiled at both of them. "Blame who really is responsible. Two bad guys who robbed a bank."

Mickey's body heaved with a sob and dropped the bottle onto the floor, covering his face with both hands, using even the injured one.

Billy stood and waved Jeff over.

Jeff sat on the couch and held Mickey, crying with him.

"It ain't easy, boys," Billy said, rubbing his injured chest. "We lose cops every fucking day for stupid shit. Shit like banks getting robbed, or worse, no fucking good reason."

Mickey kissed Jeff's teary cheek. "I'm sorry. It wasn't you. Please don't blame yourself."

"Mick, my baby. You're a hero. You are so much my hero." Jeff sobbed against Mickey's hot skin.

Billy stood behind the sofa and kissed each of them on the hair. "You think the flesh wound would be the hard part. Take my word for it, it isn't. Alex is still traumatized and grieving. He will be every time I walk out the door to go to work."

Jeff sniffled and wiped his nose with his hand. He hiccupped on his sob and held Mickey against him. "I didn't lose you."

"Okay, baby. Okay." Mickey kissed Jeff's cheek and hair.

"Call me if you need me. I'll drop everything and be here." Billy walked to the door.

"Thank you," Jeff said through his tears.

"My pleasure." Billy opened the door. "Oh, and by the way?"

Both he and Mickey looked up at him.

"Mark and Alex are beside themselves with worry. When you're up to it, can ya at least see them?"

"Yes. We will." Jeff nodded and felt Mickey doing the same against him.

"Bye." Billy smiled and let himself out.

Jeff faced his man and wiped at his tears. "I love you. So much."

Mickey choked up and went for a kiss.

Jeff cupped his jaw and kissed him, tears rolling down his cheeks.

~

Between the vodka and the painkillers, Mickey was high. He cupped Jeff's head through his hair with his good hand and opened his mouth for his tongue. A tingle of pleasure rushed through Mickey's groin. Against Jeff's lips he said, "Suck me, you dirty pig."

Jeff smiled over Mickey's mouth. "You're kidding right?"

Mickey flipped his dick out of his briefs.

After a look of complete shock, Jeff shoved the coffee table back, set the vodka bottle on it, and knelt on the floor in front of Mickey's legs.

Mickey held Jeff's head and stared into his red rimmed blue eyes. "Wanna come."

"You are unbelievable, Stanton." Jeff smiled and held the base of Mickey's semi-erect cock.

With slow steady force, Mickey lowered Jeff's head to his lap. Jeff kept laughing as if he were amazed and enveloped Mickey completely into his mouth. Mickey moaned and rested his head on the sofa. "If you think this shit is going to slow my sex drive down, think again, bitch."

Jeff chuckled with his mouth full and said, "Mmm," drawing strong suction on Mickey's cock, making him harder.

Opening his eyes, Mickey watched Jeff, meeting Jeff's gaze and then feeling Jeff tug Mickey's briefs down, then off. Mickey straddled wide and Jeff went for his balls. "That's it. Suck me like a whore, ya prick."

Jeff reacted as if he was highly stimulated and knelt upright, rubbing under Mickey's balls and jerking him off into his mouth.

Mickey closed his eyes again from the pleasure, then opened them to watch, seeing Jeff working hard at pleasing him.

"Gonna taste like vodka and painkillers, Chandler."

"Mmm hmm," Jeff agreed.

Mickey held his left arm against his own chest, keeping it still, and started thrusting his hips up into Jeff's mouth. "Yeah. Oh, that's it…"

Jeff wet his finger and went for Mickey's rim. Mickey threw his head back and came, stunned he actually could through all the chemicals he'd ingested, and thrilled at the same time.

Jeff milked him and massaged his balls and the root of his cock. When Jeff sat up he smirked. “Damn, I wanna fuck you good, Stanton.”

“I’ll bet you do,” Mickey said, completely spent and his spirits most definitely higher.

“You’re lucky you’re in a sling or I’d throw you off this couch and fuck you.”

“Yeah. That’s me. Lucky SOB.”

Jeff crawled up over Mickey’s lap and kissed him. Mickey swirled his tongue around Jeff’s and said, “Don’t taste like vodka to me.”

Jeff cracked up and shook his head. “You are one crazy motherfucker.”

“Never forget that.” Mickey pointed at him.

“Let me get you to bed. You look like you’re about to fall asleep right here.”

Mickey reached for Jeff and was helped to stand. They made their way to the bedroom and Mickey lay down and closed his eyes. “Love you, Chandler.”

“Back at ya, Stanton.”

Mickey smiled and fell asleep.

Chapter Sixteen

"You are so drunk."

"Shut up, Hunter. He has a right to be."

"They both do," Tanner said.

"I'm so glad you don't do that job any longer, Steven." Mark Antonious Richfield ran his fingers back through his long hair.

"I do not want you doing that job. *I do not want you doing that job!*"

"Shut up, Alex," Billy said.

"Aww, don't yell at pretty Alex." Josh pouted.

"You're all drunk," Jeff laughed as he spoke, looking around the pool at Billy and Alex's home. He and Mickey were side by side on two lounge chairs, while the rest of the gang were either sitting around the circular glass table under the umbrella or in folding chairs close to them.

"Give them more booze," Adam Lewis, the hotshot Hollywood agent said, filling their empty glasses with margaritas.

Big handsome blond Jack Larsen, Adam's attorney husband, shook his head. "Mickey, you look out of it."

Mickey held up the drink Adam had just poured. "Booze and painkillers. Cheers." He gulped the drink.

Jeff glanced at Mickey. He was in a pair of shorts, his left arm still in a sling, his sunglasses on his nose.

"What's Cochran's condition?" Steve asked.

"Who gives a fuck?" Jeff replied, sipping the drink, totally drunk.

"Can't believe we were off duty that day," Blake said, shaking his head.

"Yeah!" Mickey sloshed his drink as he gestured to Blake with it. "What's up with that?"

Hunter said, "Lousy timing."

"Good. Feel guilty." Mickey finished the drink and set the glass on the patio beside him.

Mark stood and, like a feline, walked over to Mickey's lounge chair. His long full hair framed his face like a lion's mane, and his green eyes were hidden behind his sunglasses. Tight white shorts, a black tank top, Mark's lean muscular figure was spectacular. But, he was the nation's top male model, so Jeff never got enough of him.

Mark gestured to the foot of Mickey's lounge chair. "May I?"

Mickey immediately spread his legs and placed his feet on the ground.

"Go, Dad, go!"

"Be quite, Alex," Steve said, giving him a scolding glance.

Josh said, "Why? I was about to say the same thing."

Jeff watched the lovely British model sit near his man. Mickey seemed to swoon.

Mark relaxed on the lounge chair with him and ran his hand up Mickey's thigh teasingly. "Tell me where you hurt, my lovely."

"Here." Mickey pointed to his dick.

"I saw that coming," Hunter said.

"I wanna see *it* coming." Alex shifted in his chair.

With his index finger, Mark ran a line up Mickey's leg to his hip and up his good arm.

"Christ," Mickey said, leaning his head back. "Sorry, Jeff. He's making me really hot."

Adam laughed. "He's making us all hot."

"Officer Stanton doesn't want to talk about the flamin' incident, or work," Mark said, scooting closer, caressing Mickey's chest and neck.

Jeff could see the outline of Mickey's hard cock through his shorts.

"Incident?" Mickey moaned. "What incident? You mean the group sex we all had at your mom's estate?"

Jeff laughed as the men around him did the same.

"Richfield," Steve said, "You are the cure for everything."

"I'd blow Mickey." Alex shrugged.

"Me too," Josh said.

"Oy!" Mark wagged his finger at them both. "Your men are right there."

"And I'm right here," Jeff said, loving the attention Mickey was getting from Mark. Though Mickey was reluctant to come and hang out with their friends, Jeff was glad he convinced him to. He could tell their love and friendship was helping Mickey, and it was doing wonders for him as well.

"Give us a kiss." Mark leaned closer to Mickey.

Mickey let out a low whimper and parted his lips.

Mark reached his hand over Mickey's shoulder to the chair to brace himself, and they met lips.

"I'm gonna cream." Hunter stuck his hand into his own shorts and seemed to be adjusting himself.

Jeff became distracted by the reactions of the men watching, and then looked at his lover, who was kissing the prettiest man Jeff had ever seen. Jealous? Never. Mark shared his affection equally. And Mark's police fetish kept him extremely attracted to all things in uniform.

Mark parted from the kiss and touched under Mickey's jaw. "How you feel now, love?"

"Like I've died and gone to heaven."

Mark reached for Jeff's hand and placed it on Mickey's erection. "Mm. My two top men."

Jeff gave Mickey's cock a nice squeeze and rub.

Slowly Mickey opened his eyes. Jeff could see his eyelashes flutter beneath the sunglasses.

"Love you, Officer Stanton." Mark cupped Mickey's cheek.

"Love you, Mark Antonious." Mickey leaned forward and dug his fingers into Mark's hair, drawing his mouth to his again.

Jeff felt Mickey's cock throb and heard a few sexy whimpers from the gang who watched.

"Why does Dad get to play with Mickey and I don't?" Alex asked.

Mark parted from the kiss gently and looked at his son. "Mickey can get anything he wants. He has a free pass." Mark winked at Jeff.

Jeff smiled wickedly. "What do you want, Stanton?" Jeff asked, rubbing Mickey's stiff cock through his shorts.

"All of you to shoot your load on me." Mickey closed his eyes and appeared spent. Booze and pills. He was about to fall asleep.

Josh hopped to his feet and flipped his erect cock out of his bathing suit.

Mark started laughing. "Of course Joshua is willing. Who else would be the first in line to accept that offer?"

"You really want that, Stanton?" Billy asked.

Mickey smiled sleepily and reached out to Jeff. Jeff held his hand and kissed it. "Yeah, in a couple of days. But it's hilarious you'd all do it."

Josh stood over him, holding his dick and said, "Then no?"

Tanner reached for him. "Josh, put that away."

"Before you poke someone's eye out," Blake laughed.

"I can't. I'm too horny." Josh was notorious for his solo performances when they were gathered for parties.

Jeff expected him to do it.

Mark gave Mickey another peck to his lips and walked back to his seat by Steve. The ex-LAPD cop, Mark's husband, Steve Miller, immediately drew Mark to sit on his lap, claiming the prize.

"You tired, baby?" Jeff asked Mickey softly.

"Drunk."

"In pain?"

"No. I'm not."

"Good." Jeff held Mickey's good hand and when he heard a splash he looked up in surprise.

Tanner had picked Josh up and thrown him into the pool, most likely in an effort to cool him off.

When Jeff heard Mickey laughing loudly, his heart warmed. With all the dark thoughts they had dealt with the past week, Jeff wondered if he would ever hear Mickey laugh again, but of course, that was insane. And with the help of their good friends, Mickey's laughter was back one day after the ordeal. Jeff couldn't ask for more.

As if Josh getting tossed into the pool was a cue, one by one the men jumped in, roughhousing and playing.

Jeff knew Mickey couldn't swim with his injury, but watching the men enjoying themselves was wonderful tonic for the soul. He moved to sit where Mark had been and faced Mickey, straddling the chair. "How you doin', copper?"

"Come 'ere." Mickey drew Jeff to his mouth and kissed him, moaning at the passion. Jeff scooted closer, trying to get their cocks to touch and couldn't quite manage it. So he massaged Mickey's erection through his shorts as they kissed.

Jeff asked, "Do I kiss as good as Richfield?"

Mickey pretended to put on a thinking face and tapped his chin. "Hmm."

"Shut up, ya dork." Jeff laughed and dug his hand into Mickey's shorts as the laughter and splashing continued behind them.

"Ya wanna join them?" Mickey asked.

"Nope." He held Mickey's cock in his fingers and kept kissing him.

Cold water began to run down Jeff's back, so he sat up abruptly and glanced over his shoulder. Alex was standing there, purposely dripping water on Jeff, and peered at the action between them.

"Mm." Alex licked his lips. "Don't stop playing with Mick's dick on my account."

"Alexander, you are too much," Jeff said, smirking.

"Alex!" Billy called from the pool. "Leave them alone!"

Alex pouted comically and then reached to kiss Mickey's cheek. "Love you."

"You too, Alex." Mickey smiled.

"And you," Alex said, kissing Jeff's cheek next. Then Alex rubbed Jeff's hand where it was placed in Mickey's pants and groaned.

"Alexander," Mark admonished.

"Coming." Alex winked at the two of them. "I would be too if I were you!" He took a running leap and did a cannon ball into the pool, splashing everyone.

Jeff smiled at his lover, still massaging his cock gently. "We've got a lot to be happy about, Mick."

"No kidding." Mickey shook his head and stared at the men in the pool. Withdrawing his hand from Mickey's pants, Jeff sat in his own chair and waved Mickey over to him.

Mickey got up and joined Jeff, leaning his back against Jeff's chest so they could both watch the fun together.

Jeff kissed Mickey's neck, then slipped both his hands into Mickey's shorts again, playing with him.

Mickey leaned his head on Jeff's shoulder and Jeff felt him let out a loud sigh.

"You still gonna test, Chandler?"

"Nope." Jeff opened the button of Mickey's shorts to make more room for his hands.

"How about in a year, we talk about it."

"Deal." Jeff gently pulled on Mickey's cock. "You going into SWAT?"

"Nope."

Jeff smiled and repeated the line Mickey had said, "We can discuss it in a year."

"Deal." Mickey bent his knees and pulled his zipper down. "Make me come, ya dirty cop."

"Ya want me to jack you off in front of all our friends?"

"Yeah."

"Dirty, dirty cop." Jeff laughed and held Mickey's cock in both his hands, outside his shorts, jerking it vigorously.

"Who you staring at, Mick?" Jeff loved the sight of the scantily clad men enjoying the pool.

"Staring at them all…"

"Mm." Jeff pulled harder on Mickey.

"Thinking of you…getting fucked…"

Jeff felt chills rush over him with Mickey's words.

"By me…in uniform…on duty…Oh, Christ, Chandler."

Mickey came and Jeff looked down at his spattered pelvis and abdomen. "Nice. Ya got spunk on your sling." Jeff milked him gently.

"Good." Mickey rubbed the cum with his fingers.

Jeff tucked him in and zipped his shorts. He hugged his man tight and kept kissing him on the neck and good shoulder.

Josh climbed out of the pool and left wet footprints as he walked over, his hair dripping down his face and eyes. "Good one, Mick?"

"Mm. Yup." Mickey shifted against Jeff, snuggling.

"You guys are so nice. I can't believe you're cops."

Jeff laughed and shook his head. "Shut up, Mr Elliot."

"Now that's more like it!" Josh pointed to them and laughed.

"Damn lifeguard," Mickey teased. "Go save someone from a shark."

Josh bent down and kissed Mickey. "Stupid cop."

"Moron lifeguard," Mickey replied as Josh flipped him off playfully, then exposed his bottom, mooning them.

"Don't show that off unless you intend to use it!" Mickey yelled after him.

Tanner reached for Josh from inside the pool and yanked him down into it.

Jeff laughed and Mickey glanced back at him. "We're surrounded by maniacs."

"Yeah, but the off duty ones I like a lot more than the ones we encounter on duty." Jeff ran his hand over the stickiness on Mickey's skin.

"I'll drink to that, Chandler…"

Jeff knew Mickey had survived that shooting because he had been in the exact same situation as the drill they had enacted in their nighttime survival training. Though tough and ruthless, the tactical training had saved Mickey's life. So the nightmare of training, training, and more training, had turned Mickey into a fighting machine. Jeff couldn't be more proud and wondered if he would have reacted as well as his lover.

Jeff closed his eyes and held Mickey tight, hoping this time next year, they would still be together, in a car, in uniform, Eight-Adam-One, fighting crime together. *Screw it. There's only one Mick. And he's mine.*

The End

About the Author

Award-winning author G.A. Hauser was born in Fair Lawn, New Jersey, USA and attended university in New York City. She moved to Seattle, Washington where she worked as a patrol officer with the Seattle Police Department. In early 2000 G.A. moved to Hertfordshire, England where she began her writing in earnest and published her first book, In the Shadow of Alexander. Now a full-time writer, G.A. has written over ninety novels, including several best-sellers of gay fiction. GA is also the Executive Producer for her first feature film, CAPITAL GAMES. For more information on other books by G.A., visit the author at her official website. www.authorgahauser.com

G.A. has won awards from All Romance eBooks for Best Author 2010, 2009, Best Novel 2008, *Mile High*, and Best Author 2008, Best Novel 2007, *Secrets and Misdemeanors*, Best Author 2007.

The G.A. Hauser Collection

Single Titles

Unnecessary Roughness

Hot Rod

Mr. Right

Happy Endings

Down and Dirty

Lancelot in Love

Cowboy Blues

Midnight in London

Living Dangerously

The Last Hard Man

Taking Ryan

Born to be Wilde

The Adonis of WeHo

Boys

Band of Brothers

Rough Ride

I Love You I Hate You

Code Red

Marry Me

Timeless

G. A. HAUSER

The Farmer's Son

One Two Three

COPS

Three Wishes

Bedtime Stories

Lie With Me

Enemy Mine

L.A. Masquerade

Dude! Did You Just Bite Me?

My Best Friend's Boyfriend

The Diamond Stud

The Hard Way

Games Men Play

Born to Please

Of Wolves and Men

The Order of Wolves

Got Men?

Heart of Steele

All Man

Julian

Black Leather Phoenix

London, Bloody, London

In The Dark and What Should Never Be, Erotic Short Stories

COPS

Mark and Sharon

A Man's Best Friend

It Takes a Man

Blind Ambition

For Love and Money

The Kiss

Naked Dragon

Secrets and Misdemeanors

Capital Games

Giving Up the Ghost

To Have and To Hostage

Love you, Loveday

The Boy Next Door

When Adam Met Jack

Exposure

The Vampire and the Man-eater

Murphy's Hero

Mark Antonious deMontford

Prince of Servitude

Calling Dr Love

The Rape of St. Peter

The Wedding Planner

Going Deep

G. A. HAUSER

Double Trouble

Pirates

Miller's Tale

Vampire Nights

Teacher's Pet

In the Shadow of Alexander

The Rise and Fall of the Sacred Band of Thebes

The Action Series

Acting Naughty

Playing Dirty

Getting it in the End

Behaving Badly

Dripping Hot

Packing Heat

Being Screwed

Something Sexy

Going Wild

Having it All!

Bending the Rules

Keeping it Up

Making Love

Staying Power

Men in Motion Series

Mile High

Cruising

Driving Hard

Leather Boys

Heroes Series

Man to Man

Two In Two Out

Top Men

G.A. Hauser

Writing as Amanda Winters

Sister Moonshine

Nothing Like Romance

Silent Reign

Butterfly Suicide

Mutley's Crew

Other works by G.A. Hauser:

Marry Me

What happens when you have a reputation as a cad and you hire the perfect man to work in your office? Surviving the rough patch in the economy, Braxton Todd's LA PR firm was flourishing. Braxton hires someone to give him relief from the hectic non-stop phone calls and emails from his demanding clients. And not only was Braxton going out of his mind with too much work, his love life had taken a dive ever since he had gotten the reputation as a hit & run lover, which he was; 'A one-date-wonder'.

Fabian Rhys was sick of temp jobs and when he received the offer from Braxton Todd, the infamous PR man whose reputation was a splattered all over the tabloid press, he knew one thing. He could not be attracted to a man who had a notorious reputation as a one-hook-up cad. But when Fabian started working for Braxton, and could see the press had painted Braxton in a terrible light, the two men began to dance around each other at work, terrified of ruining a good thing.

When a pair of A-type individuals find working with each other a breeze, what will it take for them to jump the divide into each others' arms?

Maybe it was two simple words. *Marry me.*

I Love You I Hate You

Parker Douglas started his new job at *Judas' Rainbow* as a sex and style columnist for the LGBT magazine. After one week he was learning the office politics and gossip. It didn't take long to figure out two of the men who worked beside him were having an on-again-off-again, fiery relationship.

Forty year old group advertising manager, Mason Bloomfield always had bad karma for being attracted to Mr Wrong. It seemed to Mason, no matter how hard he tried he was drawn to very young pretty men who treated him badly, and the hunk, Dack Torington, was no different. Mason was smitten by the twenty-six year old man's looks and physique, but inevitable, Mason was let down, again and again.

When Valentine's Day hits the couple hard, and thirty-five year old Parker witnesses some firsthand drama between the two men. Parker's impulses are at first to stand clear of the mess- but his second thought was…complete empathy for Mason, who is clearly the loser in the scenario.

Can the end of one relationship signal the beginning of a new one? Or are love and hate truly tied together like a bow on a box of Valentine's chocolates?

I Love You I Hate You!- Parker knew which emotion he preferred, and soon it became clear to Mason, Hate was not a virtue, nor did it have a place in a healthy relationship.

G. A. HAUSER

Code Red

Thirty-five year old, African American Noah Hopkins loved his job as a nurse. He worked late nights and long hours, so that wasn't conducive to meeting and dating. But inevitably on his shift, the paramedics from the Los Angeles Fire Department would bring in victims from accidents or illnesses to their trauma center and the female nursing staff would put out the alert. 'Code Red'. It was a silly phrase they used when a hot fireman would be spotted in the ER. And everyone who worked at the LA Medical Center knew, fire-fighter Keegan Vance was 'Code Red' indeed!

Noah had to tolerate the female staff circling Keegan like buzzards when he showed up, and Noah and Keegan were always friendly and professional to each other when they met.

Tough, masculine, Keegan Vance was ex-army, and in a career where homophobia was rife, the LAFD, so he kept his private life private. He was not out to anyone, not even his family. Only one person knew his secret, his housemate Karen. But there was a man he kept meeting at the ER who had already captured his heart.

Seeing the care and professionalism Noah used with everyone he contacted, Keegan was already smitten with the handsome nurse. But he had no idea how he was going to date him without the gossip and information getting out and making his life miserable.

It was a risk Keegan would have to take if he took the leap and wanted a man in his life. A man as incredible as Noah.

Both men were used to trauma and high stress on the job, thought they could handle anything. But when it came to love, it was anything but easy. It was 'Code Red' all the way, and the two men had to handle putting out the fire or learn to enjoy the burn.

Revisit some of your favorite GA characters from the *Hero Series*, *Happy Endings,* and *Living Dangerously!*

BOYS-

BOYS WHO LOVE BOYS WHO LOVE GIRLS

Twenty-five year old Jag Huntington loved straight men. He couldn't help it. Something about their macho-allure intrigued him. But Jag had never even managed to have a straight man as a friend.

His best friend Tyson Hopper, and Tyson's boyfriend Howard Steinman invite Jag out for a night with the gay-boys and Howard's sister, Virginia.

When Virginia brings her straight boyfriend, Carson Phelps, Jag's attraction to the thirty year old stud was instant. But there was not mutual attraction, not even curiosity.

It wasn't until Virginia insinuated that Jag and Carson should be friends, 'close' friends, that Jag began to wonder if he had a chance.

Carson liked hanging with gay men. They were fun. His straight buddies didn't get into dancing, music, or anything he really wanted to do. The idea of having a great gay friend appealed to Carson. Self-assured, Carson didn't flinch at the racy conversation nor sexual overtones of his gay companions' conversation. He liked it.

There was something which intrigued both men into crossing the line of friendship into a physical relationship, but for Jag, it was devoid of any emotional attachment, which he craved from Carson.

Would Jag and Carson's friendship ever evolve into anything more than a couple of friends; one gay and one straight?

Or was there really something extra special about a boy who loves boys, who loves girls?

G. A. HAUSER

BAND OF BROTHERS

Two young men in their early twenties, Austin Shelby and Henry 'Woody' Woodcliff, had somehow lost their way. Living in Albuquerque, petty thieves, neither man had family or hope of becoming anything more than inmates in the county jail.

Orlando Ancho had other plans. Working in his family restaurant, going to med-school, Orlando meets the two young men one night when they come to the restaurant for a meal. Immediately Orlando suspects they are living on the street, and may dine and dash. But what Orlando doesn't expect, is to find a common bond with these men.

Being deep in the closet, living with a brother who was a harsh critic of Orlando, and extremely homophobic, Orlando had no intention of coming out. Hiding from intimacy, Orlando led a lonely life. When Austin and Woody, exchange a 'blood' vow with him one night, Orlando admits his sexual attraction to the fair-haired Austin, craving his love and touch.

But jealousy and violence becomes inevitable, and disaster strikes one of the trio.

What had begun as a friendship between three very different men, turns into a journey for this Band of Brothers; blood brothers…who are put to the ultimate test of trust and loyalty.

ROUGH RIDE

In this sequel to *Cowboy Blues*, we find out about the sexy but proud gay rodeo star, Dean Houston. Though Dean came across as a larger than life superstar, immersed in both gay porn and one of the big players in the Tex-Ass Rodeo league, at thirty-one, Dean is nearing the end of both his careers, and struggling to accept the changes that are coming in his life; no longer being the prime star of the rodeo and top dog of the gay porn circuit.

And Dean was going to be handing his rough stock bull riding crown over to the new stud in town; Clint Wolcott.

To everyone around him Clint looked like the next big sensation of the gay rodeo scene, but his partner Cheyenne Wheeler and close friends, Rob Grafton and Victor Sarita knew his secret.

Will the end of the line for Dean be the beginning of a new life with a potential new partner?

And will the beginning of Clint's career and stardom end with disaster?

Whichever way they boys get bucked, its going to be a Rough Ride.

G. A. HAUSER

COWBOY BLUES

Gay cowboys? Gay rodeos?

Rainbow Rough Riders Rodeo, is a small, newly formed group made up of a diverse selection of gay men who each have their own reasons for wanting to compete in the rodeo challenges and enjoy the fun of the celebration of the wild west.

Follow three couples; Ken Marsh, the forty-one year old founder of the group, his forty-five year old country music singer lover, Lyle Jackson; the two bearded cuddly bears who are the perfect couple, Rob Grafton and Victor Sarita, and the youngest of the bunch, Mike 'Clint' Wolcott and the object of his desire, Cheyenne Wheeler.

Six men, three complicated relationships, and all the thrill and hardship that goes with life on the road, moving town to town, riding bareback and enjoying a good hard buck! And that doesn't even include the rodeo competitions!

Cowboys. The new macho sex symbols, or maybe not 'new', maybe just the sexiest men around. But being a cowboy sometimes is a hard road, and even Cowboys get the blues.

Midnight in London

Thirty-one year old Ted Mack, the high-school ‘geek’, was on the cusp of developing the next mega social-network-for-one. His group of techno-philes worked day and night to create a unique computer network that would astonish the world.

Twenty-three year old Kevin Moore, Jeremy West’s straight roommate from the novel ‘Teacher’s Pet’, has graduated college with honors and is now working on his own creating websites. His idol? Ted Mack.

When the two meet during an IT convention in London, the connection between the handsome college jock and the geek is electric. With the chiming of Big Ben signaling the midnight hour in the background, Ted and Kevin kiss, altering their lives from that moment on.

Can that one moment in time make a connection that will last a lifetime? Or will their colliding worlds pull them apart?

Both Ted and Kevin knew their relationship would not be easy. And if it fell apart? They always had Midnight in London.

G. A. HAUSER

Happy Endings

Twenty-seven year old, Kelsey 'Kellie' Hamilton was caught up in the economic housing disaster. Losing his home, his job, and having to reinvent himself, Kellie went back to school for his certificate in massage therapy and is hired by an elite spa in West Hollywood. Though Kellie had experienced 'happy endings' in the past while getting massages from older men, he was going to abide by the rules and not get sexual with his clients.

Montgomery 'Monty' Gresham, ex Navy SEAL plans to open up a SEAL training boot camp for civilians, and decides getting referrals from a celebrity club in LA would be a perfect idea. While Monty recruits members to his military training center, he meets the handsome massage therapist, Kellie Hamilton.

The contact between Kellie and Monty while Monty is on the massage table instantly sends both men into a state of pure sexual arousal. In this heightened state, where two opposites certainly are attracted, Kellie needs to decide if the tough thirty-eight year old ex-military man will be his Happy Ending, or if living happily ever after is just a fairy tale.

The Crush

Straight thirty-two year old Cooper McDermott knew marrying an eighteen year old pageant queen was a mistake. And after two years, his young wife began a spree of cheating on him, breaking his heart.

Newcomer from New York City to the Los Angeles area, Blair Woodbury joins the staff of the law office where the stunning Cooper McDermott works. Blair considers himself 'bisexual', but has just ended an affair back in New York with a man. It didn't take long for Blair to get a full blown crush on Cooper, especially when he was asked to represent Cooper in his divorce. Blair knew getting emotionally involved with a man on the heels of a bad breakup was bad enough, not to mention the object of Blair's desire was straight-

As their friendship grew and they became best buddies, Blair's crush on Cooper became extreme. When Cooper agrees to go for a 'boy's' weekend in Las Vegas, as his sexual curiosity began to emerge, Blair knew he was in for a wild ride!

Can Blair convince Cooper that his feelings for him are real? Or will this fantasy of Blair's be simply just a crush on his co-worker. All Cooper kept hoping was that what happens in Vegas stays in Vegas!

G. A. HAUSER

Lancelot in Love

Still working through an upset of a romance gone bad, thirty year old Lancelot Sanborn escapes to an old haunt; the bungalow colonies of the Catskill Mountain Resort. As a child Lance remembered the comfort and simplicity of his summer vacations, lazing by the lake and enjoying everything upstate New York had to offer. A stark contrast from his hectic life in the Big Apple.

Twenty-three year old Keefe Hammond and three of his friends from Rutgers decide to rent a cottage at the resort for a Labor Day weekend of non-stop partying. Keefe was deeply in the closet and had no intention of stepping out. Until…

The two men meet as they became temporary neighbors in the bungalow resort and soon Keefe began testing his own desires for sex with a man, against his terror of revealing who he is to his friends.

One place Lancelot never expected to find true love was during a retreat to escape from it.

In the end, love always finds a way and for Lancelot, he finds the love of his life in a young man named Keefe.

Capital Games

Let the games begin...

Former Los Angeles Police officer Steve Miller has gone from walking a beat in the City of Angels to joining the rat race as an advertising executive. He knows how cut-throat the industry can be, so when his boss tells him that he's in direct competition with a newcomer from across the pond for a coveted account he's not surprised...then he meets Mark Richfield.

Born with a silver spoon in his mouth and fashion-model good looks, Mark is used to getting what he wants. About to be married, Mark has just nailed the job of his dreams. If the determined Brit could just steal the firm's biggest account right out from under Steve Miller, his life would be perfect.

When their boss sends them together to the Arizona desert for a team-building retreat the tension between the two dynamic men escalates until in the heat of the moment their uncontrollable passion leads them to a sexual experience that neither can forget.

Will Mark deny his feelings and follow through with marriage to a woman he no longer wants, or will he realize in time that in the game of love, sometimes you have to let go and lose yourself in order to *really* win.

Capital Games- soon to be a full length feature film

G. A. HAUSER

Secrets and Misdemeanors

When having to hide your love is a crime...

After losing his wife to his best friend and former law partner, David Thornton couldn't imagine finding love again. With his divorce behind him, he wanted only to focus on his job and two children. But then something happened, making David realize that despite believing he had everything he needed, there was someone he desperately wanted—Lyle Wilson.

Young and determined, Lyle arrived in Los Angeles without a penny in his pocket. Before long, however, the sexy construction worker nailed a job remodeling the old office building that held the prestigious Thornton Law Firm. Little did Lyle realize when he gazed upon the handsome and successful David Thornton for the first time that a door would be opened that neither man could close.

Will the two men succumb to the tangled web of societal pressures placed before them, hiding who they are and whom they love? Or will they reveal the truth and set themselves free?

Naked Dragon

Police Officer Dave Harris has just been assigned to one of the worst serial murder cases in Seattle history: The Dragon is hunting young Asian men. In order to solve the crime it's going to take a bit more than good old-fashioned police work. It's going to take handsome FBI Agent Robbie Taylor.

Robbie is an experienced Federal Agent with psychic abilities that allow him to enter the minds of others. You can't hide your secrets and desires from someone that knows your every thought. Some think what Robbie has is a gift, others a skill, but when the mind you have to enter is that of a madman it can also be a curse.

As the corpses pile up and the tension mounts, so does the sexual attraction between the two men. Then a moment of passion leads to a secret affair. Will their love be the distraction that costs them the case and possibly even their lives? Or will the bond forged between them be the key to their survival?

G. A. HAUSER

The Kiss

Twenty-five year old actor Scott Epstein is no stranger to the modeling industry. He's done it himself between acting jobs. So when his sister, Claire, casts him in a chewing-gum commercial with the famous British model, Ian Sullivan, he doesn't ask any questions. He's a professional. He'll show up, hit his mark, say his lines, and collect his paycheck. Right?

Ian Sullivan is used to making heads turn. Stunningly handsome, he's accustomed to provocative photo shoots where sex sells everything from perfume to laundry soap. Ian was thrilled when Claire Epstein cast him in the new Minty gum commercial. He has to kiss his co-star on screen? No problem. Until he finds out Scott is the one he has to kiss!

Never before has a commercial featured two men, kissing on screen. Claire knows that the advertisement will be ground-breaking, and Scott knows that his sister needs his performance to be perfect. As the filming progresses and the media circus begins around the controversial advertisement, the chemistry between Ian and Scott heats up and the two men quite simply burn up the screen. Is it all an act? Or, have Ian and Scott entered into a clandestine affair that will lead them to love?

For Love and Money

Handsome Dr. Jason Philips, the heir to a vast fortune, had followed his heart and pursued his dream of becoming a physician. Ewan P. Gallagher had a different dream. Acting in local theater, the talented twenty-year-old was determined to be a famous success.

As fate would have it, Jason happened to be working in casualty one night when Ewan was admitted as a patient. Jason was more than flattered and surprisingly aroused by the younger man's obvious attraction to him. The two men entered into a steamy affair finding love, until their ambitions pulled them apart.

Now, one year later and stuck in a sham of a marriage that he entered into only to preserve his inheritance, Jason is filled with regret. Caught between obligation and freedom, duty and desire, Jason finds that he can no longer deny his passion. He plans to win Ewan, Hollywood's newest rising star, back!

G. A. HAUSER

The Vampire and the Man-eater

Love at first bite!

Stock broker Brock Hart's idea of fun was playing at the local gay nightclub every weekend with someone new. He imagined the Rules of Relationships didn't apply to him, and his best friend thought his nonchalant attitude towards sex was crazy. Until one night his playboy image was put to the test.
Spying Brock in a crowded club, Vampire Daniel Wolf sets his sights on the handsome 'man-eater' businessman. Sparks literally fly, between the two, and with one bite from the sexy vamp Brock is hooked.

Never did Brock ever imagine falling for anyone, especially not a man from Sixteenth Century England! The only problem is, he's a vampire. Can love conquer all? It will be a challenge, but one Brock is up for, in so many ways.

Murphy's Hero

Sometimes...being a hero isn't about putting on a cape.

Alexander Parker has always been painfully shy and his job at the British Museum keeps him busy. Dedicated and serious, no one is more surprised than Alexander when the replica of a Greek warrior's helmet he impulsively places on his head suddenly transforms him from mild-mannered clerk into something else entirely.

Adrian Mackenzie, the editor of a famous erotic gay magazine, is about to get the scoop of the decade. The crime ridden city seems to have a savior, a mysterious man who is righting wrongs, protecting innocents, and as luck would have it… is extremely hot.

When Adrian happens to stumble upon the Good Samaritan in action he falls hard and fast discovering love *and* Alexander's true identity. Now, if he can only get Alexander to come out of the closet. But is the world ready for a gay superhero?

Let bestselling author G.A. Hauser take you on an unforgettable fun-filled adventure and discover the story that inspired Ewan Gallagher's famous movie roll in G.A.'s *For Love and Money.*

Exposure

Exposure...the truth will set you free

In politics for twenty years, Senator Kipp Kensington knows that even a whisper of suspicion about his sexuality could jeopardize his aspirations for the Presidency. Kipp thought he could be content living a lie in a marriage of convenience. Then he met Robin Grant.

Leather-clad, motorcycle riding Robin isn't accustomed to hiding what he is or denying himself who he wants. The instant he meets Kipp, the sparks begin to fly and what started as a chance encounter soon turns into a full-blown affair of sizzling proportions.

When the contract Kipp has had for nine years with his now alcoholic, bitter wife begins to crumble and he's threatened with blackmail, the senator needs to make a decision. Should he hide who he really is in order to avoid losing his career, or reveal the truth and set himself free?

Mile High

Book One in the Men in Motion Series

Divorced accountant Owen Braydon spends his weeks working in Los Angeles and his weekends in Denver with his daughter. Straight-laced and mild mannered, he normally looks at the weekly flight to and from Denver as an opportunity to get some extra work done. But then he found himself on the same plane as the luscious Taylor Madison.

Texas-born Taylor is from Denver, but for several months he's been flying back and forth to Los Angeles where he works as a project manager on a major construction job. Charismatic and confident, Taylor is a man who knows what he wants and isn't afraid to go after it. The second he lays eyes on bi-curious

Owen, he knows he wants him.

What starts out as a smoldering no-strings-attached initiation into the Mile High Club quickly turns into a weekly ritual that both men look forward to over all else. Soon their desire for one another deepens and both men find themselves wanting and needing more.

When a possible change in work assignments threatens to end what they have, both men are faced with a decision. Can the heights they soared together in the air be maintained on the ground? Only if Owen and Taylor are willing to cast aside their doubts, open up their hearts, set aside all inhibitions, and go the extra mile.

Cruising

Book Two in the Men in Motion Series

Brodie Duncan expected to be taking a week-long Alaskan cruise with his girlfriend. But when she ended their relationship just moments before boarding, he ended up on the ship alone. Determined to make the best of a bad situation, Brodie considers a no-strings-attached fling. What he didn't bargain for was a man as appealing as Julian Richards. Trapped in his own bad relationship with a selfish woman he was starting to resent, the charismatic Julian is shocked by his reaction to tall, dark, and handsome Brodie. Instantly attracted to each other, the men create enough heat on their trip to the Inside Passage to melt the Glaciers in the bay.

In the end, on a vacation full of surprises, Julian and Brodie discover that not only do they have strong feelings for one another, by *Cruising* they just might have found their soul mates.

Driving Hard

Book Three in the Men in Motion Series

They met on the highway. It was the beginning of ride they'd never forget...

Texan Jude Rae Clark hit the road in his pride and joy, a jet black International big rig, searching for a new life after his divorce. Unfortunately the long, lonely hauls provided little comfort until just outside Houston on Interstate 10 a blue-eyed stranger asked for a lift.

Yale Law School graduate, Logan Bleau, set out to explore America and escape his past by hitching his way across country to San Francisco. When he meets up with a handsome stranger in his eighteen-wheeler, a physical attraction blooms and the two men end up taking a detour.

When what began as sexual exploration on the open road turns into something deeper, the pair find themselves reevaluating their lives and Jude is faced with a decision. Give up his career of cruising the highways or pass up on the love of a lifetime.

G. A. HAUSER

Leather Boys

Book Four in the Men in Motion Series

Start your engines, mount up, and get ready for the ride of a life-time...

Sexy gay fiction author Devlin Young donned his helmet, black leather jacket, and jeans. Then he mounted his Kawasaki and set off for what he anticipated would be a wild ride to Sturgis.

There were thousands of motorcycles, thousands of men, but only one Sam Rhodes. When web-designer Sam Rhodes joined a local group called The Leather Boys, he wasn't quite sure what to expect, but he knew what it was he wanted. Amidst the decadence and insanity of the monster event, all Sam could think about was what it would be like to share an erotic experience with the deliciously naughty Dev Young.

Never one to apologize for who he is, or who he desires, Devlin doesn't understand Sam's reluctance to openly explore their relationship or his wish to keep their liaisons confined to the darkness of their tents while at the rally. Then he crosses swords with a tough-as-nails biker who both taunts and tempts him, unleashing a potentially dangerous craving and pushing Dev to make a choice.

The Boy Next Door

Brandon Townsend and Zachary Sherman were best friends and next-door neighbors. Growing up together in a cozy suburban town in New Jersey, they were inseparable and thought nothing could tear them apart. Then one night something happened between them, something that brought them even closer together…

They didn't anticipate that what began as youthful sexual experimentation would lead them into an affair of the heart that would rock them to the core. Nor did they expect the danger of being discovered and separated by their families. At the time, neither Brandon or Zach realized that life would give them another opportunity.

Now, ten years later, a chance meeting brings them together again. Let best-selling gay fiction author G.A. Hauser take you on an unforgettable journey. A coming of age story about faith, about courage, and about trust…you'll never forget The Boy Next Door.

G. A. HAUSER

When Adam Met Jack

Attorney Jack Larsen may not have everything he wants, but between his successful career and best friend Mark Richfield, he's content. But when Mark comes out of the closet only to declare his love for ex-LAPD officer Steve Miller, Jack is devastated. Months later and still wounded, he's not looking to be swept off his feet, but it's hard to say no to handsome

Hollywood hotshot Adam Lewis. Adam Lewis has made a name for himself representing some of today's brightest stars. But when his business partner is accused of unethical behavior, he finds himself in need of legal advice. When Adam walks into the law office of Jack Larsen, it's strictly business until he sets eyes on the powerful and sexy hero that's about to rescue his reputation.

When Adam Met Jack is an amazing new novel by Amazon best selling gay fiction author G.A. Hauser featuring characters from Love you Loveday, For Love and Money, and Capital Games. It's got the glamour of the entertainment industry, the drama of the courtroom, and the amazing passion that you've come to expect from every G.A. Hauser book.

Love you, Loveday

Angel Loveday thought he had put his life as a gay soft-porn star of the 1980's behind him. For seventeen years he's hidden his sexuality and sordid past from his teenage son. But when someone threatens Angel's secret and Detective Billy Sharpe is assigned to his case, he finds himself having to once again face them both.

Since his youth Billy Sharpe has had erotic on-screen images of Angel Loveday emblazoned in his mind. Now Angel is there in the flesh, needing his protection and stirring up the passionate fantasies that Billy thought he'd long ago abandoned.

As the harassment continues and the danger grows, Billy and Angel become closer. What began as an instant attraction turns into an undeniable hunger that unlocks Angel's heart. It's a race against time as Billy tries to save the man of his dreams from a life without love and the maniacal stalker hell-bent on destroying him.

G. A. HAUSER

To Have and to Hostage

When he was taken hostage by a strange man Michael never expected he'd lose his heart...

Michael Vernon is a rich, spoiled brat with a string of meaningless lovers and an entourage of superficial friends. With no direction in life, he wastes his days spending his father's money and drowning himself in liquor…until he crashes into a man even more desperate than himself, Jarrod Hunter.

Jarrod Hunter grew up on the wrong side of the tracks. Out of work, about to be evicted, and unable to afford his next meal,

Jarrod thought he'd reached the end of his rope and was determined to take his life. Then fate intervened delivering him

Michael Vernon. Why not take him home, tie him up, and hold him hostage to get the money he needs?

Two men from two different worlds…one dangerous game. Trapped together in close quarters, Jarrod and Michael find themselves sharing their deepest thoughts and fighting an undeniable attraction for each other. As the hours tick by, the captor becomes captivated by his victim and the victim begins to bond with his abductor. This wakeup call might prove to be just what Michael needs to set himself free. To Have and to Hostage…sometimes you have to hit bottom before realizing that what you need is standing right in front of you.

Giving Up the Ghost

The visit from beyond the grave that changed their lives forever...

Artist Ryan Monroe had everything he wanted and then in a blink of an eye, he lost what mattered most of all, his soul-mate, Victor. Tortured by an overwhelming sense of grief and unable to move on, his pain spills out, reflected in the blood red hues of his paintings.

Paul Goldman thought he'd found the love of his life in Evan, his beloved pianist. Their mutual passion for music was outweighed only by their passion for one another. They were planning a life-time together, but then one fateful night Evan's was taken. Drowning in sorrow, unable to find solace, the heartbroken violinist has resigned himself to a life alone.

Now it's two years later and something, someone, is bringing them together. Two men, two loves, two great losses… and one hot ghost. Giving up the Ghost by G.A. Hauser, you won't be able to put down!

If you enjoyed this book you may enjoy 'GRIT' from Patricia Logan:

Book Blurb:

Grit is a kid who's run the gauntlet. Suffering tragedy at a tender age and coping with it the only way he knew how, the boy has lived a lifetime in his eighteen years. Forced out of the only home he's ever known and onto the mean streets of Los Angeles, Grit must find the means to survive but does he have the will anymore?

When two unlikely heroes step into his life, Grit reluctantly accepts the safety they appear to offer. Thrust into a world where he can only observe and not participate even if he'd wanted to, Grit learns to cope—with his past and his future. After all, he always lands on his feet.

A chance meeting with an incredible dominating man turns Grit's world upside down. Where Grit has always made his own rules, this Master wants to control him, and Grit's desire to please this tender-hearted man shifts his tightly controlled world on its axis. Can Grit embrace the changes in his life, and will the control of this Master lead Grit to the freedom he searches for?

Sample Chapter for GRIT:

Fifteen minutes later, there was a knock at Zack's door.

"Come in," he called. The door opened and Jimmy McNamara walked in. Jimmy was as tall as a tree, towering over Zack's height by several inches. Zack was well over six feet himself. Jimmy's Scottish roots showed through in his height, his barrel chest and his bright blue eyes. His hair was buzzed into a short brown flat top but he had a full beard and a hairy chest, back and arms, a true fuzzy bear in every sense of the word. Tasteful tribal tattoos circled both biceps, just peeking out from under his tight tee shirt which covered his thickly muscled midsection like a second skin. Jimmy wasn't fat by any means but he was a very meaty man. He wore tight black leather pants and thick silver rings in both ears. He looked like he walked right off the boulevard at the Folsom Street Fair, a massive leather and fetish fair held every year in San Francisco at the end of September. Zack liked his ready smile and his jovial personality more than anything. He walked right up to Zack's desk, that charming grin plastered on his face, and reached out his hand, dwarfing Zack's large hand in his bigger mitt. Zack detected the light fragrance of the Cuban cigars the bear liked to smoke on his time off. It was somehow attractive, unlike the cigarette smoke a past receptionist had clinging to her all the time.

"You wanted to see me, boss?" He flopped down into a chair in front of Zack's desk before Zack had the chance to ask him to have a seat. Zack grinned.

"Hey, Jimmy thanks for taking the time to come by this morning. I know you have a session shortly but I have a question for you," Zack began. Jimmy nodded, his face serious as he leaned forward in the chair, placing his elbows on his knees and resting his chin on his folded hands.

"Sure, boss, anything."

"Well, you may have noticed that we have some new submissives around lately. You even played with one of them. Jett?" Zack said.

"Oh, that kid is amazing. What a gorgeous boy," Jimmy answered. "And, in answer to your question, I was wondering a bit, just what I'd gotten myself into here. You seem to be running a home for wayward subs." Jimmy said, humor in his expressive clear blue eyes. Even though Zack knew it was said tongue in cheek, he knew that Jimmy was absolutely right. He was turning the studios into a charity. Not that he could turn any of the kids away. He could never bring himself to do that and if he were honest with himself, Wade, Jett and Kaden had all begun to find themselves with the help of their loving Doms. The boys were content and the studios were making money. What was not to love about these young subs? He blew out a breath and sat forward, burying his face in both hands as he leaned his elbows on his desk. He shook his head back and forth and then looked up into Jimmy's compassionate expression.

"I'm sorry, Jimmy. I know this isn't what you signed on for," he said honestly. The big bear stood up and leaned forward, landing a giant paw on Zack's right shoulder as he stared into Zack's face.

"It's fine, Zack. I am really happy to be here and to be honest, I don't think I would ever want to work in a place where the Doms don't take a real interest in the subs that they care for. The last club that I worked in New York, *Gayle's* was run by two brothers, nice guys, but in it for the profit only, sometimes at everyone's expense. He limited our time with the subs, so aftercare was a real issue at *Gayle's*."

When Jimmy mentioned aftercare, Zack completely understood what he was talking about. One of the most important aspects of BDSM was aftercare. By its very nature, BDSM brings with it, tremendous intensity to whatever scene is being played out in the playroom at the time. Whether it is a flogging, a caning, a violet wand, or Shibari, the sub and the Dom go into subspace or topspace while in a scene. The Dom is responsible to make sure that the sub is not pushed to the point where pain is so unbearable that they are actually physically harmed. Once the human body has been pushed to its limits, it must be cared for. The simplest analogy that Zack could think of was exercise. As a cool down after an intense work out at the gym or a nice long run, the muscles must be cared for. Whether that is a hot shower and a massage or simple stretches and time to cool down, the human body requires a time to recuperate afterward.

Aftercare in BDSM is much the same. Subs can easily dehydrate during an intense scene. They sweat, they pant and they are pushed physically so that their electrolytes can become off balance which is an incredible risk of heart attack. And with an abundance of adrenaline running through them, it is extremely important for them to hydrate afterward. In addition, there will be redness, and often bruising when a sub is flogged, paddled, caned or has the crop used on their bodies. There are creams like Arnica which help to prevent bruising. A good Dom will make sure that their sub is cared for in whatever ways they need. Sometimes that is a simple bottle of water and a loving touch. Sometimes it requires that the Dom speak softly to their sub, bringing them out of their subspace and back into the world, before they walk out of the doors of DOMZ.com. The last thing Zack or any Dom wanted was to watch a sub whose just been through an intense scene, walk out the doors and disappear to their car, being left raw and still in subspace.

"Well for that I am glad, Jimmy. I am happy to have you here too. I've watched you with your submissives since you first came and to be honest, you are probably one of the softest hearted people I've met. That's why I have a special favor to ask of you," Zack said. Jimmy sat back down and gave Zack his full attention, leaning back in the leather chair and clasping his fingers across his belly.

"Shoot, Zack," he said with a grin.

http://naughtypassions.blogspot.com/?zx=81f3e99425678df2

https://www.facebook.com/ploganauthor

Made in United States
North Haven, CT
19 April 2022

18401624R00137